THE
BLADE HEIR

The Blade Heir

Daniel Adorno

Lost Coin Press, LLC

ISBN 978-0692273166

Printed in the United States of America
First Printing, 2014

Cover design by Sevenlives Designs

Lost Coin Press, LLC
534 Tamarack Trail
Farmington, MN 55024
http://lostcoinpress.com

Table of Contents

To my wife, Ariel. Your unfailing love and support have been invaluable in realizing a lifelong dream.

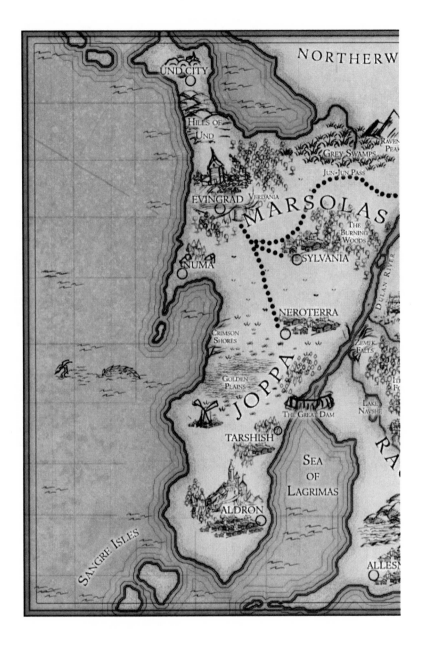

THE
CONTINENT OF
AZULEAH

ONE

Into the Deep

The blue mist permeated the air once more and enveloped Lucius in the darkness of the land of Azuleah. Before him stood a great fortress, once prominent and awe-inspiring but now an empty shell of its former glory. Its towers stood ominously above him, dark sentinels beside the massive gate of the fortress known as Arkadeus. It was a sight to behold, both awe-inspiring and fearsome to Lucius.

From the outside, Lucius saw mist emanating from the open gate and he walked closer, entering the place where darkness dwelled and awaited him. He passed slowly through the mold-ridden doors. Once inside, he found himself at the outer edge of a massive courtyard with a fountain at its center. The blue haze surrounded him and radiated a surreal light within the courtyard. On each side of the front gate there were stairs rising up to the ramparts of the stronghold where tattered flags hung lifelessly from the sentry posts along the inner wall. Broken spears and arrow shafts lay strewn on the courtyard floor, evidence of a grand battle fought long ago. Beyond the aged fountain, there was an arched doorway leading deeper inside the halls of the old fortress. Every few seconds, the fog would billow out from the doorway like smoke from the mouth of a pipe. Lucius made his way to the entrance, fearing what lay within the bowels of Arkadeus.

He peered inside and saw a long corridor with oak doors on each side. The mist floated above the floor and cast an eerie light on the cracked and moldy walls. A stench hung in the air, and as Lucius continued inside, it grew fouler, causing his stomach to wrench. He tried to open the doors within the corridor, but they were locked. And after the third door, he gave up and followed the mist toward the end of the hall.

Lucius stepped through another arched doorway and found himself inside a room full of overturned tables, shattered pots, and broken chairs. The mist was thicker inside this room and the stench stronger. A doorway to the right led to a descending staircase, while the one to his left ascended to some upper level of the dark fortress. Another doorway straight ahead was blocked with rubble and refuse. He glanced to his right and saw the fog billowing from that doorway, so he crept closer toward it. The putrid stench filled his nostrils and nauseated him. His uneasiness intensified as he descended the spiral staircase, but he could not retreat—some force beckoned him further down. The blue, hazy light seemed to brighten more with each step he took. Deepening dread began to overtake him, and he feared what evil lay at the end of his descent.

The staircase ended in a narrow hallway where the blue light shone steadily. Lucius heard a faint whisper calling to him from a glowing chamber at the end of the hall. He reluctantly drew closer to the light. Its gleam enticed him, pervading his every thought. The walls of the hallway bore arcane inscriptions and runes unknown to Lucius. He stopped just outside of the room and peered inside.

The stench was now burning his nostrils, and he fought to keep himself from retching. Within the round room, a blanket of fog covered the entire floor. He examined the walls of the chamber in the blue glow and noticed dark stains along the porous stone surface. Rusty hooks and chains hung from many places in the room. In the center of the room, Lucius noticed a small bump protruding from the mist. He squinted his eyes to examine the object in the dim light and soon realized it was glaring at him. The bump had two unblinking, dark eyes peering above the mist, keeping a steady gaze on Lucius. He wanted to run and hide from the bump's relentless stare, but his legs were frozen in place. The bump did not move, and Lucius did not look away, fearing any movement might bring about his end.

His fear kept him motionless. But after a few minutes, Lucius broke his stare and quickly looked around for any kind of weapon. He saw nothing except the swirling fog around him. His eyes darted back to the shadowy eyes at the center of the room. They had not stirred in the slightest. Lucius crouched down, keeping his eyes fixed on the creature before him. He ran his fingers along the cold, damp floor hastily searching for a weapon. His hand felt something hard. He quickly snatched it up and gripped it with his right hand, eyes still trained ahead. The object was light, but felt hard enough to inflict some damage to the creature with a powerful thrust.

He hesitated a moment before attacking the unblinking bump challenging him within the dancing blue cloud. With a yell, he dashed forward, raising his right arm over his head, ready to strike. But before he could smite his enemy, Lucius stopped abruptly and, to his horror, finally realized what lay at his feet.

A human skull upon a pile of bones stared blankly at him as he lowered his weapon. His heart thumped rapidly in his chest. He had never seen the remains of a man before, and it soon became apparent the chamber he had wandered into served a dark purpose. The round room was a dungeon of some sort, and the stains upon the walls were the blood of those unfortunate souls who had ventured inside. Panic swelled within him. He raised his arm to wipe the sweat from his brow and gasped when he saw his weapon was a thigh bone. He dropped it and frantically wiped his hand on his vest. The sound of hoarse laughter from above startled him.

Lucius looked overhead, but only saw a dark expanse. The laughter subsided, and a faint whisper called out his name. A chill ran down his spine as he searched the piercing darkness.

"Who goes there?" Lucius cried. There was no response. He trembled while he searched for movement of any kind. Nothing stirred.

Lucius stepped away from the center of the room, heading toward the staircase slowly. A metal squeak overhead followed by a thundering flap of mighty wings alarmed him. Strong gusts of air from above rushed all around his body. The fog was blown off the floor momentarily, revealing scattered bones and bloodstains throughout the dungeon. Lucius' knees buckled, and he hit the floor hard.

A guttural bellow resonated in the darkness. The foul stench finally caused Lucius to vomit. And as he did so, a huge beast descended upon him. Its large talons crushed the pile of bones underfoot with a thunderous crack. Lucius looked up to meet the behemoth's glare. Its eyes were intense sapphires shining through the dimly lit room. The monster stood upright on its back legs, spreading its wings at a span that nearly touched the opposite walls of the room. Its breath reeked of death and decay. Large fangs inside a jaw the size of a man's body formed a wicked smile on the creature's face. Black scales adorned its body, save for the monster's belly, which was a pinkish hue. The scales shimmered in the dark. And as the creature craned its long neck, they lifted to reveal gills like those of a fish. With a sudden jerk, the creature folded its wings and inhaled deeply. It opened its jaw and released the blue mist from its gaping gills. The mist floated down above the floor and once again filled the halls of Arkadeus.

"Lucius, you have come to me," the creature said, lowering its head and staring at him.

"What do you want with me, demon?" Lucius said, cowering before the monster, which let out another laugh.

"I am no demon. I am a dragon, fool! Kraegyn is my name, Lord of Arkadeus and of all the aeries of Ghadarya. Fear my wrath, *Ellyllei.*"

A dragon? Tales of such great beasts had been told to Lucius as a child, but he thought the dragons had vanished long ago. "Please, Lord Kraegyn, have mercy. What does a dragon desire from me?"

"Mercy?" Kraegyn grunted. "Mercy shall do you no good, *Ellyllei*. Your flesh shall burn from the sapphire flame I spew, and none will remember Lucius again!"

Kraegyn reared up and spread his wings. The dragon's nostrils opened wide as he breathed in the fog in the air. He let out a fierce growl, and blue fire erupted from his jaw into the cavern above. The chamber's immense height was revealed in the crackling flame. The walls climbed nearly fifty feet, ending in an iron grate where the night sky peered through. Between the grate and the room below, dozens of steel perches protruded from the walls. Then they disappeared into darkness when the dragon exhaled the last of its fire and quickly crawled on all fours before Lucius.

Lucius ran toward the staircase, but Kraegyn anticipated his plan and slashed at the foot of the steps with the long claws of his wing arm. Lucius jumped back to avoid the swipe and stumbled, falling backwards on the bones of Kraegyn's victims.

"Foolish boy! You will not escape this chamber, save through dust and ash!" Kraegyn thrust his claw upon Lucius and pinned him with all his weight. Lucius yelled in pain at the monstrous weight. He struggled to free himself, but to no avail.

He quickly realized he would die in the dark chamber and endure the same fate as those he now lay upon.

"Be still now, *Ellyllei*. You will be one with your fathers and share their doom!" Kraegyn said. The black dragon inhaled the remaining mist in the room and snarled as his jaws gaped open.

Lucius felt the blood drain from his face as flames ignited inside the dragon's mouth. Kraegyn lifted his talons from Lucius' chest and propelled the flame at his body. The fire singed his face and chest, delivering torrents of agony throughout his body. Lucius screamed, but his voice was drowned out by the sound of Kraegyn's laughter. Seconds later, darkness overtook him.

Siegfried Silverhart woke up abruptly when he heard his brother's scream. With elven swiftness, he jumped from his bed and snatched the elf dagger, *Riome*, from the wall. He ran outside his bedroom into an elegantly decorated hallway, well lit by the moonlight cascading from open slits in the ceiling. His brother's yells persisted as he dashed to the last door at the end of the hall. Siegfried quickly opened the door, dagger at the ready, and lunged inside. He saw his human brother struggling on the bed, tossing his head wildly from side to side. A violent nightmare was upon him. Siegfried set the dagger down and lit a candle on his brother's wall. He stood beside the bed and placed a hand on his brother's shoulder trying to shake his brother awake, but he continued to suffer in his sleep.

"Brother, please wake!" Siegfried cried. "Lucius! Wake up!"

Lucius gasped loudly and finally opened his eyes. He looked up at the elf standing over him, not recognizing him at first. He examined Siegfried's silver locks of hair, his fair face, and the pointed ears characteristic of his race.

"Siegfried?" Lucius whispered.

"Yes, Lucius. It is I," he said smiling.

"Did I have another nightmare?"

"Yes. This one more terrible than the last," Siegfried said. The elf grabbed a glass pitcher from a nightstand and poured water into a small cup then handed it to Lucius.

Lucius sat up and drank the water. "It was worse than any of the previous dreams."

"We should talk about it in the morning. For now, you should rest for tomorrow. It shall be a busy day for both of us."

Lucius sighed. "Yes, I know. Please don't tell Father about this. I know how worried he can get over a foolish dream."

"I won't say a word." Siegfried took the cup from Lucius and set it back on the stand. "Rest now, Lucius. The light of D'arya shall be upon you."

Lucius nodded and lay down, pulling the velvet covers to his shoulders as his mind sank to rest. Siegfried walked out of the room and quietly sang an elven song of protection before closing the door. He returned to his bedroom where he lay on his bed pondering the nature of his brother's dream before drifting to sleep.

TWO

A Test of Skill

Lucius awoke to a knock on his door. Despite his long sleep, he felt tired and uneasy. The ghastly images of his dream were still clear in his mind. The knocking continued as he quickly put on his tunic. He opened the door and saw Siegfried, fully dressed in an emerald tunic and a brown jerkin. He wore a quiver made of tanned hide; in his left hand he held a long bow with a crescent moon embossed on its handle. He greeted him in the elven language and smiled.

"I see you are not yet prepared for our contest today."

Lucius' face flushed. "No, I just woke up. I'm sorry. I didn't mean to oversleep."

"No apology is needed. I will go to the archery grounds and shoot a few targets while you prepare yourself."

"I'll meet you there, Siegfried."

Siegfried bowed slightly then exited the hallway. Lucius dressed himself hurriedly and grabbed his bow and quiver from the hooks on the wall. He walked into the hallway and turned left through an arched door that led into a grand atrium where sunlight poured out from a circular hole in the ceiling onto ornate pillars and marble benches. At the center of the atrium stood a stone monolith with a crescent moon and tree carved on its surface—the crest of the Silverhart family. Lucius walked up to the monolith, admiring the fine craftsmanship of the elves. On the carved tree's trunk, there was a symbol: three dashes in a column with a single vertical line running through them. It was the rune of D'arya, the elf spirit of Azuleah.

Lucius walked to the southern entrance of the atrium and stepped into a large courtyard. The sun shone brightly outside, giving warmth to the plants and saplings around the stone path he walked on. The path curved around the house and ended at a stone arch, beyond which stood the city of Evingrad. The city rested upon *Breninmaur*, the Great Tree of Verdania—a centuries-old elvish oak rising seven hundred feet from the ground. Many of the Great Tree's topmost branches were burned in the Ancient War, allowing the D'aryan elves to erect a circular stone foundation in their place. During the construction of Evingrad, the elder elf sages used all their powers of healing to restore the tree and its lower branches. The branches grew in a distinct way, curling around the foundation like a giant, spindly hand tightly grasping the newly constructed city. These supporting branches grew hundreds of feet high, and the myriad of leaves provided substantial shade to the elves living within *Breninmaur*. The city became a living monument built to honor the last of the ancient elvish oaks.

Lucius ran through the stone arch and onto the western road of Evingrad, hastily making his way to the archery grounds near the city square. He passed many lichen-covered houses formed by the elvish wood that sprouted from the trunk of *Breninmaur*. The elves would coax the sprouts to form their dwellings by singing their ancient songs to them. The elf houses, known as *egini*, were the common dwelling, but a few houses were also constructed of marble. As Lucius passed several *egini*, he remembered as a child witnessing the coaxing ritual, where many elves sang day and night to form a house from a sprout no larger than a flower. The result of such patient labor was a beautiful home complete with lattice windows and elegant buttresses rivaling those of great lords and kings. The greater houses built of marble and glass belonged to elves who held great honor and esteem among the elf clans. Siegfried's clan, Silverhart, was held in such regard.

Lucius saw his brother at a distance, shooting arrows with impeccable accuracy at sacks filled with straw. Lucius approached the archery grounds through a gap in the wooden fence surrounding the area. Siegfried continued to shoot the sacks as his brother walked up beside him. Lucius chose not to disturb his practice, but even if he had, the elf's concentration would not waiver—each shot was as precise as the last.

Lucius strung his yew bow and pulled an arrow from the leather quiver over his shoulder. He nocked the arrow, taking steady aim at one of the five sacks dangling from a branch overhead. Marked circles painted on the surface of the sacks corresponded to critical targets on an enemy's torso. Lucius aimed at a circle marked where an enemy's heart would be. He took a deep breath and listened to the twang of Siegfried's bow before releasing the arrow. It whizzed through the air and landed on its mark.

"Very good, Lucius. Your skills are improving," Siegfried said, aiming and shooting at his target while he spoke.

"Indeed they are, Siegfried," he said, nocking another arrow. "Though I doubt I can ever be as good as an elf."

"I dare not question the abilities of a young man like you, but I am confident your potential will surprise many elves."

Lucius laughed. He took aim and shot another arrow, hitting a critical mark. "Let's hope this potential you speak of will help me in today's contest."

"You need not trouble yourself with worry, brother," Siegfried said. He shot his last arrow and hit the target's heart without looking.

"That isn't what troubles me the most," Lucius said, missing his target. "Last night's dream still troubles me."

Siegfried lowered his bow and furrowed his brows. "Was it ... *him*?"

"Yes. The dragon appeared in my dream again—darker and more menacing than before. Kraegyn's fire burnt my flesh."

"Do not speak his name—not here. I do not know what these dreams entail, Lucius. But perhaps you should tell Father about it."

"I don't want to worry him about this. He always secludes himself in his study when I share my dreams with him. I feel as if I've brought a great burden on him ... and to you also by arriving as I did," he said.

"Lucius, you have been a blessing to both my father and I, you know this. If Father worries about your dreams, it is merely because he cares for you. Neither he nor I would allow any evil to cause you harm."

Lucius nodded. "I know. Perhaps I should tell him, then."

"It can only help you, brother. And as for this matter of your arrival, you know that could not be helped. You were a mere infant when you were left at the Marble Gate," Siegfried said, placing his hand on Lucius' shoulder.

"Father still believes it to be a sign of some sort," Lucius scoffed. "But the only sign I see is that of uncaring parents."

Before Siegfried could speak, a horn sounded nearby. They both looked toward the city square. "Has the tournament started?" Lucius asked nervously.

"No, but we must not tarry any longer. Come!" Siegfried grabbed a second quiver of arrows leaning on the fence and rushed toward the western road.

Lucius quickly gathered his gear and tried to keep up with his brother's swift pace. They hurried along the road that ran through the outskirts of the city in a semicircle, eventually connecting with the eastern road. The eastern and western roads were split by an intersecting lane known as the Royal Road. Lucius and Siegfried ran along the eastern road for a few feet before they turned right onto the Royal Road, which led them to Evingrad's center. The cobblestone path was lined with the marble houses of the most honored families. The Royal Road descended a few feet as they neared the Tower of *Breninmaur*, a tall spire used as a post for the elven warriors patrolling the city. The tower also housed the entrance to the Hollows of *Breninmaur*, long tunnels descending into the world below.

The elves of Evingrad were all gathered in the oval court on the eastern side of the Tower. A dais had been erected at the end of the courtyard, and all members of the *Cyngorell*, the governing council of Evingrad, were seated upon it. The *Cyngorell* were sages, judges, alchemists, and healers who led the elves of Evingrad with their ancient wisdom, seeking peace for all peoples of Azuleah. Helmer Silverhart sat at the right end of the dais and watched his sons, Siegfried and Lucius, run toward the crowd. He winked at Lucius as he lined up with the rest of the assembly.

Lucius stood behind some elder elves in long, velvet robes. He was out of breath, and some of the elves looked at him with raised eyebrows. Siegfried was as calm as ever, standing tall among his kin and waiting for the leader of the Council, Quetulya, to speak. A tall elf dressed in a flowing scarlet robe rose from the center of the dais. His eyes were fierce, but his demeanor was tranquil as he looked upon the crowd before him.

"D'arya be with you all as we gather here today. The *Cyngorell* is pleased to see so many of you here today willing to compete in this year's tournament. As many of you well know, those who claim victory today will become Protectors of Verdania and join our kin in the forests below to safeguard our land from the evils plaguing Azuleah. But this honor cannot be bestowed on any elf ... or man," he said while glancing at

Lucius, whose eyes lowered to the ground. "Only those whose skills with a bow and a sword surpass the challenges ahead will be deemed worthy by this Council to serve the Great Tree."

A brief applause came from the crowd as Quetulya sat down. An elf with braided blonde hair and thin eyebrows stood up beside him. He stretched out his arms and recited a poem in the elven tongue honoring D'arya. Then he opened a scroll set on the dais and called out the names of those competing in the tournament. Lucius straightened his posture when his name was called.

"Please step forth from the crowd and join Kiret and Athri on the green seal," the elf said, gesturing toward the large green circle just a few feet from the dais.

Lucius and Siegfried moved through the crowd to the seal where two elves with long, slim swords stood. They wore light armor with a dark green elvish oak emblazoned on the front and back of their torsos. Their greaves gleamed in the sunlight and revealed elven inscriptions. Lucius was most impressed at the artistry of the Protectors' weapons. The elven blades were a curved shape, and the brown leather scabbards bore the rune of D'arya.

Lucius watched as both Kiret and Athri bowed their heads slightly when the competitors assembled on the seal. Kiret, a shorter male elf with brown hair tied in a knot, motioned to one of his kinsman holding two swords to come forward. Kiret sheathed his sword and took the two swords from the elf's hands. He then signaled Athri with a nod to address the assembly.

"D'arya be with you all who compete here today," the darker-skinned and slender female elf said. "To begin we shall test your efficiency and grace with these elvish swords in combat. Your opponent shall be Kiret. Whoever deals the fatal stroke shall be considered the victor, but the graceful control of your swordplay will be taken into account above victory by the *Cyngorell's* ruling. Let the first warrior step forward."

A young, ruddy elf stepped forward and took hold of one of the swords Kiret handed him. They quickly squared off against each other, Kiret leading the first offensive blow. The young elf parried it gracefully. Kiret thrust his sword at his opponent's chest with ferocious speed, but the elf sidestepped the attack and swung his blade toward Kiret's neck. Kiret anticipated the move and quickly brought his sword up to his face, parrying the swing with a resounding clang. He then lunged forward with his shoulder, catching the young elf off guard, and swept him with his right foot. As soon as the elf hit the ground, Kiret's blade hovered just an inch above his throat. "Next competitor!" he shouted, then helped the defeated elf to his feet.

Lucius and Siegfried stood quietly observing Kiret make quick work of the competitors, each hoping to gain victory and the acceptance of the *Cyngorell*. Many elves eagerly met the elven warrior in combat and came close to defeating him, but neither their graceful sword strokes nor their phenomenal speed could match Kiret's prowess with a D'aryan blade.

"This is madness. No one will overcome Kiret," Lucius whispered into Siegfried's pointed ear.

"Do not fret, Lucius. A battle is not always measured by victory. Put trust in your skills as a swordsman and the grace in which you enter combat. These will aid you in dealing the fatal blow. Search for the gap in his defense," Siegfried advised. The elf scrutinized every parry and thrust made by Kiret.

His words did little to boost Lucius' confidence. He watched each match with dread, knowing his name would soon be called and he might suffer the same defeat as his peers. Practice in elven swordplay had become a ritual for him in the past year. He had sparred with Siegfried for countless nights, learning every thrust, swing, parry, and counterstrike known to the elven masters of the D'aryan blade. Despite his diligence, Lucius had never scored a victory over his brother. Siegfried was more cunning and graceful with a sword than any elf Lucius had known. If anyone could defeat Kiret in a contest, it would be Siegfried.

Athri suddenly called Lucius' brother to the center of the seal where Kiret had just vanquished Isis, the daughter of Quetulya. She stood up in shame as her father glowered at her from his seat. Siegfried approached the Protectors calmly without any hint of emotion. Lucius rubbed the back of his neck as Athri handed Siegfried a sword. The blade's edge was dull, and should the competitors fail to restrain an attack, the weapon would not cause serious injury.

"At the ready!" Athri yelled. Both elves drew up their swords and took their stances, glaring at each other with restrained intensity. In an instant, Kiret charged toward Siegfried with an upward swing of his blade. Siegfried gracefully blocked the charge and dashed behind Kiret, to his bewilderment. Kiret quickly turned to face Siegfried, who arrogantly smirked at the Protector. Kiret scowled and swung his sword at his side, but it was a feint. As Siegfried hurried to parry it, Kiret immediately arched his blade and swung at Siegfried's other side. With little time to react, Siegfried jumped backwards, but the edge of Kiret's blade still slashed the surface of his jerkin, exposing his undershirt. Lucius and the crowd gasped. Siegfried did not let his opponent's move deter him. He quickly charged Kiret with a series of short thrusts, but the Protector was able to block them. And after parrying the last of the strikes, he sidestepped then placed his right foot behind Siegfried's and tripped him. Siegfried fell on his back, and Lucius knew Kiret's next move would be the last if his brother did not act swiftly. Kiret drove his D'aryan blade downward, aiming at Siegfried's neck, but Siegfried shifted his upper body to the side. He then grabbed the hilt of Kiret's sword with his left hand and pulled the elf's sword to the ground. The blade struck the stone floor with a clash. With one swift move, Siegfried brought his blade up with his right hand and the tip stopped just an inch below Kiret's throat. Kiret's eyes widened as he realized he had been defeated.

Athri looked at them in surprise and announced, "Siegfried is the victor!" The previously silent crowd erupted in applause and cheered enthusiastically for the younger Silverhart elf. Siegfried was helped to his feet by Kiret, who looked rather flustered. Siegfried turned to face the dais and bowed before the Council and his father. Helmer smiled at his son, but only for a brief moment to avoid any suspicion of partiality among his fellow councilors.

Siegfried walked back to his place beside Lucius, who expressed his joy at the victory more than anyone else did. But Lucius' wide grin quickly turned to a frown when Athri called him to the seal. Siegfried reminded Lucius to trust in his abilities, but his brother's words did not prevent the knot forming in Lucius' stomach. He took a deep breath and walked up to the Protectors who glared at him. They saw a young, dark-haired human—one incapable of defeating a Protector of the Great Tree and unworthy of the respected role. The race of men had been a thorn in the side of the elven realms for centuries, and no victory or kind words from Lucius would change the intense disdain he sensed coming from Kiret and Athri.

Athri handed him the D'aryan blade. "Prepare yourself."

Lucius grabbed the sword and faced his opponent, who was still anguished at his previous defeat. Lucius took a defensive stance and breathed calmly. Kiret's stare bore into him, whether to intimidate him or communicate a deeper dislike, Lucius could not tell. Athri yelled for the match to begin, and Kiret immediately dashed forward. His first attack caught Lucius off guard, but he managed to parry the elf's vicious strike.

Lucius reared back, took a breath, and charged at Kiret with a broad swing to the elf's shoulder. Kiret ducked beneath the blow and thrust his sword at Lucius' neck. Lucius leaned back, away from the tip of the blade and desperately blocked the thrust. The move annoyed Kiret, who expected a quick victory over him. The Protector took a few steps back and twirled his sword with both hands as Lucius watched.

Kiret was taunting him.

Lucius scowled, then with a cry swung his sword at Kiret's side, anticipating a parry. Kiret did so, and Lucius quickly whipped his sword at the elf's head. The Protector barely blocked the ambitious swing, but lost his balance for a second. Lucius capitalized and swung his blade in a downward arc that caused Kiret to fall backward while blocking the force of the blow

A sudden silence fell upon the crowd, and everyone watched in anticipation of a human besting an elven warrior. Lucius swiftly tried to position the dull point of his sword at Kiret's heart, but the elf was too quick. Kiret rolled from his prone position with cunning grace, lifted himself to his knees, and flicked the edge of his blade beneath Lucius' jaw all in a matter of seconds. Lucius sighed in frustration and dropped his sword.

"Kiret stands victorious," Athri announced.

The audience applauded Lucius and Kiret's spirited contest, but Lucius felt unworthy of any applause. He sauntered back to where Siegfried stood, glancing at the Council dais toward his adoptive father. The white-haired elder Silverhart nodded slightly at him without a hint of disappointment.

Siegfried stood with his arms crossed and a smile on his face as Lucius approached. He knew what Siegfried wanted to say. *My technique was rushed and too erratic to defeat a Protector.* But his brother said nothing. He only bowed his head at him and continued to watch the remaining contests.

Only two more elves were able to score a decisive victory over Kiret when the tournament was over. The short Protector looked flushed after the fighting had finally ended. When the entire assembly of competitors had lined up as Athri commanded, the *Cyngorell* spoke quietly amongst each other. Lucius felt more than a few glances from the Councilors on him while they conversed. After a few minutes, the whispers atop the dais ceased and Quetulya stood up.

He looked at the row of prospective Protectors before him solemnly. Lucius felt uneasy whenever Quetulya's stare fell upon him. The wise elf sighed deeply and looked to the heavens for a brief moment before he finally spoke.

"I congratulate every one of you for competing in this tournament, which has been a tradition of Evingrad for ages. You have all fought with great honor and valor this day. Nonetheless, the *Cyngorell* has come to a decision on whom among you are worthy to guard the Great Tree of Verdania," Quetulya said. The councilor paused briefly and let the anticipation in the crowd reach its full limit. "Siegfried, Mora, and Isis step forward!"

The three elves stepped forward in near perfect sync, arms at their sides. Lucius grumbled in disappointment as Quetulya began to speak again.

"You have all been deemed worthy of defending the Great Tree and land of our ancestors. Your grace and skill with a sword has placed you above your kinsmen. However, in order for the burden of the Protector to be bestowed, you must now prove your skills with a bow. For the rest of you, the archery tournament will be a chance to redeem yourselves. The D'aryan bow is the heart of an elf on the battlefield, and a Protector of the Great Tree is required to wield it proficiently. The bow always precedes the sword. After a brief rest, you will all compete, and we shall determine who will join Siegfried, Mora, and Isis in the ranks of the elite."

Quetulya signaled to Athri and Kiret. The two Protectors dismissed the competitors for a short time. The elves dispersed, talking among themselves and their family clans who stood watching a few feet behind the green seal. Lucius walked up to Siegfried and patted him on the back.

"Well done, brother. It is quite an honor, and I see no elf more worthy of it than you."

Siegfried nodded solemnly. "Thank you, Lucius. But I have yet to bear the armor of *Breninmaur*."

"I have no doubt you will after this next contest," Lucius admitted.

"Have you not seen what is happening here, Lucius?" Siegfried's tone grew serious. Lucius looked at him quizzically. "Isis was chosen over you."

"So? What of it?"

"Isis is Quetulya's daughter, Lucius. She suffered a quicker defeat than you."

Lucius followed his logic. "You're suggesting the Council was biased in their ruling?"

"Yes. You fought more valiantly than she did. Go present the matter to our Father, or Quetulya himself. The honor is rightfully yours," Siegfried persuaded.

"No, Siegfried, I don't wish to get involved in the *Cyngorell's* decision. It's not my place ... I am not even of elven blood." His voice trailed off.

Siegfried shook his head and walked toward the dais where the councilors were chatting and laughing. Lucius realized what his brother planned to do and he reached out to stop him, but it was too late. Siegfried called to his father.

Helmer abruptly stopped his conversation with one of the councilors and turned to his son. Quetulya, who had been writing on a piece of parchment, looked up at the fair-skinned elf.

"I do not agree with the *Cyngorell's* decision," Siegfried said, eliciting a few gasps from those nearby.

"Why not, my son?" Helmer asked.

"Father, it is clear to me that I should be honored by this Council for worthy display of skill with a D'aryan blade and the defeat of a Protector. But it is unclear why Lucius, who displayed the same skill and valor as I, should not also be bestowed this honor."

Before Helmer could answer, Quetulya interrupted, "young Silverhart, it is not your place to question the rulings of this Council. We alone will judge who is worthy of recognition for such a prestigious honor as that of a Protector of the Great Tree."

"As a descendant of the great sage Ellyllei of the ancestral line of Silverhart and heir to my father's seat in the *Cyngorell*, I have every right to question your ruling, Quetulya Elvinstar," Siegfried challenged.

Quetulya stood from his seat and turned to Helmer. "Is this the manner of respect you have taught your son, Helmer?"

"Siegfried speaks for himself, Quetulya. He is not a child anymore. The decision has been challenged. Now what does the Grand Councilor suggest?" Helmer retorted.

Quetulya clenched his jaw. "The decision to honor Siegfried, Mora, and Isis was fair—"

"Fair?" Siegfried interrupted. "How fair was it that your daughter, Councilor, should gain honor when she was defeated quicker than any other elf who faced Kiret? Surely, if she is worthy of the Protector's armor, then so is my brother."

"Enough!" Quetulya snapped. "One more insolent word from you, Siegfried, and your honor shall be stripped of you."

Lucius swallowed hard and put his hand on Siegfried's shoulder, pleading for him to stop. But he did not.

"There is no need, Quetulya. I forfeit my honor since you have chosen to withhold my brother's."

The faces among the crowd of elves who had formed behind them looked on, aghast at Siegfried's words. Lucius couldn't believe what his brother had just done.

"Very well, Siegfried," Quetulya said with noticeable satisfaction in his tone. "You will no longer be considered for the role of Protector—unless, of course, this Council nominates you again after your performance in the archery tournament."

Siegfried scoffed. "Even if I shoot my bow with the grace of a seabird of Und, you will not nominate me again, nor will you consider Lucius, who I dare say, shoots an arrow with skill rivaling the best archers of Verdania."

"Alright, Siegfried," Helmer spoke before Quetulya had a chance to chide his son. "You have had your say in this matter. Go and compete, if you so choose."

Siegfried sighed and glared at Quetulya one last time before he clutched his bow and walked away from the green seal. Lucius followed him reluctantly, asking whether he would compete or not. Siegfried didn't answer and kept walking away from the square toward the Royal Road. Lucius stopped at the edge of the seal and watched him for a while until the blast of Kiret's horn filled the air. The archery tournament was about to begin.

The elves grew silent and hurried to their positions, both spectators and competitors. Lucius did not wish to compete without Siegfried present. But he knew this would be the last chance to show Quetulya and the Council he was worthy of being chosen to be a Protector. He hurried toward the green seal, grabbing his bow from the spot on the floor where he had left it. He pulled the bowstring a few times to prepare his arm muscles for the contest while he listened to Kiret and Athri state the rules of the tournament. It was nothing new to him. Various targets would be set up at differing distances and had to be hit within a predetermined time limit. Accuracy, speed, and grace were of the utmost importance.

After another poem to D'arya was recited by one of the *Cyngorell*, Lucius and the rest of the competitors lined up. Athri commanded them to nock their arrows and aim. The tall, attractive elf raised her hand as the contestants readied themselves. A few seconds later, her hand dropped and Lucius released his arrow.

THREE

Revelations of Lineage

Your skills were unmatched, Lucius," Helmer complimented as they walked down the western road.

"If that is so, then why didn't the Council nominate me, Father?" Lucius replied, knowing the answer.

Helmer looked up at the Great Tree's high branches as they passed underneath, perhaps seeking an answer hidden among the leaves. "Lucius, you know the sensitivities of the elf-folk of Evingrad. There is a marred history between the elves and men."

"Yes, the Battle of Verdania, I know," he confessed.

"Then you should also know that the elves have not yet forgotten the savagery of such times."

Lucius looked down and kicked a twig on the road. "But I wasn't present during those times! Why am I looked upon with such contempt?"

"It is not you whom they have contempt for, Lucius. It is your people. Since the time when mankind stepped into Azuleah, they have only shown the elves their insatiable lust for power over this land." Helmer turned a corner behind a moss-covered house onto the northern lane that led to the Silverhart house.

"I understand the bane my people have been to this world and to the elves, but have these qualities been seen in me, my lord?" He stopped at the intersection of the roads.

Helmer turned around to face him, "No, Lucius. They certainly have not. I daresay you are unequaled among the men of this world. And it is for good reason that I embraced you into my house eighteen winters past. You may not yet know it, Lucius, but your life is of great value to the elves and to your kin."

Lucius raised a brow. He had never heard his father speak of him this way. When he attempted to get more answers from the wise sage, his father dismissed them. Helmer put his hands on his shoulders affectionately and said, "The answers to the questions you seek are soon coming, like the dawn of a winter's night. Have patience, my son. Come, I am curious to see what Siegfried has been up to in these passing hours."

They continued to walk down the road, walking past many elves who were on their way to the oval courtyard to see the three newest Protectors of Verdania: Isis, Mora, and Thrinmiel. The sun was beginning to descend in the western sky, and a gilded hue fell upon the verdant houses of Evingrad and the narrow road they traveled.

They soon arrived at the stone arch of the Silverhart estate and saw Siegfried sitting in the courtyard playing his wooden flute. Birds in the bushes and branches of *Breninmaur* chirped along with the notes of his joyful melody. Some fluttered away when Lucius walked up to him. Siegfried appeared to be in a trance while he played his song with fluidity and grace. Each note filled Lucius' ears with peace, and he found himself unconsciously swaying to the rhythm of the enchanting song.

Siegfried opened his eyes after a few more notes and looked up at Lucius and Helmer in surprise. "You've arrived! How great it is to see you both," he smiled.

"That song was beautiful, Sieg. I didn't know you were so skilled in playing the flute," Lucius said, still in a slight daze from the enchanting music.

"I have played the *telyn* since my mother still walked this land. She taught me the song of Prince Mervenyon. But it has been almost an age since I last played it," he said sorrowfully.

"You have played it with the grace and skill that she once did, Siegfried," Helmer walked up from behind Lucius to greet him. They grabbed one another's forearms and slowly pulled each other closer, until their foreheads pressed softly together—the common greeting among the Evingrad elves.

"Tell me, Lucius," Siegfried turned to face him, "how did you fare in the archery tournament?""

Lucius looked down and tugged slightly on his bowstring, "Not well."

Helmer took a deep breath, "I shall be inside my study should any of you need me. Siegfried, make sure you tell Peniel to serve some pomegranate mead tonight at the table."

Siegfried nodded, and Helmer walked toward the house and disappeared inside the atrium. Siegfried looked over at his brother and asked him about the contest. Lucius was hesitant at first, but with some gentle persuasion, he finally told his older brother what had occurred.

There were fifteen archers at the ready when Athri signaled for them to shoot. All of them released their arrows at the sacks of hay and hit their marks. Lucius was confident his arrows would find their mark on the next two targets.

The next target was a wooden cube, which had been enchanted to dodge all of the archer's shots as it flew wildly in the air. Lucius had missed his first two shots, but his last shot struck the small cube. Only a few elves had been able to land their arrows on the marked sides of the cube, which included Isis, Mora, and Thrinmiel. There were only six competitors left to participate in the final round after the others had been dismissed by the *Cyngorell*. Quetulya watched intently as Athri and Kiret brought the last target out into view. It was around six feet tall and covered with a silk cloth. The two Protectors pulled the silk cloth from it and revealed a cage with a banshee inside. The banshee floated inside like a surreal mist and watched them with shiny red eyes. Her face was gray and luminescent with a mouth full of jagged teeth. Though banshees pass through physical barriers with ease, this one could not leave the confines of her prison because it was constructed of *efydd*—an exquisite metal imbued with magical properties and created by the elves long ago. *Efydd* was one of the few substances in Azuleah capable of killing banshees, and the tips of each of the competitors' arrows were made from it.

Kiret and Athri opened the cage doors without warning, and the banshee flew out in haste. Her scream pierced the air, greatly distracting Lucius and the others who tried to shoot the nightmarish creature above their heads. The banshee avoided all of the arrows whizzing past her spectral form, dodging with fiendish speed. Lucius nocked another arrow in his bow as the banshee spiraled down toward him, mouth gaping wide and ready to tear into his flesh. Lucius fumbled with his bow, trying to take aim at the banshee's head, but before the creature finished its ferocious dive, Isis landed an arrow in its side. The banshee howled in pain and ascended into the sky. Mora and Thrinmiel both shot at the creature's heart as it twirled into the tangled branches above. Their arrows found their target, and with a sharp cry, the banshee fell from the air, her ghastly corpse evaporated before hitting the ground. A loud cheer came from the crowd, which had watched the spectacle in apprehensive silence from the moment the banshee escaped her cage.

Lucius stood with his head hung low as the Cyngorell congratulated the three elves who felled the banshee and were now Protectors. One moment had cost him victory and a place among the great elves of Evingrad. Though he was merely a man, he desired greatly to be accepted by the D'arya elves, just as Siegfried and Helmer had accepted him. But perhaps such thinking was folly and his kind would never find a reconciliation or acceptance among the elves.

Siegfried nodded his head throughout the recounting of the tournament, "A banshee is not an easy opponent to strike with arrows, my friend. However, you have proved your bravery and skill in battle"

"How can that possibly be? I was not chosen to be a Protector of the Great Tree. I was not worthy, Siegfried," he said, walking past him and entering the atrium of the Silverhart house.

"You know so little about your worth, dear brother," Siegfried said quietly as Lucius entered the house.

Night descended upon Evingrad like a velvet curtain falling from the heavens revealing the blue light of the stars in the vastness of the summer sky. Lucius, Siegfried, and Helmer sat in the dining hall of the Silverhart estate around a long, oval table. Helmer sat at one end while Lucius and Siegfried sat across from each other. They all delighted in the feast Peniel, the housemaid, had prepared for them. The table was decorated with an array of colors, delicious aromas, and exquisite delicacies that Lucius reveled. He particularly enjoyed the loaf of omer bread made from the sap of *Breninmaur*'s branches. A single slice tasted sweeter than honey and nearly satisfied his appetite. A roast of Verdanian sheep and fresh apricots also lay upon the table on silver platters. The large spread reminded Lucius of the grand banquets Aldronian kings hosted in the epic stories Helmer had shared with him as a child. Rounding out the feast lying on the table was a pitcher of pomegranate mead, which was highly favored by the D'aryan elves. It was poured on special occasions and rarely drank otherwise. Lucius could not imagine what occasion this might be, considering both he and Siegfried had failed to become Protectors of Evingrad.

When they had finished the main course and their mead, Peniel entered the dining hall with a small silver platter in her hands. She had the appearance of a young girl: fair skin, auburn hair, and sparkling emerald eyes. Despite her appearance of youth, she was an elf maiden who had served her masters generations before even Helmer was born.

She placed the small platter in the middle of the table and bowed her head slightly, "An elderberry torte for my lords before they retire?"

Helmer smiled, "Thank you, Peniel."

She bowed her head again and silently walked out of the room and into the kitchen.

Helmer cut the pastry and served his sons. The torte had a delectable taste and put Lucius' mind at ease as he ate it. They finished their dessert in silence, and Peniel stepped in again to gather their dishes. Siegfried departed to his room after bidding Lucius and his father goodnight. Lucius sought to do the same, but Helmer asked if he would join him in the study.

Lucius followed the elf sage inside his private study for only the second time in his life. The first time, he was eleven years old and stepped inside without permission. He remembered seeing Helmer and Siegfried arguing about something. He had entered thinking they had called his name, but later learned the argument had been about him, the details of which have eluded him ever since.

Once inside, Helmer asked Lucius to take a seat in a wicker chair in front of a large desk adorned with the Silverhart crest on its side. The desk was piled with dusty tomes and scrolls. At the far end of the room stood large bookcases lining the entire wall, and mysterious runes inscribed on parchments hung on the wall closest to the door. Beeswax candles flickered on an ornate candelabrum beside a lattice window where the moonlight shone through and into the study. The combination of candlelight and moonlight gave the room an ethereal glow. There was a heavy smell of aged paper and leather inside, but it was a pleasing aroma to Lucius.

"It has been eight years since you first stepped into this room unannounced, Lucius. Do you remember?" Helmer questioned behind twinkling eyes.

Lucius looked around, "I do remember."

"It has been with great apprehension and excitement that I have awaited your entry again into this study for a revelation that will surely change your life."

"I don't understand, my lord," he furrowed his brow.

"Lucius, have I told you how you came to be in Verdania?"

"Yes, of course. I was left on the steps of the Marble Gate inside a woven sack. You and Siegfried found me upon returning from an errand in Numa," he said proudly.

Helmer shook his head. "I'm afraid it isn't true, Lucius. Tonight I wish to reveal the true account and why your arrival to Evingrad was more than mere fate."

Lucius leaned back on the chair, anxiously awaiting the truth that had been withheld from him. Helmer took a seat in the large chair behind the desk and fixed his gaze on Lucius. For a moment, Helmer hesitated to speak. But after a heavy sigh, he leaned forward and began.

"It was not I who found you nineteen winters ago, Lucius. Nor was it Siegfried. The Protector whom you fought in combat today, Kiret, he found you beside the Marble Gate during that chilly night. You were wrapped in bundles of wool blankets inside a woven sack, crying desperately into the night for someone to find you. Kiret was keeping watch on the outskirts of Verdania that night when he heard your shrill cries. He thought it was some trick of an unknown enemy to leave an infant at the steps of the Marble Gate. But when he realized it was not, he had pity on you. He fed you some of his rations and brought you back to the Great Tree and to Evingrad. He saved you, Lucius."

Lucius furrowed his brow. *The elf who nearly killed me in combat saved me?*

"He did not know what to do with you at the time," Helmer continued. "It is within the nature of elves to help any creature in need, even a child of men."

"Kiret brought you before the *Cyngorell*, placing your fate in their hands. Quetulya believed your arrival at Evingrad was a great omen to the elves and in direct defiance of D'arya. He admonished Kiret for his irrational act and demoted him of his rank as Chief Protector. The Council argued for days, not sure whether to send you to Joppa, the land of men, or to care for you until the time when you would return to your kin. Quetulya was clear on what he wished to do with you. He would not stand for a man's son to live among the elves and taint the sacred ground of *Breninmaur*, and so he argued vehemently that you be cast out of Verdania immediately. His own family had not been spared by the men of Joppa during the great Battle of Verdania."

Lucius understood now why the leader of the *Cyngorell* held him in such low esteem. The thought of his patronizing voice suddenly angered him.

"But despite his objections, you would not be turned aside so easily," Helmer confessed with a smile. "Unlike many of the Councilors, I viewed your arrival as a blessing to this land. I chose to defend you, Lucius, and desired for you to have a place in my house equal to a son of the Silverhart line."

Lucius slouched in his chair and pondered Helmer's confession. "Why, Father? What deemed me worthy of such an honor?"

"Nothing, Lucius. I saw your vulnerability as an infant and, like Kiret, I had pity on you. You see, like many of my kinsmen, I have long grieved for the children of men and the world they inhabit. So much war and malice wrought by their hands when they are capable of loftier pursuits. And I did see a lofty pursuit in keeping you among us." Helmer stood up and walked to the lattice window. He looked at the moon for a few moments in silence, contemplating how to phrase what he wanted to say next. "The *Cyngorell* did not easily concede to my wishes for you to have a place in Evingrad. They needed to be convinced you would not be a threat to Verdania or to the peace of D'arya. It proved difficult to sway them, considering you were not only a child of man, but also a royal heir of Aldron."

Lucius' eyes widened and his posture straightened. "What? An heir? How can you be certain of this?"

Helmer placed his hand inside his garment and pulled out a flat, stone octagon the size of his palm. He handed it to him for closer inspection. The seal was lighter than Lucius expected and had a slight sheen in the candlelight. On its surface was a carving of an eagle with wings outspread, clutching a sword with its right talon and a scroll with its left. Above and below the carving there were words inscribed in an ancient language of men, but Lucius could not decipher their meaning.

"'In the Lord Yéwa do we stand and in his son, Yesu, do we trust.' This is their meaning," Helmer said.

Lucius raised his brow and searched the stone for any further meaning, "I don't understand—"

"How this pertains to you?" Helmer finished the question. "The stone carving you hold is the crest of the King of Aldron, Cervantes Nostra. Kiret found it among the blankets you were clothed in."

Lucius knew little of the legendary king, Cervantes, who had reigned in the kingdom of Aldron nearly a millennia ago. In those days, elves and men fought together against the Draknoir of the east before their alliance faded into gloom. The current ruler of Aldron, King Alfryd Dermont, was not from the line of Nostra. The third generation of Cervantes' line had been hunted down and killed off by the Draknoir and various enemies of the throne. A servant of the Nostra house named Gareth inherited the throne of Joppa and established his dynasty in the southern province of Azuleah. Knowing the Nostra line had been wiped out for years before his birth, Lucius saw the stone as nothing more than an artifact and not evidence of royal status.

"This stone proves nothing, Father. The house of Nostra has been desolate since before I was born. I am no heir to the kingdom of Aldron or the province of Joppa," he said, setting the stone on Helmer's desk.

Helmer laughed, which slightly annoyed Lucius. "Desolate? Who told you it was desolate? Siegfried?"

"Well ... yes," Lucius admitted.

"My son, Cervantes had many sons and daughters. When the Draknoir invaded Joppa ages ago during my youth, Cervantes ordered his family to be evacuated in a caravan led by the king's servants. Cervantes died in the ensuing chaos the Draknoir inflicted upon the city of Aldron, but his children were hidden throughout Azuleah secretly. The Draknoir have an intense hatred of the Nostra line—and all of mankind for that matter. They have forever cursed the day when men settled on the southern shores and challenged their dominance of the region.

"After King Cervantes fell, the Draknoir searched Azuleah for his scattered heirs and descendants. Many were found and killed, including women and children. The long hunt for the remaining survivors of the Nostra line lasted for centuries. Eventually, rumors began to spread throughout Azuleah that the great royal line had been completely destroyed by the Draknoir. But many believed a few descendants were still alive and lived as nomads in the far north, constantly on the move to hide from their enemies," Helmer said. He walked up to the desk and picked up the Nostra seal. "This seal proves you are indeed a descendant of Cervantes and heir to a great dynasty. Seven of them were made for each of the Nostra heirs and were passed down over the generations. You are of noble blood, Lucius."

Lucius let the truth of his past sink in. An heir to the throne of Aldron? He could barely imagine himself taking the role of a Protector of *Breninmaur*, much less of a king over thousands of subjects. The responsibility of such a position was far beyond his imagination at this point in his life. "What does all this mean? Am I to return to Joppa and challenge the rule of Alfryd?" he asked apprehensively.

Helmer shook his head. "No, Lucius. There will be a time for that, but I do not believe it is now."

He sighed in frustration. "Then what is to become of me, Father? I feel a sudden burden from all these revelations you bring me."

"I am sorry, my son. I did not wish to make you sorrowful over all this. But you are of paramount importance to your people. You would not have been left on the threshold of Verdania if it were not so." Helmer sat down again and began looking through the assortment of papers on his desk.

A question lingered in Lucius' mind as the wise elf foraged through the tomes and scrolls. "Does the Draknoir know I am here? You said the descendants of Cervantes were hunted and killed by them. Could they have followed whoever left me here?"

Helmer looked up at him with serious eyes, "I'm not sure. But I can assure you no Draknoir fiend would dare enter the sanctuary of Verdania, lest a swift descent to the grave be their desire."

"What are they?" Lucius asked curiously.

Helmer's countenance turned grim, "They are a fallen race of the *ellyll*. An ancient race of elvish warriors who were once highly favored by D'arya, but their lust for power led to their downfall. They abandoned the ways of the Elf Queen and embraced the detestable dragon god, Nergoth. Through Nergoth and his dark magic, they were given an abominable power, which consumed them and, in the end, transformed them. They are no longer elves, but beings of darkness. No more do you see fair-skinned folk seeking peace, but scaly, monstrous beings waging war and yearning for blood.

"In the years after their fall, the Draknoir allied themselves with the dragons of Ghadarya paying tribute to their lord," Helmer paused abruptly and whispered, "the Black Dragon, Kraegyn."

Lucius felt the blood drain from his face. The blue fire of the great dragon consuming his flesh immediately filled his thoughts. His heart raced in fear of the hypnotic blue stare of the Black Dragon's eyes.

Helmer sensed his sudden burden, "What is it, my boy?"

Lucius hesitated, "It's nothing."

"Tell me, has another dream or vision disrupted your mind?" Helmer asked.

He wished to remain silent, but his father's incredible foresight would determine the answer at some point. "Yes."

Helmer nodded his head. "I feared you would have another one. Was it more vivid than the last?"

The Black Dragon's hot breath burned in his mind. "Much more vivid."

Helmer sighed and started digging through the clutter on the desk again. He pulled out a withered tome and quickly searched the pages. His eyes gleamed in the candlelight, darting from side to side as he read the text.

"Ah, here it is," he whispered. "Read this page, my son."

Helmer handed him the book, pointing at the inscription. It was written in the common language of Azuleah. The text was very faded and written with quick pen strokes. It read:

Yéwa, the deliverer of the race of men has spoken to his prophet. He has found favor in Joppa through Yesu, the Great King to come. A star has fallen on Azuleah and spread through the land. Men have partaken of the land and have lost their way. Yéwa has seen the evil of Nergoth; his time is coming.

King Yesu has chosen the line of Cervantes, in whom the Lord Yéwa was pleased, to lead the men who fell from the sky. One like a king will rise from the house of Nostra and serve. He will lift Yéwa's name in Joppa and a song for Yesu will be heard from the North. Nergoth and all who follow him will tremble at the sound of his footsteps and know Yéwa is with him. He will not forsake him nor allow harm to come upon him if he trusts in Yéwa with all his heart.

These are the words of Yéwa, our Deliverer, and Yesu, our King.

"Is it a prophecy?" Lucius asked, looking over the text again.

"Yes, Lucius, it is. It was inscribed by a man named Zebulun, one of the servants of the king and a loyal follower of Yesu."

"I know of Yéwa, the god men worship, but who is this Yesu?"

"I could probably speak all night to you about him, but perhaps you should figure that out for yourself, my son," Helmer opened the top left drawer of his desk and fetched a scroll. "I have been saving this for a very long time, Lucius. It is a near perfect copy of a great heirloom in the kingdom of Aldron. The answers to many of your questions can be found here."

Lucius leaned forward and took the scroll. He unrolled it, revealing many small characters in elvish script. The scroll was about the length of his arm. But because of the complexity of the elven language, it would take a day or two to read it completely.

"There is something more I wish to reveal before you go and rest."

Lucius closed the scroll and listened attentively, anxious to know what else the wise sage could reveal in one night.

"Zebulun's prophecy correlates very well with an elven prophecy foretold many ages ago. I reminded the *Cyngorell* of it when we debated years ago whether you should stay with the elves or be cast out. The words of the prophecy read thus:

'Behold, a light will fall on D'arya's doors

Unknown to the fair folk of old

A child without home among the poor

But with a quest told once before

A sword and scroll he will hold

On his way to quench the flame

Which defiles *Ellyllei's* name'"

Lucius sighed deeply, his hands shaking slightly. This morning he had been an ordinary young man, wishing only to become a Protector of the forest of Verdania—the limit of his aspirations for greatness. But now his path was leading to a place he did not wish to go. The daunting role of *Ellyllei* already burdened him as much as the chilling prospect of facing the Black Dragon.

"Your path has been foretold, Lucius. Your people need you, and even the elves need you, though they may not yet know it," Helmer said softly.

"I do not know if this is the path I wish to take, Father. Fear overtakes me at what may meet me on this path. Why must I rise to such responsibility? Why was I chosen? My mind is full of questions, and my mind is unwilling to hear the answers," his head sank.

Helmer stood from his chair and walked to his son's side, placing a hand on the young man's shoulder to comfort him. "I know there are many things that have not yet been answered, my son, but do not be discouraged. It is best now if you rest. We shall talk further in the morning."

Lucius wanted to object, but he suddenly realized how tired he was from competing in the tournament. He stood up at Helmer's request and went to his room.

For the first few minutes, he laid on his bed, afraid to sleep. Kraegyn's piercing stare was still vivid in his mind. Eventually, sleep overtook him, and he dreamed of a great palace on a golden plain.

Four mighty bastions stood high on each corner of the palace, along with two spires jutting into the air: one from the northern wall and one from the southern wall. Large doors stood in front of him, adorned with a golden eagle whose wings were outspread. A voice from inside called his name. It was soothing and beautiful to his ears.

The doors opened slowly, and a light brighter than the sun illuminated from inside the palace. Despite its radiance, Lucius found no need to cover his eyes. An elegant lobby lay ahead with polished marble floors and gleaming white walls. A tall statue of a bearded man holding a scepter stood at the center of the lobby. The man wore a crown on his head and a flowing robe draped over his muscular frame. His face held a stoic, determined gaze. Behind the tall effigy, there was a wide, double banister staircase rising to a wooden door below a gilded archway. A large elm tree was embossed on the door. He was compelled to go up the stairs and into the door, but the voice spoke again before he took his first step onto the staircase.

Lucius. The voice spoke from inside his head, but somehow he sensed its source came from overhead. He looked up and saw a ball of light pulsating from the ceiling above. He cowered at the immensity of the light.

"Here I am," Lucius said, his voice cracking.

Lucius ... the time has not yet come for you to enter the door.

"When will it be time?" he asked curiously.

Soon, but now you must forge the Requiem Sword. Go and seek counsel in the swamps of the north. The light began to ascend and fade within the ceiling.

"Wait! Why must I do this? I don't understand!" Lucius cried, but the light did not respond and continued to fade away. The regal lobby began to fade as well, and Lucius heard a faint call in the distance.

FOUR

The Path of the Ellyllei

Lucius woke with a start when he heard the knocking on his door. Siegfried had been calling his name on the other side and knocked several times to wake him. He got up, still half asleep, and opened the door. Siegfried stood outside with his arms crossed and a stern expression on his face.

"What's wrong, Siegfried?" Lucius asked.

"It's Father. He's gone to the Cyngorell to request our departure from Evingrad," the elf replied calmly.

"Departure? Whatever for? Does he mean to cast us out?"

Siegfried smirked. "No, Lucius. The time has come for us to go outside of Verdania and fulfill Zebulun's prophecy.

Lucius swallowed hard. "I do not think I am ready to embark on such a quest, brother."

"My father believes you are up to the task, which is why he has faced much opposition from the Council. We must go, Lucius," Siegfried said earnestly.

Lucius quickly got dressed and set out with Siegfried to the Council House where Helmer's appeals were taking place. Siegfried explained to Lucius the main cause for concern if they were not allowed to leave Evingrad. The Cyngorell considered it treason for any elf to step outside the forest of Verdania, except for those who bore the rank of Protectors or who were sanctioned by the Council. Quetulya was presiding over the proceedings and was against the idea of allowing anyone to leave the sanctuary of Evingrad, even Lucius. Lucius found it odd that the Councilor suddenly had a change of heart concerning a man dwelling among the elves. He could hardly wait to hear the Grand Councilor's reasoning for preventing his departure.

There was a slight chill in the morning air, and the grass was still wet from the dew overnight. Siegfried led him through the narrow winding roads to the center of the city. The sunlight gleamed in the east and trickled through the canopy of *Breninmaur*'s branches. The few elf-children of the city played their wooden flutes and lyres on the rooftops of their houses and in the branches overhead. The sweet music they played was lost on Lucius, whose thoughts were on his adoptive father and what penalty he might face for confronting his fellow councilors. But as they neared the Tower of Evingrad, Lucius pondered his own fate and the revelations of the previous night. It seemed as though the whole land of Azuleah depended on him now— a frightening prospect. The music overhead began to crescendo, accompanying the growing anxiety Lucius felt at the thought of being cast out from Evingrad. *Will I ever hear such beautiful music in Azuleah again?*

The Council House was a large marble building with a stained-glass, domed roof. The building stood a few feet away from the green seal where the tournament had been held the day before. Lucius and Siegfried ascended the long staircase of the Council House and opened the oak door. Inside there was a small amphitheater where the Cyngorell sat listening to Helmer. Daylight shone brightly in an array of colors through the stained glass onto Helmer, who stood behind an ornate podium as he spoke to his fellow Councilors. Quetulya stood behind a similar podium nearby and watched impatiently as he spoke.

Lucius and Siegfried sat down on marble benches designated for the general populace of Evingrad. They both listened closely as their father explained his case to the elves of Evingrad.

"I believe it is highly imperative we send Lucius and Siegfried to Sylvania to forge the Requiem Sword. My fellow councilors, I stand before you today to declare the time our elders spoke of has now come. Dark days are on the horizon for all peoples of this land ... for Kraegyn has returned to our world," Helmer said, his voice echoing through the room as the crowd gasped in response to the Black Dragon's name.

Quetulya's eyes studied the audience. "The Lord of Ghadarya was defeated ages ago at the hands of our ancestors, Reyeon and the King of Aldron in Arkadeus."

"Yes, but the Draknoir sorcerer, Scipio, uttered an incantation before his dying breath that sealed the Black Dragon's soul into the ruins of Arkadeus. Since that time, Scipio's descendant, Memnon, has succeeded him. Who can say whether he has aided the beast in garnering its full strength or not?" Helmer asked indignantly.

Quetulya scoffed, "It is not the purpose of this Council to consider possibilities, Lord Helmer, only realities. Even if what you say comes to pass, what does your son and Lucius have anything to do in the matter?"

Lucius straightened in his seat, eager to know the answer to the Councilor's question. Helmer grabbed a scroll from the top of his podium and unrolled it. He recited the elven poem Lucius had heard last night, but there were additional verses at the end he had not heard. The poem spoke of a vanquished evil rising from an ancient ruin and enslaving the world with a force greater than D'arya herself could muster. The four corners of Azuleah would fall in its wake, and blue fire would consume all life. He shuddered at the image of searing flames engulfing his body. Helmer continued reading the prophetic poem solemnly. A man will be chosen by the peoples of Azuleah to banish the evil once and for all, but he will not do so of his own accord. Yesu will accompany the man and all who stand with him. The enemies of the chosen man, known as the *Ellyllei*, will fall from the blade he carries. The blade will be forged by an elf's hands and possess great power over the dark forces of the world. The sword will not be forged from a common metal, and specific instructions for its creation will be revealed to a seer of D'arya.

"In light of all this evidence, Councilor," Quetulya uttered, "you still have not determined the reasons as to why Siegfried and young Lucius should be permitted to leave these sacred woods to Sylvania. There is no prophecy concerning that city. Why, then, does this quest to vanquish evil start there?"

Helmer smiled, undaunted by Quetulya's question. "Sylvania has long been a sanctuary for all peoples of Azuleah, most notably, elves and humans—"

"Vagabonds and criminals, Lord Helmer," Quetulya interrupted.

"Some, yes," Helmer retorted. "But there are many skilled blacksmiths within the city, many of which are elves. It would be the opportune place to forge the sword to slay the Black Dragon. More importantly though, Sylvania is home to a D'aryan seer by the name of Lumiath."

The Councilors seated in the rows ahead of Lucius began to whisper to each other and shake their heads in disapproval of the D'aryan seer.

"I know there is much controversy over Lumiath within the Cyngorell—"

"Councilor, Lumiath is an exile of Evingrad and has disassociated himself from D'arya," an elf with blonde, shoulder-length hair spoke from the second row.

"He cannot be trusted," another elf blurted out, and others began to join in.

Quetulya raised his hand to quiet them, "Peace, Councilors. Surely Councilor Silverhart has a good reason for suggesting a firebrand such as Lumiath."

"I believe in his ability as a seer and a loyal follower of D'arya, Quetulya," Helmer admitted proudly. "And if he is not the elven seer the prophecy speaks of, then he will undoubtedly lead us the right way."

Quetulya disagreed, and many of the Councilors were divided on Lumiath's reliability. The debate continued on for an hour. Siegfried slipped outside while Lucius continued to wait on the Cyngorell's decision. In the end, the Council sided with Quetulya. They did not believe Helmer's plan to send Lucius and Siegfried to Sylvania was the only option concerning the prophecy. Many suggested when the time was right, D'arya would reveal the identity of the seer to the High Elves of the Cyngorell, only then should Lucius be sent out.

Quetulya did not believe Lucius was the man prophesied to seal Kraegyn's fate. His resentment towards Helmer was evident, and Lucius disliked him all the more for it. Before the decision had been made, Lucius felt a slight reluctance to be sent to unknown parts of the world on some wild adventure, but when the opportunity had slipped away from him, he eagerly desired it.

When the final deliberations were made, Lord Helmer stepped down from his podium and dismissed himself from the audience in the Council House. He walked past Lucius, bearing a sullen look in his eyes completely uncharacteristic of the sage. Lucius followed him outside, after glancing back toward the amphitheater where his gaze met Quetulya's smug expression.

Siegfried met them outside on the steps of the marble building. His face did not display any hint of anticipation or curiosity about the outcome of the proceedings. Lucius was certain he knew the outcome before he had walked out, just as his father did. Their incredible foresight had always amazed him, but at the moment, both father and son probably wished their predeterminations had been wrong. The three walked down from the Council House and headed for their home in silence. Lucius felt a growing need to say something—anything—to lighten the depressing mood, but he failed to find any words.

"I suppose we should move forward with our next move, Father," Siegfried broke the silence.

Lucius raised his brow and eyed his brother quizzically, "Next move?"

Helmer chuckled. "I suppose it is time to employ more forceful measures upon the situation, Siegfried."

"What?" Lucius shot his head to the right, meeting Helmer's eyes.

"You didn't honestly think this was our only plan in sending you to Sylvania, did you?" Helmer asked.

"I thought it to be the most reasonable," Lucius answered.

"Indeed, it was," Helmer agreed. "But you are the *Ellyllei*, Lucius, the Elf Son prophesied about long ago, and we cannot sit idly waiting for any intervention from the Council."

"What are you suggesting we do, then?" he questioned anxiously.

"We must sneak outside of Verdania unnoticed and travel to Sylvania," Siegfried said confidently with his usual calmness.

Lucius' eyes widened. "Sneak outside? We shall be arrested for treason and imprisoned. And if by some miracle we make it to the bottom of *Breninmaur's* trunk, the Protectors would capture or kill us before we could ever come within a mile of the Marble Gate."

"Do not trouble yourself over such matters, Lucius," Helmer placed a hand on his shoulder. "I have meticulously planned your escape from this enchanted city. You shall fulfill the quest that Yéwa, your God, has placed before you—unless, of course, you willfully choose to stay behind."

Lucius stopped on the road to ponder the choice before him. The idea of this adventure to rid Azuleah of a vile terror excited him, but frightened him to death as well. He envisioned facing an enemy as hellish as Kraegyn, and the fear swept over him again.

"The decision is still yours to make, brother," Siegfried said emphatically.

He took a deep breath, expelling fear and doubt from his mind, "My heart is willing. Tell me what must be done."

FIVE

A Grand Escape

The stars above Evingrad shone brightly in the darkness of the city as a chill wind wisped through the narrow roads between all of the *egini*. Lucius walked outside from within the warm confines of the Silverhart estate carrying a full backpack with supplies for his long journey. Siegfried followed him, carrying their weapons and a bag with scrolls slung on his shoulder. Lucius frowned as the wind whipped his hair. He buttoned the collar of his coat and threw the hood of his cloak over his head. The chill weather surprised him since the cooler autumn season was still months away.

Siegfried handed him his yew bow and sword. He took them, placing the sword in its leather scabbard and attaching the bow to his backpack. Helmer suddenly appeared at the top of the steps of the atrium. He held a scroll Lucius immediately recognized. It had been the duplicated heirloom of the Nostra house since the time of Cervantes. Lucius had studied its opening passages, which chronicled the dawn of man at the hands of Yéwa. But time had grown short, and in his haste, Lucius had forgotten to pack it.

"Remember to take the eastern tunnel once you've reached the Great Tower." Helmer handed him the scroll.

Lucius tucked the scroll inside a sown pocket in his cloak. "How will we get past the sentries inside the Tower?"

"Leave that to me," Siegfried said as he wrapped himself in a dark green cloak.

Helmer looked at them solemnly, and Lucius saw a slight sadness in his eyes. "This quest will be perilous. Trust only those whose hearts seem worthy to you, and look to each other for help in desperate times. The light of D'arya and the grace of Yéwa be upon you both."

They both bowed in his presence and set off down the narrow lane leading toward the western road. Lucius recalled Helmer's instructions to veer off the road when they reached the intersection. He and Siegfried cut through the houses and stayed within the shadows lest they be seen by anyone. Siegfried jogged swiftly ahead of him in absolute silence, a difficult skill for Lucius to mimic as he avoided the crunch of leaves underfoot.

A few yards ahead of them the Tower of *Breninmaur* loomed in the moonlight. Sentries making their rounds stood inside the tower, watching the stillness of the city from diamond-shaped windows. Torches lit the inside of their posts and revealed their faces to Siegfried's far-reaching gaze.

"Six sentries are keeping watch from inside. Their sight will catch our movement in a yard or less," the elf whispered. He crouched behind a tall bush and signaled Lucius to stay behind him.

"How will we ever get past them?" Lucius asked, calculating the odds of successfully escaping the sight of six trained elf-warriors and not liking the result.

"Fear not, Lucius, the magic of D'arya will deliver us from their sight," Siegfried said.

"I do not know any of the magical elven songs, Sieg. And even if I did, men do not inherit the magical abilities of the elf clans," he said resentfully.

"No songs are needed." Siegfried pulled out two transparent spheres from a pouch on his belt and handed one to him. "Put this in your mouth, but do not swallow it."

Lucius raised his brow, but at Siegfried's insistence, he took the small sphere and placed it in his mouth. He immediately felt a slight prickling on his tongue, which surprised him. The feeling spread throughout his mouth and his insides. He began to panic, wanting to spit the sphere out of his mouth, but Siegfried assured him nothing was wrong. The prickling reached all of his insides and then his skin. His right arm itched from the prickling effect, and he reached with his left hand to scratch it. But as he looked down, he realized his hand was gone. They had disappeared from sight. The itching spread to his left arm, and he watched it vanish before his very eyes.

"Do not worry, brother, you will be restored once the diaphanousphere has been removed from your tongue," Siegfried promised. "Once I have disappeared, I will go down to the door of the Tower, while you stay here. Keep your eyes fixed on the door. When it opens, run quickly and enter."

Lucius nodded his head, forgetting Siegfried could not see him.

Siegfried placed the diaphanousphere inside his mouth and in seconds disappeared from sight. The bush they hid behind suddenly moved as Siegfried ran through it, making his way through the last stretch of *egini* and into the open square of the Evingrad.

Lucius watched the empty square, searching for any trace of Siegfried's flight, but found none. He looked up at the sentries inside the Great Tower. Their pale faces showed no sign of alarm, and they continued to watch the cityscape in complete ignorance. Lucius smiled mischievously. He steeled himself and darted across the darkness.

He looked up at the sentry watching the main square. The elf didn't flinch in the least as Lucius reached the green seal and hurried inside the opened door. The door entered into a large chamber inside the Tower. A spiral staircase at the center of the room climbed up to the guard room where the sentries kept watch. Small torches were placed all along the circular room, which gave it a warm, inviting light despite the fact they were unwelcomed visitors.

Suddenly, the door closed behind Lucius. He turned quickly and saw a diaphanousphere appear from thin air. It hovered in the air for a few moments and was quickly swallowed up by Siegfried's right hand. The rest of the elf's thin figure soon reappeared.

"You may release the diaphanousphere, Lucius," Siegfried said as he tucked the small sphere in his pouch and approached him.

Lucius grabbed the transparent sphere from his mouth and, to his surprise, found it was neither wet nor warm to the touch. The prickling feeling, which had emanated from his insides, began to fade and his entire body came into view.

"That's quite a tool." He handed the diaphanousphere to Siegfried, who slipped it in his belt.

"We must go down the east tunnel, through that door," he pointed to an arched door nestled at the rear of the chamber.

"Where are all the guards?" Lucius looked around suspiciously.

Siegfried walked past him to the door, "There are none assigned to this room since the door is always locked, but I managed to pick it with relative ease."

"Do your skills know no bounds, brother?" Lucius shot him a wry smile.

Siegfried ignored the witty remark, "If Father is correct, there will be one or two elves guarding the exit of the tunnel below, but we must not tarry any longer."

Siegfried opened the arched door slowly and crept inside, motioning for Lucius to follow. He looked up at the spiral staircase, wary of any sentries who might descend or look down. When he saw none, he ran to the door quietly and followed his elf companion.

They entered a small room with two large holes in the floor. Unlike the last room, the interior of this room was not marble, but entirely wood. A small torch hung on the far wall past the holes and flickered as a breeze blew from the openings. The top rungs of ladders stuck out from each tunnel, allowing passage to the descending hollows of *Breninmaur*.

"Which is the east tunnel?" Lucius asked.

"That one," Siegfried pointed his slender index finger toward the tunnel on his left. He grabbed the small torch from the wall and began to climb down the wooden ladder.

Lucius followed him and peered into the dark pit. He swallowed hard, fears pouring into his mind. *What lies at the end of this dark tunnel, I wonder?* His hands clutched the topmost rung, and he began to descend into the darkness.

The descent was shorter than he had expected. The tunnel was humid and filled with the smell of wood and tree sap. In the torchlight, he saw the knotty walls of *Breninmaur's* trunk. Beetles and other small bugs crawled in and out of crevices in the wood. The wind howled inside the tunnel from the entrance hundreds of feet below. It would take them about a half hour to get to the forest floor, but Helmer had told them to make it out of Verdania before dawn lest they be caught.

Siegfried led the march down. The tunnel descended in a spiral, but at some points leveled out. It was a dreary walk due to all the bugs and sticky tree sap Lucius kept stepping on. They both remained silent as they walked. Lucius' thoughts were scattered most of the time. For a while, he thought about Aldron and the great kings who had reigned in the legendary city. *Would he ever be accepted as a king?* He seemed so insignificant and unfit to sit on the throne of Cervantes Nostra, but if it was Yéwa's will for him to do so, then perhaps the role of authority would come naturally.

Lucius ... the time has not yet come for you to enter the door.

He recalled the words of the light in his dream, who he understood to be Yéwa. When would the time come for him to assume the kingship as the prophecy foretold? Perhaps the elven seer, Lumiath, would know the answer. Helmer had been very discreet in revealing any details about the D'aryan exile; a fact that raised questions about Lumiath and whether or not the seer could be trusted.

"We are nearly there," Siegfried said, interrupting his thoughts.

"How can you be sure?" he peered ahead, seeing no change in the winding hollow they'd traversed for the last few minutes.

"I can smell the grass and humid air in the forest below. A few yards more and we shall be at the bottom." Siegfried quickened his pace, and the torch flickered wildly, casting eerie shadows along the tunnel walls.

Lucius followed in suit with a sudden surge of adrenaline. He was excited to see the world below Evingrad and perhaps meet another human for the first time in Sylvania.

As they hurried onward, the tunnel walls began to widen around them, and the ceiling rose above them. Lucius saw a dim light forming at the end of the tunnel. The torchlight quickly became useless as the wooden walls were swathed in the fading moonlight coming from *Breninmaur's* large entrance.

Siegfried muttered something in the elven tongue, and the torch's flame immediately dissipated, leaving a small trail of smoke.

The elf stopped a few steps before the entrance, peering through the fading darkness outside. Lucius crept beside him, seeing nothing but trees and shadows.

"What do you see, Siegfried?" he asked quietly.

"There are two Protectors in the forest, ten paces south and twelve paces east," his eyes twinkled in the dim light

"Should we use the diaphanouspheres?" He cringed at the thought of the prickling sensation the small sphere caused on his body.

Siegfried remained still and quiet for a moment. "No. The diaphanouspheres will not aid us."

"Why not?" Lucius looked out into the forest, thinking he saw a flicker of movement.

"They already know we're here."

Lucius searched the forest, looking for any sign of the Protectors. How had they spotted them so easily? And while they still stood inside the dark tunnel?

"We must go, Lucius—now!" Siegfried dashed outside in a split second, heading for the nearest tree.

Lucius quickly ran after him, adrenaline pumping in his veins. They ducked behind the nearest tree as an arrow whizzed by them, hitting the soft grass near their feet. Lucius grabbed his dagger, but Siegfried grasped his wrist.

"These are my brethren. They are merely serving Evingrad and protecting this sacred place," Siegfried tightened his grip as he said it.

Lucius snapped his hand free. "Well, who's going to protect us?"

Another arrow flew by them, landing a few inches from Lucius' torso into the tree trunk.

"We must flee to the Marble Gate. It is a few miles from here. The darkness can aid our escape, but not for long—the dawn is nigh. Follow my pace, brother." Siegfried ran from behind the tree and into the gray forest ahead before Lucius could protest.

He followed his elf brother, trying hard to keep up. Trees and dense foliage whipped past him, leaving small cuts on his face and arms. He looked behind him a few times during the chase, searching for their pursuers. They remained hidden in the shadow of the trees, but he heard the sound of arrows piercing the cold air and smacking on the barks of the trees all around him. Siegfried was swift, ducking to and fro in a zigzag pattern. Several times he lost sight of his brother's flittering green cloak among the trees, but seconds later he would reappear in front of him.

The sky overhead was beginning to illuminate with the coming dawn. The verdant colors around him burst into view, and for the first time, Lucius saw the beauty of the forest of Verdania. He wished he could sit and marvel at the landscape, but it would have to wait for another day.

A few yards ahead, he saw a small clearing rapidly approaching as they ran full speed. He looked behind him, fearing to spot an elf with a bow fixed on him, but he saw no one. They reached the clearing, and Lucius stopped abruptly. His knees ached, and he took labored breaths, feeling as though he might collapse at any moment. Siegfried continued to run through the clearing, but stopped a few feet away when he noticed his brother stooped over at the edge of the clearing.

"Have you been hit?" He ran over to him, keeping his eyes on the trees they had run through seconds before.

"I'm alright; I just needed to catch my breath." Lucius continued panting and looked up at the sky. The stars and moon had disappeared, and the sky was erupting with the sun's orange glow just below the horizon.

"The dawn is approaching, Lucius. Let us fly." Siegfried sprinted through the tall grass of the clearing.

Lucius, still out of breath, followed, despite the immense toll the chase was bearing on him. He hoped such long distance pursuits would not become common on this journey. The ability to sprint over long distances without experiencing fatigue was a natural gift endowed only to the elves, but he sorely desired it right now.

As he and Siegfried approached the center of the clearing, a sudden jolt struck Lucius in the back. The force of the blow knocked him to the ground. He realized he'd been shot with an arrow, but no pain accompanied it. The arrow was lodged in his backpack and hadn't pierced all the way through to his back. Siegfried helped him up, pulling out the arrow in one quick motion. Lucius looked toward the edge of the clearing and saw the shining armor of two Protectors. He could not make out their faces, but one was unusually short for an elf. Lucius immediately recognized him; it was Kiret.

He ran hastily, with Siegfried leading the way once again. They entered the claustrophobic space of the forest once more, hoping to gain some distance from their pursuers. Protruding roots from the ground and dense thickets were more abundant on this side of the forest, and Lucius found himself stumbling many times over them. He continued to follow his brother at a breakneck pace, afraid another arrow would find its mark more accurately than before.

"How much more?" he puffed at Siegfried, who did not seem tired at all.

"A mile or less," the elf said, avoiding a low branch in his path. "They will not continue the chase once we've reached the doors. Their concern is only for Verdania, not the lands beyond it."

"That's a relief." Lucius glanced over his shoulder again.

The sun suddenly came into view in the east, and its light splintered through the forest canopy. Lucius knew they would be easy targets for the Protectors now if they chose to slow their pace or stop before reaching the Marble Gate. A horn sounded behind them.

"What was that?" he gasped.

"More Protectors have joined the hunt, probably from the North." Siegfried pulled an arrow from his quiver and nocked it.

"I thought—"

"If it comes to it, I will only wound them," Siegfried cut in, darting his head from side to side.

Lucius hoped it would not come to that. His lungs burned from labored breathing, and his leg muscles ached tremendously. He worried he might collapse at any moment. A glint of white light became visible through the gaps of the trees. At first, he thought it was the sun, but as they raced closer to it, he realized it was the gleaming white marble of the Gate of Verdania. The Marble Gate was about a quarter of a mile away, and it joined with a great marble wall surrounding the southeastern border of the province of Verdania. The Gate stood on a hill just outside the forest's edge.

Lucius sped his pace, nearly matching the swiftness of Siegfried. "We are nearly there," he shouted excitably.

"Yes, but ascending that hill may prove treacherous. We shall be easy prey to the Protector's arrows," Siegfried said.

Lucius wanted to glance back and see how close the Protectors were, but he decided running as fast as his tired body could take him would be a better option.

The forest finally came to an end and poured into a small meadow before the hill. Wild daisies and corn poppies adorned the grass of the meadow—a tranquil scene immediately disturbed as they raced toward the hill. The incline of the hill was steeper than Lucius thought, which caused him to slow his pace as he ascended to the top. Siegfried climbed the hill without losing a step. Lucius clambered up to meet him, breathing hard and completely exhausted when he finished his ascent.

While he stood hunched over, attempting to catch his breath, he gazed at the splendor of the Marble Gate. They were around twelve feet in height and equally wide. Leaf shapes and elven runes were carved on the Gate's doors along with the crest of Evingrad, which was divided symmetrically where the Gate split in two. Two spherical posts rested on the top of the Gate where each side joined with the marble wall.

As he stood examining the structure, Siegfried was crouched at the foot of the wall, fiddling with something.

Lucius limped beside him and saw he was tying a noose on a silver rope. When the knot was finished, Siegfried quickly lassoed the noose over one of the posts. He tugged on the rope to make sure it was secure.

"We must make haste. Climb the rope, brother," Siegfried cried.

Lucius didn't hesitate. He grabbed the rope and began to hoist himself onto the stone door. But he easily lost his footing on the smooth marble and struggled to climb up.

"Is there no way to open this gate?" He strained as he ascended and slid again.

"No. The Protectors are the only elves who know the words that will open the doors," Siegfried replied, exchanging glances between Lucius and the edge of the forest.

Suddenly, an arrow smacked the wall beside them and startled Lucius. Siegfried instinctively swirled around, taking aim with his bow at the direction where the arrow had flown from. At the foot of the hill, they both saw Kiret. His bow was fixed on Lucius, and his forehead creased as he stared at them.

"Drop your bow, Siegfried. I do not wish to harm you," he said, unflinching.

Siegfried hesitated for a moment, but then lowered his bow and let it fall on the ground. Lucius felt a nauseating feeling building up in the pit of his stomach. Their journey had come to its end prematurely. Kiret slowly walked up the hill, keeping his bow level with his target. The shorter elf reached the top and stared at them with fierce eyes. No sympathy seemed to dwell in his glaring blue eyes. Lucius felt uneasy from the awkward silence between them, and the fact no other Protectors had come out of the forest worried him. It was unlikely Kiret had easily forgotten the humiliation Lucius brought upon him or the untimely defeat at Siegfried's hand during the tournament. *Will he kill us here on this lonely hill?* The sound of a horn in the distance broke the silence.

"The others are coming for you," Kiret spoke softly. "There will be no escaping that way."

Lucius looked at the rope and the manner of escape he was referring to. He was right. There would be no escape.

"But there is another way." Kiret uttered some words in the elven tongue, and the Marble Gate creaked to life. The doors slowly opened toward them and revealed golden plains stretching for miles.

"Why are you doing this?" Siegfried asked, knowing the punishment Kiret would suffer for his insubordination.

Kiret lowered his bow, suddenly looking tired and old. "I believe in the prophecy. I always have. Nineteen winters have passed since I found you in the shadow of this gate and took you in. And now, here you are whence you came. I am ready to let you go."

Lucius looked at the Protector with newfound respect. He had completely misjudged Kiret. This honor bestowed on them was beyond anything he would have expected from the elf warrior. "Thank you," he simply replied.

Kiret bowed his head. The horn sounded again, closer this time, "You must go now. The doors must be shut before the others arrive. Run!"

Siegfried quickly grabbed his bow and summoned the silver rope. The noose loosened, and it dropped in Lucius' hands. He ran with Siegfried to the other side of the great wall of Verdania, but not before looking back. Kiret stood visibly in the opening as the Marble Gate began to shut, lifting an open palm to wish them farewell. With a low boom, the doors shut, and for the first time in his life, Lucius was outside of the realm of the D'aryan elves.

SIX

Dragon Slayers

Lord Memnon, dressed in his ceremonial garb, stood at the altar of his ancestor, Scipio, speaking in *shak'teph*—the dark tongue of the necromancers and sorcerers of the Draknoir. Each word hissed from his forked tongue and echoed in the hall situated at the heart of the Nasgothar fortress. The interior of the sorcerer's hall resembled the inside of a cavern; it was dark and rocky protrusions filled the floor, walls, and ceiling. At the center of the room there was an octagonal table where a hand-drawn map of Azuleah lay. On the opposite wall to the hall's entrance stood a brazier where Memnon knelt with his arms outspread. He had been meditating continually the past few days, trying to summon the spirit of his ancestor in order to master the black arts as he once did. His concentration was interrupted when the chamber doors swung open.

Genghis Ikben, his trusted general, entered the sacred altar with a gallant stride that displayed his willful haughtiness. Memnon turned to face him, noting his appearance. His face was a dark green hue with scales covering his entire body. Plated armor with sharp spikes protruding from the shoulders shielded his torso and thick leather greaves covered his legs along with ironclad boots. The warrior's eyes were yellow with dark pupils at the center. Two rows of half-inch horns ran from his forehead to the back of his head—a sign of high rank among Draknoir warriors. Memnon didn't have the rows of horns; instead, he bore two long horns just below his lower lip that curled inward beneath his chin. The horns, along with his darker scale pigment, were the mark of a great sorcerer.

"My liege, I have tidings from our encampment at the mouth of the Feilon River," Genghis hissed.

He raised a brow, which was nothing more than a few tiny spikes above his eye. "Tidings? Well, I would very much like to hear it."

"My lord—"

"After you've told me why you chose to enter this domain so brusquely," Memnon interrupted with pleasure.

Genghis frowned, trying to find the right words. "The tidings were of great importance—"

"Wrong! It matters not to me if this fortress is being attacked by Dermont's entire army. You will not enter this sacred lair unless I order you to. Is that understood, Genghis?" Memnon chided, his eyes piercing into the younger Draknoir.

"Yes, my lord. Forgive me." Genghis bowed his head.

Memnon lifted his chin in victory. "Good. Now, tell me your tidings."

"Three nights past, a scout from our encampment near the bank of the Feilon spotted a battalion of Aldronians marching through Ithileo Forest. There were fifteen men, all on horseback and carrying the flag of the Drachengarde." Genghis bared his teeth as he spoke the name.

"Dragon slayers?" Memnon asked, gritting his sharp teeth. "Have they camped in Ithileo?"

"We believe so, my lord. There is no doubt that they are headed to Ghadarya by following the Dulan River northward," Genghis said confidently.

It seemed foolish for the Slayers to be traveling from the eastern side of the Dulan. Something was amiss.

"How many men did you say were in this battalion?"

"Fifteen, sir."

"That is not nearly enough men to cross into Ghadarya Vale and overtake the mighty aeries of the dragons." Memnon clasped his hands behind his back and paced the dark chamber, trying to make sense of the humans' tactics.

"The Drachengarde were formidable adversaries, my lord. One of those dragon slayers is as formidable as five Aldronian soldiers, or so it is said," Genghis suggested.

The suggestion fell on deaf ears. Memnon glared at his subordinate as if he had spoken blasphemy.

"The Drachengarde may be formidable, but they are not so foolish to believe that they will be victorious over a flight of dragons with so few in their ranks. No, Genghis. There is more to this than we are seeing."

"What does my lord suggest?"

"Monitor the dragon slayers. Have your scouts track their every move along Ithileo. If they are indeed headed to Ghadarya, attack them before they reach the Dulan. Leave none alive, if that is their plan."

"And if their intentions are not set for Ghadarya?" Genghis' eyes shone like fiery gems, the hunger for blood and war was saturated in them. It pleased Memnon.

"Report their movements to me, General. That is your order for now, if they stray from the Dulan." He turned his back on him. "Shut the doors on your way out."

"My lord," Genghis bowed his head and walked out of the sacred place, a resounding boom accompanying his exit.

What are you plotting Dermont? He sought the answer from his god, Nergoth. Memnon stood at the foot of the brazier, raising his arms before the idol of Nergoth. He dispelled all thought from his mind and began speaking in *shak'teph* again. Nergoth stood above him, carved from the black, stone wall behind the altar. His eyes were rubies, and his face was contorted in a snarl with long fangs resembling stalactites. Lord Memnon knelt before the ghastly effigy, entranced in the darkness. Images began to appear within his mind.

He saw the edge of the forest of Ithileo shaded in gray, lifeless colors. The members of the Drachengarde lay in the underbrush, resting from their long journey through the woods. Some slept, while a few tended the dying embers of the fire they encircled. His sight shifted from the encampment. Within the forest, there was a separate encampment. Nearly two hundred Aldronian soldiers hid in the forest beneath a blanket of grass and leaves. They held their swords and bows at the ready, watching the Slayers with sleepless eyes.

An ambush! How clever, Dermont. The moment I send the Draknoir scourge, you would make quick work of them.

Memnon opened his eyes, pleased by the revelation from Nergoth. He looked down and saw the bloodstained brazier upon the altar. A gift was in order for this generous foresight. He pulled out a hooked dagger tucked under the sash of his garb. And after rolling up his sleeve, he made a deep gash in his reptilian skin. Violet blood oozed from the cut as he positioned it above the brazier. The sharp pain from squeezing his arm so the blood could pour onto the brazier gave him an unnatural pleasure.

When the brazier was half-filled with the dark blood, Memnon sucked his wound until the blood stopped flowing out. He uttered a few words in *shak'teph* and suddenly the brazier lit with a roaring fire. Flames danced just below Nergoth's chin, casting an eerie shadow on the idol's face. A foul smell of burnt blood filled the chamber. Memnon sniffed the pagan incense with delight.

"Let the blood of your subjects burn as it has on this altar, Dermont, for invading my lands and opposing Nergoth's power," he uttered to himself. Joppa's end was nigh, and soon the ashes of the Black Dragon would be rekindled to a great blue flame. Soon his bloodlust would be satiated, and darkness would sweep the land beneath Nergoth's black wings.

Crickets chirped all around the outskirts of Ithileo forest and created a soothing melody that tempted Silas to fall into a deep, peaceful slumber, but he forced himself to stay awake. The success of their mission was at stake. For days they had been encamped in the wilderness, waiting for a Draknoir raid. He had seen the Draknoir scouts in the hills and knew an attack was imminent. The other Slayers had seen them too. Asher was the first to spot a speck of movement on the bluffs just below the Onyx Mountains and anxiously reported it to him. Perhaps they were mobilizing an attack from Nasgothar, which could take days or even weeks. Nonetheless, something was amiss. The Draknoir were bloodthirsty fiends who did not hesitate in hurling a siege on their enemies. Could they have seen the king's army in the forest? It was too great a distance from the bluffs to Ithileo for a scout to catch sight of the army, especially hidden as they were. Maybe he was thinking about it too much, but it continued to add to his uneasiness.

The night air was arid, and a slight chill in the breeze caused him to shiver. He unfolded the blanket in front of him and wrapped it tightly around his shoulders. He pulled out a gold ring attached to a silver necklace beneath his armor and turned it many times between his fingers. It was a comforting habit he often succumbed to when worry gnawed at him. The ring belonged to his mother, but he forced himself not to think of her. She would be unhappy to know her son lacked courage. Silas knew he had to be brave.

The loud snoring and shuffling bodies around the camp interrupted his thoughts, and he quickly tucked the ring back inside his chainmail shirt. Moonlight shone on the camp like a bright torch revealing their positions. They were naked out here in the wilderness. Silas stood up and threw another log in the fire. He peered into the dark gloom of the forest. Somewhere inside the Aldronian, warriors watched the Drachengarde in seclusion. Their protection did not comfort him. He looked eastward, toward the black bluffs at the foot of the Onyx Mountains. There was not the slightest movement, save the swaying branches of the fir trees at the edge of the camp.

Silas, you worrisome fool.

He sighed and lay down beside the fire. The slow crackling of the flames put his mind at ease while he stared at the stars above. Their glimmering light caused his eyelids to droop. An owl hooted from within the forest, and he quickly sat up, gripping the hilt of his sword. He cursed under his breath and lay down again. Something else stirred in the forest, but he ignored it and set his mind on his sleep. Eventually, darkness overtook him, and he drifted into disturbing dreams of swords clashing upon shields.

A loud horn blast sounded in the camp, and Silas awoke from his slumber. The men all around him stood up and unsheathed their swords. He looked toward the edge of the forest and saw them. Ranks of Draknoir poured out from within the dark forest. They carried serrated blades and wooden shields with the insignia of Nasgothar—a black face with jagged teeth and crimson eyes—seared on the surface. Their blades were wet with blood, and their yellow eyes glowed in the darkness.

Silas rose to his feet and picked up his broadsword from the ground. It was longer than most swords and made from *efydd,* ideal for cutting through the thick scales of dragons. He unsheathed the sword from its scabbard and joined his fellow Drachengarde. At his command, the men formed a defensive line to meet the first wave of Draknoir invading the camp.

"At the ready," he yelled. The Slayers took their battle stances and held up their shields. They were all superior swordsmen, more strenuously trained than any Aldronian soldier. But the upper hand belonged to the Draknoir, whose numbers were staggering.

The first wave hit them hard. Silas and his second-in-command, Asher, fought beside each other, fatally slashing many of the ungodly beasts. Asher, an older man with a graying beard and steel blue eyes, wielded his sword with ferocious vigor. Two Draknoir warriors attacked him simultaneously from his right and left. He blocked the right one's sword and stabbed the left one in the neck before the Draknoir warrior could strike. Silas then beheaded the creature on his left with a swift swing of his sword. More Draknoir approached them, but they quickly disposed of them in minutes. The Drachengarde survived the first wave without any casualties But as Silas looked toward the forest, he saw dozens of Draknoir assembling and preparing to attack them. He looked all around, desperately searching for the blue and white colors of the Aldronian army's uniforms. But he only saw the scruffy, worn tunics and breastplates of the fourteen Drachengarde around him. He feared the worst, either the Aldronian soldiers had not heard the sound of their horns or they had been wiped out by a Draknoir ambush. The bloodstained swords of the evil minions of Nasgothar a few yards away confirmed the latter.

The Draknoir charged toward them, and in seconds an eruption of clashing steel was heard throughout Ithileo. Silas and his men were surrounded by the cruel beasts. Asher stood behind him, flailing his sword in every direction and avoiding every Draknoir attack. Gradually, their defensive line was divided, and Silas could not see any of the Slayers, except for Asher. He fought harder, slicing and tearing each Draknoir fiend close enough to touch. Asher did the same. Their combined ruthlessness held the ground, and the few Draknoir left retreated to the forest. Blood and carcasses lay all around; he felt nauseated at the growing stench. The victory seemed theirs for a moment, until Silas realized he and Asher were the only two Slayers still standing. The other thirteen men had fallen and laid among the dark corpses of their enemies.

Before Silas and Asher could grieve for their fallen friends, a horn was sounded from the edge of the forest. His heart sank at the sight of two ranks of Draknoir archers lined up behind the warriors who had retreated. They had not retreated, as he thought, but had reassembled their line and now had the advantage of long bows.

"My lord, we must flee," Asher wheezed as his chest heaved from exhaustion.

"There is nowhere to run, my friend. This is our last stand," he gripped his broadsword tight and held it up in view of the Draknoir. The sword shone in the moonlight and many of the dark fiends growled at the sight.

The archers fixed their bows on the two warriors and fired. The arrows whizzed in the night toward their targets but did not find their mark as the two veteran warriors dodged and parried them with their swords. Draknoir warriors charged once more toward them and were accompanied by a second volley of arrows. Silas moved quickly to avoid the sting of the enemy's shots. But he was not fast enough, and an arrow struck him in his right shoulder. He cried in pain and fell to his knees. To his right, he saw Asher stumble to the ground and fall on his back with a solitary arrow standing erect from his chest. Tears welled in his eyes as he crawled to his friend's side.

The Draknoir warriors slowed their pace towards them, knowing his plight was grave and there would be no escaping the impending doom. Silas held up Asher's head and looked into the old man's eyes. The once vibrant blue he had remembered was quickly fading away, as the old Slayer breathed in short, erratic spurts. He gripped Silas' hand in his cold, clammy fingers with what little strength he had left, fighting the unwelcome darkness ahead.

"You fought bravely today, my lord ... you've brought no shame to the King or me," Asher gasped.

"Be still, Asher, old friend. Do not let the darkness take you, please."

"My time has come, my Prince. You must flee ... to the Feilon River ... all hope is lost if you die beside me ... go."

"I cannot leave you here." Silas looked up to see the Draknoir slowly approaching down the hill at the foot of the forest. Their yellow eyes glared at him like vultures encircling a carcass.

"You must go now, my lord ... fly. Fly to the Feilon," he said with a strained voice. Then his grip on Silas loosed, and his body grew limp. A final rasping breath escaped his lips as his eyes looked toward the night sky.

Silas felt rage and sorrow fill his mind as he held onto Asher's hand among the hewn bodies of Draknoir and Drachengarde in the night. His mentor and friend had been taken away by the demonic beasts who now wished to lay a final blow upon him. Everything within his soul urged him to fight them to avenge Asher's death and the death of so many innocents slain by their filthy hands. But he could not deny Asher's last request. He must flee to Feilon River. If he died in this field, there would be no one left to avenge his fallen friend, his fellow Slayers, or more importantly, his sister. He fought back the painful memory of her death so many years ago and willed himself to stand—to run.

Silas stood amid the stench of blood and death around him. The glowing yellow eyes of Nergoth's followers gleamed as they gathered a few feet from him. They watched him with crooked smiles that revealed jagged teeth. Their mouths uttered foul words he could not understand, but their eyes and movements revealed their intentions.

"You will not bring me down this night, nor any night, before the blood of your kind runs fresh on my sword," Silas growled. He grabbed the arrow lodged within his shoulder and yanked it out in defiance.

The Draknoir warriors snarled and raised their swords, ready to pounce on him. Silas gripped his sword tight in his right hand, and with his left he searched for a smooth, iridescent pebble inside his belt pouch. He clutched the pebble in his hand and whispered the words, "*qui cum coram caeco.*" He then threw the stone near the Draknoirs' feet. A bright flash engulfed the unsuspecting fiends, and they shrieked in horror, blinded by the light before them.

Silas ran through the night, toward the faint sound of rushing water from the Feilon. The angry cries of the Draknoir filled the air as they realized what had transpired. He heard them running behind him and felt their arrows fly all around. His heart beat rapidly through the trek downhill to the banks of the river. A thick fog suddenly surrounded him, shielding him from the sight of his pursuers. He glanced back, seeing only fog, but hearing the war cries close behind.

When his legs began to tire, he heard the rushing waters of the Feilon less than a yard ahead of him. A few feet further he saw the glimmering moonlight on the water at the bank's edge. He stopped abruptly on the bank and sheathed his sword. The current was too strong to allow him passage to the other side. *Nergoth's blood! What now, Asher, old friend?*

The Draknoir were approaching fast, and he did not have time to think. He sighed deeply.

"Yéwa, protect me," Silas cried before he dove into the murky waters of the Feilon River.

Cold, rushing water overtook him as he plummeted to the river bottom. He fought the current and rose to the surface. He gasped for air while the river pushed him westward to the roaring waters of the Dulan. At the bank where he dove, the Draknoir warriors watched him float away and cursed at him in their black tongue. The longbow archers began to shoot their arrows at him, but he was out of range.

Before Silas could allow the thought of victory to enter his mind, he felt the rage of the river's current pull him under. He flailed his arms and kicked his legs to ascend once more. Within moments, he resurfaced and realized he had reached the fierce river rapids of the Feilon. Black rocks jutted from the surface of the river and around each bend. His body was hurled to and fro on several quick drops as the Feilon narrowed within a gorge. By some miracle, he was able to keep his head above the water and fight the weariness in his body. Every muscle in his arms and legs ached in agony with each stroke to avoid drowning in the dark waters. Before he could reach the end of the river's torrents, another drop sent him freefalling beneath the water, and his head smacked a stone underwater. Pain swelled from his forehead, and a cloud of blood formed in the water. He fought to stay conscious, flapping his arms to reach the surface again. Humid air entered his nostrils as his injured head rose above the water. The river current had slowed, and he swam toward the bank, feeling nausea and pain ripple throughout his body.

Must stay awake ... please stay awake. He reached for the edge of the bank—half of his body still floating in the water. The moon shone on the bank, revealing the many scrapes and cuts on his arms and face from the fury of the Feilon. He clawed the dirt, pulling himself towards the grassy knoll beside the river.

But before he could feel the tufts of grass at his fingertips, his entire body went numb and darkness swirled all around him.

SEVEN

A New Dawn in Sylvania

The sun rose on the green fields outside of Verdania, ushering in a new day to young Lucius and his elven brother, Siegfried. The elf had been awake an hour before the dawn, plotting the best course to take on their way to Sylvania. Meanwhile, Lucius lay asleep beside a smoldered campfire wrapped in a wool blanket.

"Lucius," Siegfried shook him, "it is time for us to head on."

Lucius rubbed his eyes with his hands and yawned loudly, "Already? The sun has just risen. Don't you elves believe in a good night's sleep?"

"Why yes of course. But the sun beckons for us to wake and begin our journey. Come now, get up." Siegfried pulled the wool blanket off of him, stuffing it inside his brother's pack.

Lucius groaned as he sat up, "Fine, I'm awake. But now you have the honor of feeding me."

"Fair enough." Siegfried pulled something from his pouch and handed it to him. "I picked these while you snored on like a mountain bear."

"Berries?" He furrowed his brow. "Is this all? This is a poor substitute for what I would qualify as breakfast."

"They are Marsolan berries, easily capable of filling an ogre's stomach, even one as hungry as you," he remarked snidely.

"Very funny." Lucius crammed the berries in his mouth as he stood up. They tasted incredibly sweet, and he found himself quite satiated after swallowing them.

"Ha! You were right; these are filling," he said.

Siegfried smiled delightedly.

"So, which way is the fastest to Sylvania." Lucius looked to the east.

"The Barren Road is the fastest way to Sylvania. It heads eastward to Sylvania and splits off to Jun-Jun Pass in the north and Joppa to the south. If we head out now, we can make it to Sylvania before the noontime." The tall elf began to walk.

"Off we go, then." Lucius grabbed his pack and slung it over his shoulder.

The walk to the Barren Road was a brisk one. Siegfried always managed to keep a faster pace than Lucius and occasionally would break into short sprints, to his disdain. They reached the road before the sun was directly above them. The Barren Road was no more than a flattened dirt road, which stuck out in the green landscape all about them. Lucius noticed the wagon wheel trails embedded in the dirt and wondered if they would run into any wayward travelers like themselves on the way. A warm breeze began to blow his messy hair from his eyes and until then, he hadn't noticed how hot it was outside. It was summer after all, but in Verdania, the temperature always seemed just right, even in the winter. Never too warm or cold, he thought. But out here in the open country, he felt the perspiration on his brow and the heat of the sun upon him.

In about four hours, they had covered nearly twenty miles on foot. It was a silent walk for the most part, a few remarks here and there about the landscape or a short conversation on what they would do once they reached the city. Never anything deeper than the present matters, but Lucius had become accustomed to it while living amongst the elves. They were a quiet people, always introspective and calm. Many times he wished he could be the same, but he wanted to talk about his dreams and his fears. Helmer was the only elf who he had ever talked to about such things, but even he could not relate fully to his experiences since he was not a man. As much as he loved his adoptive elven family and his home in Evingrad, he longed to be with his own kind. *I must know my people ... my true family.* He wondered if he would ever meet his father or mother on this quest. Could they still be alive or had they fallen by the sword of Draknoir hunters? He tried not to think too much on it, but Helmer's revelations in his study had left him longing for answers.

"Look, Lucius," Siegfried interrupted his thoughts, "the city of Sylvania is within sight."

Lucius looked to the east at the faraway city of Sylvania. He could make out thatched roofs and billows of smoke coming from chimney tops. A wooden fence surrounded the small city that housed brick towers with guards sitting inside. The gateway to the city was wide open, but would no doubt close before evening.

"I hope they have some decent food; I'm famished." Lucius quickened his pace on the road.

"I'm sure their accommodations will be suitable for the both of us," Siegfried replied.

The two travelers reached the fork in the Barren Road, which split three ways: north, south, and eastward towards the city. Lucius instinctively looked to his right and left, searching for others traveling on the road, but saw none. His eyes also searched the landscape to the North. The green hills and fields continued on for miles, but beyond them, towards Jun-Jun Pass, he thought he saw a gray line on the horizon. A slight shiver ran up his spine with an uneasiness he could not shake. Siegfried felt his brother's tension and asked about it. Lucius assured him everything was fine, convincing himself it was nothing.

When they reached the gate of Sylvania, two guards patrolling each side of the gateway walked up to them. They wore heavy armor with broadswords sheathed at their sides. Bronze helmets with several dents and stains adorned both of their heads, looking rather inadequate to shield them from a blow to the skull.

"What business do you have in Sylvania?" the heavyset guard asked.

Lucius quickly tried to think of an answer, but Siegfried spoke before he could say a word.

"We are merely here for food and lodging, kind sir. Our travels have made us weary, and we are in need of rest," he bowed his head slightly.

Lucius forced back a smile, "Indeed."

The guard squinted his eyes and glanced at his younger and thinner partner who eyed them suspiciously.

"Where have you come from, my lords?" the younger guard asked.

"From Verdania. We made flight only a night ago," Lucius replied with slight annoyance.

"Verdania?" The older one looked perplexed and apprehensive. "Not a soul has come from that land to Sylvania in many years. The D'aryan elves are a secluded people. They've no desire to leave their elven sanctuaries for the likes of this place. Now stop telling lies and tell us where you're from."

"We have no reason to lie," Lucius cried. "We do hail from the realm of the D'aryan elves and would appreciate it kindly if you would let us pass."

"Let you pass?" The bigger guard placed his hand on the hilt of his sword. "We've had a great deal of trouble in this city in the days past, mostly due to wary travelers like you. Why, just two nights ago old Ren was robbed blind while he was away at the Crimson Eagle drinking a pint. All his wife's jewelry was taken, along with his pack mule, Ethyl. The thief has yet to be caught, but many believe it was an outsider that did it. I happen to believe the same, so you can understand my reluctance to let you in, friends."

"I assure you that we aren't thieves or troublemakers," Siegfried said calmly. "My friend speaks truth about where we come from. But if this is a matter of trust, we would gladly leave our weapons and belongings here with you."

"What?" Lucius failed to see his logic.

Siegfried winked an eye at him.

"Actually, that sounds like a great idea," the younger guard smirked.

"Hand over your weapons and belongings and we'll let you in," the older guard said.

Siegfried took off his quiver from his back and his bow, setting them down at the guards' feet. Lucius sighed and did the same. They both also left their swords and backpacks at the gate. Both of the guards grinned and gestured toward the entrance to Sylvania.

"Enjoy your stay, friends. You may pick up your personal items when you leave this fine settlement." The heavyset guard gave their belongings to the younger guard who scampered off into the city.

"I'll be expecting our belongings to be back in perfect condition, sir," Lucius glared at the guard.

"No need to worry, young lad. Clay is making sure of that as we speak."

"Come," Siegfried motioned for Lucius to follow him into the city.

Lucius looked back at the guard, who simply grinned and tipped his helmet at him.

"Why do I have the feeling that we won't be getting our things back?" he said.

"Don't worry about it, Lucius. Our belongings will be kept safe while we accomplish the task at hand. We won't need weapons within these walls, trust me."

"You aren't the least bit worried that one of those insolent guards will sell your bow? It's made of an exquisite wood and was given to you by your father and by his father before him. Generations of Silverharts have held that bow, Siegfried, and now some Sylvania brute might be selling it to buy a round of beers."

"Are you quite finished?" Siegfried raised a brow. "The bow is an heirloom, and it shall be returned, I assure you, either by Clay, the guardsman, or by my own intervention. Right now, we must find a place to rest and something to eat. You are still famished, aren't you?"

"Yes, I am. I could really use some fresh bread or a pint of ginger tea." He had forgotten the growls coming from his stomach.

"Well, then, let us find a suitable place to whet your appetite, brother," Siegfried smiled.

At first glance, the city looked nothing more than a big village when compared to a city as grand as Evingrad with its great spire, marble buildings, and elegant effigies. But there was a warmth in the straw-roofed, brick houses and cobblestone paths of Sylvania that Evingrad lacked. *It's so ... human.* There was no elegance in the worn clothes or tired expressions of men walking to their homes after a long day's work. Neither were the young children walking upright nor minding their manners as they chased stray chickens in the streets with jubilant faces. The differences between the D'aryan elves and the race of men were very distinct to Lucius as he carefully observed the townsfolk. All his life he had felt like an outsider among the elves, trying as best as he could to be their equal and earn their trust. Helmer and Siegfried had done their best to help him be of like mind, teaching him their ways and accepting him as one of their own. But even they realized he was a man—an emotional creature who perhaps was incapable of becoming as peaceful or wise as they.

His lack of communion with the elf spirit, D'arya, also kept him from understanding the sacred way of life exclusive to the elves. However, upon learning of Yéwa, he no longer felt alone in the world. This human God was the maker of his kind and someone—according to Helmer—who would help him on this quest, but when or how Yéwa would do so was unknown to Helmer, and even less to Lucius.

Siegfried searched the city for an inn while Lucius followed and surveyed the sights around him. They walked into a bustling marketplace before reaching the center of the city. A blacksmith's tent was set up on their left, and they heard the steel clang of a hammer beating on an anvil. To their right, was the pub known as the Crimson Eagle, from which the sweet smell of ale and beer wafted into their nostrils. Ambitious vendors selling food, trinkets, and various fabrics called out to them from their stands and parked wagons, hoping to make some money. Siegfried politely refused each of the vendors while Lucius looked at the items thoughtfully and, after a scowl from his brother, also refused.

A few feet outside the marketplace they came to Sylvania's center square where two statues stood: an elf holding the D'aryan standard and a man holding a shield with the crest of Aldron. Around the square stood two-story buildings serving as homes and businesses for residents of the city. Lucius surveyed each of the structures but could not find any that offered lodging. They walked around the square and eventually followed the city's main road up a steep hill where a few more buildings overlooked the town square. Among the buildings assembled on the hill, there was an inn with a wooden sign above the door bearing the words, "Griffin's Head." The wooden door had a burnt etching of a griffin with its wings outspread.

"It looks like a comfortable place to spend the evening, wouldn't you say?" Lucius looked over at Siegfried, trying to read the elf's expressionless face.

"I think it should be suitable for the both of us." He walked up the stone steps to the door of the inn and opened it.

Lucius sighed and followed him inside. It seemed as though he was always following his brother into the unknown, and he hoped it would not be a common occurrence on this journey. This was the first time in Lucius' life where he felt as though he should take the lead. He was the reason they had left *Breninmaur,* and it was his dreams about the Black Dragon that were intertwined with the future of Azuleah, not Siegfried's. Lucius knew Siegfried was just following their father's instructions by taking charge, but perhaps there was some way to take the lead without being forceful or offending his older brother.

The interior of Griffin's Head was rather dark for so early in the day, and it reeked of smoke. A fireplace on the far wall of the inn was burning brightly, and tables close to the fire were seated with weary travelers patiently awaiting a home-cooked meal. A young waitress with red hair tied in a bun poured drinks for the guests and simultaneously swept loose strands of her hair away from her face with her free hand. When she had finished serving a portly man with a straw hat, Siegfried called out to her. She looked over at the two figures standing by the doorway and scrutinized them, perhaps to see if she recognized them or not. When she found she had no recognition of them, she walked over with a pitcher in her left hand and asked politely how she could help them.

"We were wondering if there are any vacancies in your establishment, madam," Siegfried said in a soft voice.

The girl looked at him quizzically, "I'm not sure if there are any rooms available, my lords. I am but a servant myself. Nicole, the innkeeper, is behind the counter if you would like to speak to him."

"Thank you very much." Lucius quickly walked to the back of the inn with Siegfried following and approached the petite-woman with short-cropped hair behind the counter. Nicole was sitting on a stool counting money when Lucius appeared across the counter from her.

"Excuse me, madam. We would like a place to stay for the night if there is a room you could spare," Lucius delighted in subtly taking the lead from Siegfried, who it seemed did not mind in the least.

The innkeeper looked up at him, annoyed someone had interrupted her counting. "A room, aye? Yes, I believe there is an extra room, but only one bed to spare inside of it."

"One bed?" Lucius frowned.

"We shall take the room. How much will it be?" Siegfried pulled out a small leather pouch from inside his jerkin.

"Eh, let's see ... two solidi ought to do it," the innkeeper replied.

Siegfried set the gold coins on the countertop along with the rest of Nicole's earnings. The woman pulled out a small silver key from a pocket on her dress, handing it to Lucius who stretched out his arm anxiously.

"Go up the stairs and into the hallway; it will be the fourth room to your right. Enjoy your stay at Griffin's Head, gents." Nicole winked and returned to counting her money.

Parallel to the counter, on the opposite wall, was a wooden staircase Lucius had not seen when they had entered the dining area. The two Evingrad warriors made their way through the tables and walked up the stairs. The steps creaked, each one louder than the last as they ascended to the second floor of the inn and entered a narrow hallway with doors on each wall. Following Nicole's directions, they found their room near the end of the hall on their right. Lucius fit the silver key beneath the handle and opened the door. The room was dim, its only means of illumination seeping from the cracks within the window shutters. Lucius walked to the window, pushing back the shutters and allowing the light to bring new life to the desolate room.

The bedroom was finely furnished, more so than the dining area downstairs. The single bed inside the room was covered in a blue satin quilt with comfortable, down-filled pillows. On the floor next to the bed lay a fine knit rug with swirling designs along its edges. Perhaps imported from Joppa, Lucius thought. There was also an oak nightstand with small griffins carved on its single drawer. A silver candleholder with three unlit candles sat on the nightstand. Directly above the candles hung an oil painting of an elf lying beneath a maple tree playing an ocarina.

"I don't believe I've ever seen you play an ocarina before, Sieg," he said, flashing a smile at Siegfried who still stood solemnly at the door. "You are rather gifted with music, brother."

"Not nearly as gifted as my mother." Siegfried entered the room, staring at the portrait. "Her favorite instruments were the ocarina and the Numan harp. I remember the gentle melodies she played for me in the evenings and also the spirited overtures in my father's study. She was truly gifted as a musician. I merely carry on a fraction of her legacy with my telyn."

"I wish I could have heard her music," he admitted.

The corners of Siegfried's mouth turned upward slightly. "Yes. I wish that as well."

There was pause in the conversation as Siegfried stared at portrait.

"So, who gets the honor of sleeping on this comfortable bed?" Lucius asked, hoping to break the awkward silence.

"You may rest on the bed, brother. This rug looks comfortable enough for me to lay on," as the elf looked down at his feet.

"What? Are you sure you'd rather sleep on that dusty thing and not on this perfectly comfortable bed?" Lucius asked, jumping onto the bed with his arms spread wide.

Siegfried laughed, "Before men even set foot in Azuleah, my kind rested on the soft roots of trees and green down of grassy meadows."

"You elves, always delighting in the simple and never indulgent. I suppose there's no complaint on my part, seeing as I will be getting a good night's sleep." Lucius propped a pillow beneath his head.

"I am not so much concerned about sleep at the moment as I am a good meal. The food in the dining area smelled quite delicious; we should eat now. We have someone to meet very soon." Siegfried's voice trailed off as he walked towards the door and into the hallway.

"Someone to meet?" Lucius questioned without any response. His stomach growled, and his thoughts centered solely on food. He got up quickly and rushed to meet up with his elven brother downstairs.

After a hearty meal and some ale, Lucius and Siegfried went back into town. Lucius would have preferred resting in their room, since he was very full and satiated, but Siegfried insisted they meet someone in the city before sunset. He had been refused the identity of the mystery man or woman they were to meet, his brother quietly dismissing all of his questions.

The city was quiet and there weren't many people wandering the streets like before. He wondered if the guards' tale about trouble in the city was a reason for the early retiring of the townsfolk. He suddenly wished he had his sword, despite the fact the sun had not yet vanished into the horizon. Siegfried led the way from The Griffin's Head down the cobblestone road and into the marketplace. Vendors had gone home for the day, their stands lay barren and their wagons were nowhere to be seen. They walked toward the gate of Sylvania, which Lucius noticed from this range had been shut and bolted for the evening.

When the two arrived near The Crimson Eagle, Siegfried stopped. Laughter and commotion came out from inside the pub's opened doors. Drunks, no doubt, Lucius thought. He turned to his elven brother, but realized he had begun walking in the opposite direction to the blacksmith's tent. Siegfried peered inside the tent but saw no one inside. A black anvil stood like a miniature monolith inside the tent. Hilts, pommels, and unfinished weapons lay scattered on the floor.

"Are you looking for the old blacksmith?" a voice behind Siegfried asked.

Siegfried turned around and saw an old man with a long beard reaching to his chest looking over at him, "Yes, I am."

The old man cleared his throat and pointed a crooked finger at the Crimson Eagle. "After work, he always stops to get a pint or two ... or three," he cackled, clearly drunk himself.

"Thanks for the tip, old man," Lucius said, standing near enough to smell the ale on the man's breath.

"Love to be of help," he gave a quick gesture as if tipping an invisible hat on his ragged white head. The old man jogged away, tripping and stumbling every so often before he was out of sight.

"A blacksmith—of course. My mind has been all over the place and I forgot about that," Lucius confessed, thinking of the prophecy Helmer had recited to him.

"What sort of things were you lingering on?" Siegfried asked with inquisitive eyes.

A flash of Kraegyn's sapphire eyes entered into his mind. "Nothing. I ... I've been thinking about my family and whether or not there are any who are still alive. I've also been a bit overwhelmed by seeing my own kind wandering about rather than the D'aryan elves. It's all so new and different."

"I understand your feelings, Lucius. Do not worry. There will be much that you and I will encounter on this quest that will be different than anything either of us is used to," the elf placed his hand on his shoulder. "I assure you that if there are any relatives of yours who still live, we shall find them."

Lucius nodded, "Thank you, Siegfried."

"*Croesi,*" Siegfried welcomed him in the elven language. "Now, let us tend to the pressing matters at hand."

They approached the opened doorway of the Crimson Eagle and entered. The air inside was humid, and the tavern had an eerie glow provided by the fireplace. Drunks in the rear of the main room broke into song, hitting their mugs together and downing whole pints. Lucius and Siegfried walked up to the counter, searching for the bartender who was absent from his post. He suddenly came out from a storage room behind the counter, and they were surprised to see he was an elf. He was graceful as he walked to the end of the counter where they stood. Deep green eyes, blonde flowing hair, and pale skin made him seem like a ghost who haunted the Crimson Eagle.

"What beverages would suit my lords this evening?" the elf spoke placidly.

"No beverages for the moment," Siegfried replied, searching the other elf's face in hopes of recognition. "Tell me, what is your name, friend?"

"I am Eldred of Numa, son of Fel-alya," he bowed his head slightly.

"Pleasure to meet your acquaintance, Eldred. I am Siegfried of the Silverhart clan of D'arya and son of Helmer,"

Siegfried bowed. "If I am not being too forward, Eldred, permit me to ask what a Numan elf is doing so far from the shores of the Zephyrs?"

"Not forward at all, Siegfried. The Numan elves have experienced quarreling within the royal family of Rubiwind. The twin heirs of the Rubiwind dynasty have turned on King Sikahr and staged a coup in the realm of Numa. The coup was thwarted, but now the princes are at war with their father. And the only competing heir, Princess Avani, has gone missing. Many suspect one of the princes has kidnapped her for ransom, since King Sikahr is very fond of his daughter. Some of my people have fled Numa since the warring began two winters past. It is a dreadful time for the Numan elves." Eldred's shoulders drooped slightly.

"I am sorry, Eldred. I had not heard of this crisis before now, and I doubt any of the Evingrad elves know of it. D'arya be with all of our kind," Siegfried whispered something under his breath in elvish, but Lucius could not make it out.

"The Elf Queen will bring peace back to Numa, in that I place my trust. For now, we can only wait and see what the future holds."

"Indeed," Siegfried nodded. "Now I wonder, Eldred, if you would care to help us?"

"Of course, what is it you need?" Eldred clasped his hands together, eager to help.

"We are searching for the blacksmith who works across the road. An old drunken man told us he would be here in the Crimson Eagle," Siegfried said.

"Oh yes, he's here. His name is Castor. That would be him in the back." Eldred pointed to a table nearest to the fireplace where a man sat reading.

"Thank you very much, Eldred." Siegfried bowed his head again and thanked him in the elven tongue.

Eldred bowed his head in return, also speaking something in elvish to Siegfried, but it was spoken too fast for Lucius to understand.

They slowly made their way to the back table, walking past shaggy drunks who made lousy jokes at them and others who had completely past out on their tables.

Castor didn't move when they stopped in front of his table. The red-haired and bearded man continued to read a piece of parchment without so much as glancing at them. He puffed on a wood pipe every few seconds and annoyingly cleared his throat each time.

Lucius lost his patience. "Pardon me, sir. Are you Castor, the blacksmith?"

The man looked up at him with fierce eyes, biting the end of his pipe.

"Who wants to know?" he asked defiantly.

"Lucius of Evingrad and my elven brother, Siegfried Lockhart," he opened his palm in the elf's direction, who bowed.

Castor placed the parchment down on the table and puffed on his pipe again, "Well, Lucius, what is it that you want? In case you hadn't noticed, it's past sunset and my business is done for the day."

Siegfried interjected before Lucius could retort, "I have merely a question to ask, Mr. Castor."

"A question?" Castor coughed on the pipe smoke. "What would that be?"

"I have heard you know a certain individual who is familiar with the forging of magical alloys for use in weaponry," Siegfried's eyes narrowed and looked menacing by the fire.

"I might know such a person, Master Lockhart," Castor crossed his arms and leaned back in his chair. "However, that information comes with a price."

Lucius frowned and suddenly grew irritated at the man. "How about a drink? Will that loosen your tongue?"

Castor glared at him and looked ready to strike him, but he did not.

"Forgive my friend, Mr. Castor. I am willing to pay for whatever information you can provide," Siegfried pulled several solidi from his belt pouch and placed them on the tabletop. "Will this do?"

"Yes, that'll do," Castor slipped the coins inside his jacket quickly. "The person you wish to find is on the outskirts of the city, just before entering the Burning Woods. Take the Barren Road north until you see a deer trail on your right. Follow it to the Burning Woods. But before getting there, you'll come to a cottage with a stable. A woman named Naomi will answer the door. Ask for the blacksmith, and you'll find who you're looking for."

Siegfried thanked the surly man, who ignored him and began reading his parchment again. Lucius wanted to say something, but Siegfried gestured for them to leave. They walked toward the front door of the Crimson Eagle, but Lucius stopped suddenly, recalling something significant.

"Lumiath," Lucius burst out. "Siegfried, we need to find the D'aryan seer, remember? I had completely forgotten."

Siegfried smirked, "I had not forgotten about the exile, brother."

"Oh really? Well, thank you for reminding me," Lucius said with a slight grimace. "So did Father reveal to you where he is in this city like that Castor fellow?"

"No, I am unsure of his whereabouts."

Lucius crossed his arms and glanced around the room, looking for someone who might help them find the D'aryan outcast, but his heart sank when he surveyed the drunken rabble in the room. Before he could make a snide remark about the patrons of The Crimson Eagle, he noticed Eldred polishing some glasses behind the counter.

"What is it, Lucius?" Siegfried asked.

Lucius shot him a quick smile and walked up to the elven bartender. "Hello again, Eldred."

"Hello," Eldred smiled and picked up another glass to polish.

"Tell me, Eldred. Do you know of an elf residing in Sylvania by the name of Lumiath?" Lucius leaned on the counter, eagerly awaiting the elf's response.

"Lumiath? Oh yes, I have heard of him. Many of the locals speak of him frequently, mostly rumors or hearsay. But as I understand it, he lives in seclusion and rarely leaves his home."

"Do you know where he lives in the city?" Siegfried asked.

"He lives in the Scarlet Quarter. It's the northeastern corner of the city where the affluent citizens reside. I believe his residence is in the loft above an alchemist shop called Greimane's," Eldred answered as he finished polishing the last glass.

"Excellent," Lucius said triumphantly. "Thank you for your help, Eldred."

"Of course, my dear sirs. Now, could I interest either of you in some ale or honey mead?" Eldred extended an open palm toward the liquor cabinet behind him.

"Tomorrow, perhaps, my friend," Siegfried replied. "It is late and we really should retire for the evening."

"Tomorrow it shall be, then," Eldred bowed his head and both Siegfried and Lucius bowed in return. Lucius then handed the bartender a silver coin for his trouble, and the two brothers made their way out of The Crimson Eagle.

It was dark outside and the stars were shining like blue diamonds above them. Torches on the guard posts of the city wall flickered in the chill breeze outside. They treaded back to Griffin's Head, neither one saying anything. Lucius felt the weariness of the day's traveling all of a sudden, and he eagerly awaited lying in his soft bed at the inn. Siegfried, however, was still alert as ever and walking with the same grace and stride since the morning.

"So would it be best if we sought out Lumiath in the morning?" Lucius broke the silence between them.

"Yes, that would be wise. I doubt he'll be eager to have visitors, but if what Father says is true, the seer should be willing to give audience to fellow exiles of Evingrad." The elf searched the streets for life as he talked, but not a soul stirred in the quiet city.

"Well, I'm eager to hear what he has to say about the prophecy and the Requiem Sword, so I hope he'll acquiesce to a meeting."

"I hope that as well, brother," Siegfried replied.

"That Castor fellow we met tonight, he could really use an education in manners," Lucius abruptly changed the subject.

"I've rarely met a blacksmith who wasn't rude or obnoxious," Siegfried admitted.

"Well, that should make our next meeting with the blacksmith on the outskirts of town all the more enchanting," Lucius said, batting a mosquito away from his face.

Siegfried stopped walking, "Did you hear that?"

"Hear what?" He looked around them. They had stopped in the middle of the empty marketplace, which had an eerie atmosphere to it now in the darkness.

"There," Siegfried turned his gaze to one of the empty vendor's stands.

Lucius followed his line of sight and saw them. Two tall men crept out from behind the stands of the marketplace. They wore dark cloaks and covered their mouths with scarves. One of them held a small object in his hand as he neared them. Even in the dark of night, Lucius knew it was a dagger of some kind.

"Well, well, it seems we've found a few stragglers wandering our street," the man holding the dagger grinned wickedly.

"Indeed it does. Give us whatever valuables you be holding, mates, and we promise not to gut you," the second man sneered.

"Wonderful. A great time not to have our weapons with us," whispered Lucius.

Siegfried remained quiet and closed his eyes. He began reciting something in elvish.

"Hey. What's the elf doing? Give me your money." the thief with the dagger approached Siegfried, pointing his dagger towards the elf's chest.

Lucius lurched to stop the thief, but his partner came alongside him and held Lucius back. Siegfried opened his eyes and they glowed like amethyst stones in the night. He moved quicker than anything Lucius had ever seen. In seconds, he sidestepped the thief's stab and disarmed him speedily. In another second the man was on the ground unconscious, beaten by a barrage of punches and kicks. The other thief let go of Lucius, who was mesmerized by what he saw. The thief threw a punch, but it missed. Siegfried leapt in the air and spun with a kick to the man's face. The bandit went down hard and no longer moved except for the slow rising and falling of his chest as he breathed.

Lucius looked at Siegfried, whose eyes had returned to their normal color.

"What was that?" he felt scared and elated at the same time.

"I recited an elven song of speed, which gives one considerable prowess in close combat," Siegfried exhaled deeply.

"You there! Stop!" Clay, the lanky guard came running out of the shadows. His bigger partner followed behind with a torch in hand. "What's all the commotion here?"

"These men tried to rob us, sir," Lucius pointed to the unconscious thieves on the floor.

"How do we know it's not the other way around?" the burly guard spit as he talked.

"If you'll notice, they are the ones who have a dagger on them. Whereas, we handed over our weapons to you earlier today," Siegfried stated matter-of-factly.

Clay reached down and picked up the dagger. "He's right. This one's got a weapon. These must be the maggots that have been causing us trouble these past few nights, Ruel."

"Looks like it. A few days in the dungeon with shackles around their wrists and ankles might help them see the error of their ways," Ruel chortled.

A few more guards came running to the scene; two of them were also holding torches.

"Take these men to the dungeon," Ruel ordered his subordinates.

The men complied and dragged the battered bandits back to the guard tower by Sylvania's gate.

"We owe you both a debt of gratitude. Those two thieves have proved quite a nuisance," Clay exhorted.

"Actually, the gratitude belongs to Siegfried. He single-handedly beat them in the fight," Lucius glanced at the elf, who stood silent. "But there is a small discrepancy that must be dealt with immediately."

"Discrepancy? What are you going on about?" Ruel's brow furrowed.

"It seems to me that earlier today, you thought we would cause trouble in this city and perhaps even insinuated we were the thieves you've been attempting to catch. But your judgment was in error, and it appears to me that thanks to my brother, the streets of Sylvania are safe again."

"And exactly what might you be getting at, friend?" Clay crossed his arms in indignation.

"Well, since you both made a mistake and can now see that we are not thieves or troublemakers, perhaps an apology and a return of our belongings is in order," he grinned, clearly enjoying himself.

"An apology." Ruel's eyes widened enough for Lucius to see them clearly in the dark.

"I think it only fair," Lucius retorted.

"Calm yourself, Ruel. We will return your belongings just as soon as the thieves are locked up, but we will not apologize for safeguarding the city from likely threats," Clay said.

"Apology accepted," Lucius smiled. "Please take our belongings to Griffin's Head. Nicole will see that we get them."

Clay reluctantly agreed while Ruel grumbled as the two guards walked back to the tower.

"It has been an interesting night, my friend," Lucius rubbed his sleepy eyes with his thumb and forefinger.

"Yes, it has. You handled those guards very well, Lucius. Father would be proud," the elf patted him on the back and began walking up the hill to the inn.

"Proud of me? What about you? You're the one who took those men down within the blink of an eye," Lucius gushed, reliving the scene of Siegfried's speedy battle.

Siegfried smiled, but said nothing more of the fight. "Come, brother. Let us go and rest our weary eyes. Tomorrow will be a new day for furthering this adventure of ours."

EIGHT

The Healer and the Assassin

The sun shone brightly in the clearing of the
forest where Silas lay. Nightmares of black
creatures with glowing yellow eyes haunted him
as he slept. A few moments before one of the
demons slashed with its sharp claws at his face, Silas woke up.
He was disoriented and surprised to find himself in a clearing,
lying next to a smoldered campfire. The arrow wound on his
shoulder had been bandaged tight, and a strip of cloth was
wrapped around his forehead where he had struck it on a rock
in the raging river. Suddenly, his memory flashed back to his
turbulent night on the Feilon. He nearly drowned in the
torrents before reaching the surface and before escaping the
river's wrath; he felt the blunt force of a rock smack his

forehead underwater. The last thing he saw was the riverbank and then darkness. *But where am I now?* Trees were all around him, blocking his view of the Onyx Mountains or any other significant landmarks. And he could not hear the rushing waters of the Feilon, only the songs of birds in the trees overhead. He guessed it was mid morning from the position of the sun peeking through the forest canopy. He unwrapped some of his bandages and also examined the cuts on his arms from the rocks in the river. His bruises had begun to heal and did not look fresh, which meant he had been passed out for more than a night.

He got up and felt lightheaded at first, but after a few moments standing still, he felt well enough to walk around. His sword and armor were laid out on the opposite side of the campfire. While putting on his shirt mail and greaves, he noticed a leather bag that wasn't his own. He reached for the bag, but stopped short when he heard the sound of footsteps in the forest.

"Hello?" Silas' eyes darted back and forth, seeing nothing.

"Hello there, stranger," a female voice came from behind him.

He spun around, with one hand clasping his sword, and met the woman's gaze. She had a slender build with curly red hair and cobalt blue eyes.

"I see you're up and about," the woman said. "Would you like something to eat?"

"How did you ..." Silas stammered. "Who are you?"

The lady smiled. "My name is Violet. I'm an alchemist's apprentice from Sylvania."

"Sylvania? Are we in Sylvania?" Silas asked, wondering how far he'd ventured from Ithileo.

"No, we are only a few miles east of the Dulan River, near the ruins of Arkadeus," she bent down and grabbed something from inside the leather bag beside him.

"How did I get here?"

"I found you on the banks of the Feilon, just beyond this forest, while I was gathering winnow leaves. You were bleeding profusely and in need of healing salves. I placed you on the back of Homer, my horse, and brought you here to tend to your wounds," she said while starting the fire with two flint stones from her bag.

"How long have I been here?" Silas sat down beside her, feeling faint again.

"A day has passed since I found you. Your wounds are healing well, but it might not be wise for you to travel anywhere yet. The head wound is still tender, and you might faint again if you strain yourself," she grabbed something else from her bag. It was a small frying pan along with two raw fish wrapped in papyrus.

He wanted to thank her for her kindness, but he quickly felt dizzy and nauseous.

Violet glanced over at him, realizing what was happening. "Lay your head down, my lord. Please rest for now, and when you wake, a meal shall be ready for you to eat so your strength might be restored."

Her voice was soothing to his ears. He lay down on the grassy floor of the clearing and watched the tree branches sway in a slow breeze. The smell of frying fish along with a sweeter scent—some unknown spice—wafted into his nostrils. His eyelids became heavy with sleep, and soon he drifted into a quiet dream.

"Insolent fool!" Lord Memnon struck Genghis with the back of his scaly hand.

Genghis winced from the pain of the blow across his face, "I'm sorry, my master."

"Your warriors allowed the Prince of Aldron to escape," Memnon glowered.

"The Draknoir force were unaware that the son of Dermont would be present in Ithileo."

"Unaware? He is the leader of the Drachengarde. Where else would he be, General?" Memnon fumed. He paced his dark chamber as Genghis grasped for words.

"My lord—"

"No more excuses, Genghis; I don't have the patience for them," Memnon said, raising a hand to silence him. "Do you have scouts on the river searching for Dermont's son?"

"Yes, my lord," Genghis eagerly replied—relieved the rebuking was over. "The scouts are patrolling the Feilon as we speak and searching for any sign of the Dragon Slayer."

"Good. He is wounded and cannot have gone far, but you will bring him to me alive, Genghis," Memnon said. He turned his back to face the Nergoth idol on the wall. "The heir of Aldron must face judgment for his crimes against our kind."

"Of course, my lord," Genghis agreed.

"Do you know which of your captains led the assault in Ithileo?" Memnon turned to face him with fierce eyes.

"Lytar and his battalion led the assault, Lord Memnon," Genghis answered, sensing malicious intent behind Memnon's question.

Memnon's lower lip twitched. "Execute him, General. Make it public amongst the other commanders so they know not to make the same mistake."

"Yes, master. It will be carried out promptly," Genghis bowed.

Before Memnon dismissed the general, there was a knock on the chamber door. The Draknoir sorcerer gave permission for entry into the hallowed hall and a lithe figure walked into the dark room. At first glance, Genghis was surprised to see it was a woman, and his first instinct was to attack her, but he soon recognized the thin, dark-haired lady.

"Ravenmane, you are early," Memnon said with a smirk. "I was just finishing my discussion with Genghis."

"Pardon me, my lords, I did not mean to intrude." Ravenmane bowed respectfully. "It is a pleasure to see you again, General Genghis."

"Yes, always a pleasure," Genghis replied with curled lips.

Memnon sensed his subordinate's discomfort and grinned, "You may take your leave, General."

"My lord," he bowed again and quickly walked out the door without acknowledging Ravenmane.

"All these years and he has yet to accept you as I do, Ravenmane," Memnon said. He looked into the young woman's green eyes trying to decipher her thoughts.

"I care not what the General thinks of me, my lord. I only seek your approval and instruction," Ravenmane said unwaveringly.

Memnon laughed. "Yes, I know. Your loyalty is a trait I deeply admire, even though you are of a lesser race."

Ravenmane accepted the insult without dispute.

"I have an errand for you, Ravenmane, and it will not be bloodless," Memnon stroked the horns protruding from his chin.

"I am at your command, my liege."

"I need you to travel to Tarshish, my dear girl. Dermont will seek to retaliate against Nasgothar for the loss of his dragon slayers and, in time, his beloved son," Memnon said, crossing his arms and staring into the crimson eyes of Nergoth's idol. "We must cripple any advance he would take against us. So I need you to kill one of his inner circle. Someone crucial to military victory."

"Whom would that be, my lord?" Ravenmane asked.

"The Captain of the Royal Guard ... Baron Stendahl."

NINE

Lumiath

The morning of a new day came late for Lucius as he awoke to a knock on the door of his room around noon. He slowly crawled out from the bed, surprised to see Siegfried was not in the room. The door opened just a crack before he could answer. He feared it was another thief like the previous night, but his fears were quelled when he saw it was merely Nicole.

"Yes?" Lucius crossed his arms, unashamed at his unkempt appearance.

"Your elf partner told me to wake you at noon. He wanted you to know that he left early to gather provisions for your journey," the innkeeper peered from behind the half-opened door.

"Did he say where he would be?" Lucius asked curiously.

"No, he simply left enough money for your breakfast, which has gotten cold I'm afraid."

Lucius sighed. "Marvelous. I'll be down to eat it in a few minutes, thank you."

"Thank you, young sir," Nicole shuffled back outside and closed the door.

Lucius dressed quickly and gathered his belongings. Clay and Ruel had been kind enough to send someone to drop off their weapons and gear last night before they had gone to bed. Lucius unsheathed his sword and slashed with it quickly from side to side. After a few more practice thrusts, he sheathed the weapon and put on his belt along with the rest of his clothing. Siegfried had not left any of his items behind, which did not surprise him. Elves were seldom known for tarrying in one spot for any given amount of time, aside from the woods or their homes.

He walked down the creaking stairs and was surprised to find the dining area lacking any patrons. Griffin's Vault was empty save for Nicole, who sat behind the counter drinking, and the young waitress who was cleaning tabletops with a dirty rag.

Lucius sat down at one of the tables and was served a bowl of stone cold vegetable soup. He ate it ravenously and ordered a pint of mead to wash it down. When he was filled, he decided to go down to the marketplace and try to find Siegfried. Impatience with his elven brother was one of his flaws, but he did not wish to stay in the musty inn any longer than he needed to. After leaving a silver quintus for Nicole and the waitress, he was on his way down the hill to the marketplace.

The market was teeming with activity once again. Townspeople were all around, buying food for their families, jewelry and trinkets for loved ones, and fabrics for knitting clothing. Lucius tried his best to weave his way through the crowd, but only found himself pestered by vendors who placed unwanted goods into his hands for him to buy. One of the vendors even threw a live chicken at him, insisting he needed it for his supper tonight. Lucius handed him back the frightened bird and moved away. He saw many men, women, and even a few elves wandering about, but there was no sign of Siegfried. Frustration began to build in him as he finally escaped the marketplace. Across from where he stood was the Crimson Eagle, and he wondered if Eldred would know his brother's whereabouts.

Lucius entered the pub and recognized some of the customers from the night before sitting inside drinking their worries away or sleeping with their heads on the tabletops. Behind the counter, Eldred was replacing empty wine casks with new casks and inserting taps on each of them. Lucius found the sight of such menial labor being done by an elf almost unnatural. He walked up slowly to the counter, not wanting to disturb Eldred, but the elf became aware of his presence almost immediately.

"Greetings, my friend," Eldred's smile gleamed. "How may I serve you?"

"Hello. I was wondering if you might have seen my friend, Siegfried, by chance."

"Yes, he did stop here this morning to inquire if I had any empty wineskins for sale. He bought two and said he would return later for them," the elf replied.

"How long ago did he leave?" Lucius inquired further.

"Nearly an hour prior. He did not say where he was headed, but if you are looking for him, perhaps it would be best to wait here since he is sure to return," Eldred suggested.

"Yes, that would probably be best. I'm not really in the mood to run about in search of him. Thank you, Eldred," Lucius replied, spotting an empty table near the counter and heading for it.

"May I get you something to drink, sir, while you wait?" Eldred raised a palm in the direction of the wine casks.

Lucius hesitated for a second. "Yes, that would be fine. I'll have a small glass of your wine, please."

Eldred bowed in compliance and poured a glass of wine from the cask behind him. As the elf walked over to place the wine in front of him, Lucius set down his pack and remembered the ancient scroll Helmer had given him, which was rolled up inside of the bag. Fear of it being stolen by an ignorant guard gripped him as he realized its importance. He opened the bag and searched its contents, relieved to have found the red papyrus scroll sitting inside. He set it on the table then took a sip of wine. The drink was sweet and had a hint of peppermint to it.

After he finished his drink, Lucius unrolled the long piece of parchment on the table and began reading random passages in the text. The elvish script was difficult to decipher at first; the fine strokes of each letter were more stylized than any of the elvish books he had read in the past. Reading had never been a pastime Lucius enjoyed like his father and brother. When he learned to wield a sword as an adolescent, he cared for it even less. Most of the books in Helmer's library required an acute intellect to understand and were rather tiresome to read. However, the passages in the scroll piqued his interest.

Lucius read about the origins of mankind, created by Yéwa in eons past. The passages of the red scroll spoke of the fall of man into evil and treachery—banished from a peaceful existence in Amarna, a glorious realm, into an arduous mortal life in the island of Gezer. Lucius skipped ahead in the document and read about Yéwa's exultation of a sheepherder who helped free an enslaved people from the clutches of a tyrant. The people were known as the Terrín. They were highly favored by Yéwa, but as Lucius read on, he learned of their betrayal and rebellion against Yéwa. Further down the parchment, Lucius read about the Terrín's subsequent punishment by Yéwa: the conquest of Gezer by the enemies of men and the mass exile of all mankind into Azuleah. Many years pass when Yesu, the son of Yéwa is born and chosen to be the king who will reconcile all men to their God. The passages cover much of the king's life, focusing on his love for his people and his willingness to forgive their many ills. His humility is boundless despite his divine heritage and royal status. Not even elves are this humble. The red scroll foreshadows the doom awaiting King Yesu—an assassination plot concocted by corrupted vassals seeking to end his reign. Lucius skimmed down to the bottom of the scroll, down to the very last passage. To his shock, he discovered the humble ruler of all mankind is put to death by the very men he wished to save.

Death?

Lucius leaned back in his chair, a flurry of thoughts racing through his mind. In an earlier passage, King Yesu said he would rise again to rule the living and the dead; his death was to atone for the sins of men. But the scroll ended with his death and nothing more. *There must be something missing.* Many promises were spoken by this Yesu that remained unfulfilled. Lucius began to doubt the power of this God known as Yéwa. If Yéwa could not save Yesu, how could he save anyone else? Perhaps no higher being existed to lead the men of Azuleah. He sighed deeply and rolled up the red scroll.

Lucius stared at the empty glass on the table for a moment, deciding whether or not to call Eldred for another round. Before he could come to a final decision, his brother walked through the tavern door. Siegfried walked in carrying two small sacks in one hand and a larger sack in the other. Lucius waved to get his attention and the elf promptly strode to the table.

"Where have you been?" Lucius asked, clearly annoyed at having to wait so long for his brother to show up.

"I have been acquiring supplies for our journey, Lucius." Siegfried placed the two sacks on the table and the larger sack on the floor next to his chair. "I have bought food, cooking utensils, and additional clothing for both of us."

"You bought clothes for me? I do hope they fit, Sieg," Lucius peeked inside one of the sacks on the table.

Siegfried handed him the larger sack on the floor where the clothes were stored. "I am confident the extra jerkin and breeches will fit you, brother. However, if they are too tight on your frame, the amount of walking you will experience on this journey will surely resolve the problem."

"Funny," Lucius replied while examining the brown sheepskin jerkin and woolen pants. "I don't suppose you found any horses we could purchase for our travels?"

"Unfortunately, the stables I visited did not wish to part with their steeds, and I doubt we have enough money to afford the prices."

Lucius frowned, lamenting their means of transportation would continue to be on foot. He began to express his feelings on the matter to Siegfried when Eldred walked up to their table.

"Greetings, Siegfried. Would you care for a drink?" the polite bartender asked.

"No thank you, Eldred. But could I ask a favor?" Siegfried picked up one of the sacks on the table. "Would you be willing to store these sacks along with the wineskins I purchased until later this afternoon when we retrieve them?"

"Yes, of course, my friend," Eldred grabbed all three sacks with one hand and managed to grab Lucius' empty glass with his other hand. "Have you already visited Lumiath in the Scarlet Quarter?"

"That is where we are headed presently, dear Eldred," Siegfried shot his brother a quick glance, as if to remind him of their primary purpose in Sylvania.

In truth, Lucius had not forgotten about the D'aryan seer, but his thoughts had been temporarily diverted by what he read in the red scroll. Everything he had learned about Yesu had led him to believe the great king was either immortal or invincible, but the scroll had negated all of his preconceptions. He stood up and stuffed the scroll into his pack. "Let's go find the seer."

The streets of the Scarlet Quarter were cleaner and emptier than the other areas of the city seen by Lucius and Siegfried in the last two days. The few people they passed on the faded red cobblestone path wore luxurious clothing ranging from brightly colored doublets on the men to exquisite gowns trimmed with fur on the women. Most of the looks they received from the townsfolk conveyed disdain and superiority, undoubtedly from noticing the pair's humble apparel. The air of supremacy was stifling to Lucius and it reminded him of Quetulya's relentless condescension. Siegfried, on the other hand, seemed either aloof to the snobbish stares directed at them by the residents of the Scarlet Quarter or he simply did not care.

As they traveled on the winding road of the quarter, Lucius spotted a brick building with wooden shingles and a dark green door. Above the door hung a sign that read, "Greimane's Unguents and Elixirs." Lucius strolled toward the two-story building, and Siegfried soon followed, once he realized his brother was no longer beside him. They both walked up to the green door, and Lucius slowly turned the doorknob to check if the shop was open. The doorknob turned easily, and after a slight push, the door creaked open allowing them entry into a fragrant store brightly lit with numerous candles on the walls and on small tables. On the far right of the door, there was a long counter extending the entire length of the wall save for a gap to access a door leading to a storeroom. Behind the counter were shelves containing numerous vials, bottles, and jars filled with contents of all colors. Directly ahead of the doorway there was a staircase leading up to the second floor of the shop— presumably where Lumiath resided.

"Greetings, weary travelers," a loud voice boomed from behind the counter where a man with a bushy mustache and blue turban stood with his hands outstretched. Neither Lucius nor Siegfried had noticed the man upon entering the shop; it was as though he had appeared out of thin air. "My name is Theodore Greimane, and this is my humble store, which is positively brimming with exotic elixirs, potions, and unguents unseen in any part of Azuleah."

Lucius stepped closer to the counter, examining the merchant's wares closely. Siegfried remained near the door, uninterested in Greimane's goods.

"Do you require an unguent for wounds received in combat? Or perhaps an elixir that can cure an infectious disease?" Theodore Greimane smiled eagerly at Lucius, desiring to make a sale on the more curious of his two visitors.

Lucius could not resist his curiosity, especially if there was an item that could aid them in the wilds of Azuleah. "Tell me more about this unguent for wounds."

"But of course, my young lad." Theodore beamed and quickly snatched a small jar filled with a yellow cream. "The Unguent of Und is an excellent remedy for cuts, lacerations, and burns. It is made from the egg yolks of Und seabirds—very rare and exquisite. No warrior or traveler should venture without a jar close at hand."

"How much is a jar?" Lucius asked, aware now of the unguent's significance.

"One centen is the cost for this exotic unguent," Theodore grinned.

Lucius balked at the price. "Surely, you can't be serious? Perhaps we could barter for this exotic unguent?"

"I doubt there is anything you own that I care to barter for, my young friend," Theodore laughed at his own veiled insult. "One centen is all I desire to barter for."

Lucius scowled at the greedy merchant and nearly protested, but his brother walked up to the counter and put a hand on his shoulder.

"We are not interested in your potions, Mr. Greimane, especially if they come at such an extravagant cost." Siegfried said.

Theodore Greimane's smile disappeared and his face contorted into an ugly frown. "Well, if my prices are not to your liking, then kindly leave my store. I am a busy man and don't have time for stingy elves or children!"

"Children," Lucius snapped. "Listen—"

"Peace, brother," Siegfried interrupted. "Mr. Greimane, although we do not wish to buy anything presently, we do require your assistance. We have come here to meet with the resident above your store, an elf named Lumiath. Is he here?"

"I don't know who you're talking about," Theodore said, drumming his fingers on the counter top. "Now, are you buying anything or not?"

"Are you saying that Lumiath doesn't reside here?" Lucius asked.

"I have never heard the name in my life," Theodore replied. He turned and slammed down the Unguent of Und on a shelf behind him.

"I do not believe you, Mr. Greimane," Siegfried said plainly.

Theodore turned to face the elf, his cheeks very red now and his nostrils fully flared. "Listen, elf. There is no one named Lumiath here. Now, I will call the guards if you don't—"

A loud knocking from overhead cut off the annoyed merchant's words and they looked up at the ceiling in unison.

"What was that?" Lucius looked over at Theodore.

Theodore sighed heavily and shook his head slowly while biting his lip. "He will see you."

"Who?" Siegfried asked, a smile slowly formed on his face.

"Lumiath," Theodore replied through clenched teeth. "Now go upstairs and leave me be."

The merchant stormed away from the counter and into the storeroom.

"Well, that was pleasant," Lucius said.

Siegfried remained silent, his gaze fixed on the stairs near the entrance of the alchemist shop.

"Shall we, brother?" Lucius gestured toward the staircase.

"Lead the way, *Ellyllei*."

Lucius eagerly made his way toward the staircase with Siegfried close behind. At the top of the stairs, they entered a long hallway with two doors on either side. Paintings of serene landscapes hung on the walls between the doors. The furthest door at the end of the hallway to their right was slightly ajar. As they neared the opened door, the fragrance of citrus mixed with incense was heavy in the air. Lucius stood directly in front of the cherry oak door, unsure if he should knock.

"Please enter," a deep voice beckoned from inside the room.

Lucius gently pushed the door opened and entered a large, lavishly decorated room. The walls were painted a deep green and displayed beautiful artwork in the forms of flowers and trees all throughout. Brass candelabras with intricate designs adorned all four corners of the room and a finely woven rug embroidered with an elvish oak design lay on the floor. Next to the rug there was a wicker armchair decorated with leaves, vines, and flowers. An elf with curly black hair wearing a red tunic with gold-trimmed sleeves sat in the armchair reading a leather-bound tome. A large stack of similar tomes and books were placed next to the chair. He watched the elf, who showed no interest in acknowledging Lucius or Siegfried's presence, and noticed he wore a silver necklace with a symbol hanging from it. The symbol consisted of a large circle with a triquetra at the center. The curves and whorls of the triquetra and circle interlocked together in a complicated but elegant pattern.

"Are you Lumiath?" Siegfried asked, a hint of impatience in his voice.

The elf turned a page and did not respond to the question.

"We don't mean to disturb you, my lord, but we've traveled far to meet you," Lucius spoke as cordially as possible despite his growing annoyance. "This is my brother, Siegfried Silverhart, and I am—"

"Lucius Nostra from Evingrad," the elf snapped his book shut and studied them for a moment. "I know who you are and why you have come. I am a seer after all."

"So you are Lumiath, then," Siegfried said. "The man downstairs did not wish to reveal your residence here, why?"

"I am a private soul, Master Siegfried, and I do not like to be bothered by curious gossips who think they know who I am. Theodore and I have an agreement: I provide him with the recipes to his unguents and elixirs; he in turn allows me to reside here in quiet solitude." Lumiath leaned back in his chair and closed his eyes for a moment, as though he wished to be alone again.

"I have many questions, Master Lumiath," Lucius said. The elf opened his eyes and looked at him.

"Of course you do. You are a man who has lived with elves his entire life. But be careful, my young lord. Questions have answers you may not wish to hear," Lumiath warned.

Lucius brushed off the warning and cut to the point. "Am I the *Ellyllei*? The one foretold in the prophecy to face the Black Dragon?"

"Yes," Lumiath replied nonchalantly. "You are the Elf Son who is burdened with carrying the Requiem Sword to kill a great evil. Pardon my saying this, but I do not envy your role in the least."

Lucius exhaled deeply and felt a sudden emptiness in his stomach. I have to kill Kraegyn. He swallowed hard, trying to think of his next question, which Siegfried asked before he could.

"Do you have instructions for how to forge the Requiem Sword?" Siegfried asked.

"I do not. Not anymore," the seer responded in a bored monotone.

"What do you mean? Have you forgotten?" Lucius questioned.

"Ha! Of course not. The means of forging the sword does not lie with me, but you already know where to go for the answer to that particular question."

"The blacksmith near the Burning Woods." Siegfried glanced at Lucius, who arrived at the same conclusion.

"Astute, like your father," Lumiath said, clasping his hands together and placing them on his chest.

"You know our father?" Lucius asked.

"Of course. Why else would he defend my reputation and risk losing his seat in the Cyngorell? We are old friends, and we hold beliefs that many D'aryan elves would consider heretical."

"My father would never embrace heresy." Siegfried crossed his arms.

Lumiath grinned. "Let us speak more of it over a cup of tea." The seer grabbed a long walking staff resting on the side of his chair and hoisted himself up. When Lumiath stood, Lucius' mouth fell open when he noticed the elf was missing his right foot. Despite the disability, Lumiath walked as gracefully as any elf, with the aid of the staff to support his weight.

He walked over to a small hearth nestled in the wall directly behind the armchair. A black kettle hung on a lug pole over the fire and it began to whistle softly as Lumiath grabbed it. The seer leaned his staff on the mantle of the fireplace while balancing on his foot. He poured the steaming liquid into two teacups sitting on the mantle and then hung the kettle back onto the lug pole. Grasping both teacups in his left hand and the staff in his right, Lumiath walked over to them with little effort.

"Please sit," Lumiath said, gesturing with his head to the rug on the floor.

Siegfried and Lucius both sat on the rug cross-legged as the D'aryan exile handed them their tea.

"I hope you enjoy ginger tea, Lucius," Lumiath said.

"Oh, I love ginger tea, it's—" Lucius remembered to whom he was speaking. "You already know it's my favorite tea, of course."

"Naturally." Lumiath sat in his wicker chair with an obnoxious grin on his face.

"You implied my father is a heretic; tell me why," Siegfried demanded, unimpressed by Lumiath's sense of humor.

"Lucius, tell me what you know about D'arya," Lumiath asked, plucking a flower from his chair and sniffing it.

"Well, I know she was once the queen of all the elves and ruled with a gentle hand. She attained great power at a young age and through powerful magic became an eternal spirit. She guides all the elves who worship her." Lucius sipped his tea, unsure how the question was relevant to their father.

"And the elves do worship her, as I once did. But herein lies the truth, my friends. D'arya is not a deity to be worshipped. I know it and your father knows it," Lumiath said, twirling the flower between his forefinger and thumb.

"You speak heresy. My father does not believe that."

"Are you so certain, Siegfried? Have you ever heard your father recite a song to D'arya like the other elves of Evingrad? Is he not always at odds in some way with the Cyngorell's decisions? Did he not, after all, send his sons on a perilous quest to find a seer who is despised for his peculiar views and an outcast to his own people?"

Siegfried furrowed his brows tightly and looked into his teacup, deep in thought.

Lucius could not remember a time when his father sang a song to D'arya or even attended one of the festivals held in her honor. And most of the heated debates within the Cyngorell were usually started by Helmer. Of course, Siegfried might know something to the contrary, since he knew their father for much longer, but his hesitation to answer the question surprised Lucius.

"Siegfried, your father is a wise elf living amongst a people that has never really understood truth," Lumiath said.

"And you understand truth?" Lucius set his teacup on the floor, losing his excitement for the hot drink.

"I do, young Nostra. Let me enlighten the both of you in regards to D'arya," Lumiath said, tossing the flower in his hand aside. He leaned forward in the armchair with a stern expression on his face. "It is true that D'arya was a queen and that she acquired great power that elevated her to the likes of a demigod. However, there is not an elf alive in Azuleah who knows from where she received this power."

"Except for you." Siegfried glared at the seer, growing tired of his arrogance.

"Me and your father, Siegfried," Lumiath corrected. "D'arya received her power from an all-powerful entity the elves have largely ignored for millennia. The power to become an immortal spirit was a gift to D'arya for her humility and charity, given by a higher being. The irony is D'arya herself does not want to be worshipped. Her role is that of a leader, pointing the elves toward a greater power who is worthy of worship."

"What greater power?" Siegfried clenched his jaw muscles tight.

"Yéwa," Lumiath whispered.

Lucius' eyes widened at the sound of the name. He recalled everything he read earlier in the red scroll regarding Yéwa's role as Creator of all mankind, but the scroll contained nothing about D'arya. Siegfried stood up from the rug and walked slowly towards the door. He stopped short and stared out into the hallway, contemplating the significance of Lumiath's words.

"Do you see this symbol, Lucius?" Lumiath pointed to the triquetra hanging from his silver necklace.

"Yes, what about it?" Lucius asked. He scrutinized the symbol and noticed the triquetra in the center was gold, contrasting with the overlapping silver circle.

"This symbol represents the triune entity known as Yéwa. He is creator, king, and spirit—Yéwa, Yesu, and Ysbryd. You already know this, Lucius. You've read the red scroll Helmer gave you."

"I have read most of it, and I am troubled by the fact that King Yesu died in such a violent manner. I thought he was the son of Yéwa. How could he be killed by mere mortals, and why didn't his father save him?"

"It is troubling, no doubt—a son of an all-powerful God chained to a tree and speared to death by men," Lumiath sighed, turning his face upward to the ceiling. "But do not be anxious, young Nostra. The time will come when divine mysteries will be revealed to you."

Lucius frowned, unsatisfied with the seer's answer. "Well, if you're going to be coy about Yéwa, then at least tell me about my family. Are any of them still alive?"

"And how would I know that?"

"You are a seer of D'arya, are you not? Enough games, tell me!" Lucius cried.

Lumiath stood from his chair and grabbed his staff to steady himself. He walked over to the place Lucius sat on the rug and towered over him. At first, Lucius thought the elf might strike him, but to his surprise, Lumiath knelt down beside him. The elf's haggard features were more visible when the seer's face was mere inches away from Lucius.

"I am a seer, but not of D'arya as you no doubt have surmised," Lumiath's voice lowered to a whisper. "Your true family is out there, Lucius; they are alive. However, I would counsel you to choose your path wisely. You can choose to seek your family or forge the Requiem Sword."

Lucius swallowed hard. "And is there no other road open to me?"

"There are always roads open to you, young Nostra." Lumiath rose to his feet and his voice rose simultaneously. "Just be wary which roads you choose to travel. Now go, your brother is tired of my ramblings, and a blacksmith awaits your arrival."

Lumiath strode back to his chair, sat down, and picked up the same tome he read when they came in. Lucius stood up and watched him for a few moments, waiting for the elf to say something more, but he continued to read as if no one else was in the room. Lucius turned to the door to join Siegfried, but his brother had already left. As Lucius entered the hallway, Lumiath's deep voice called out to him.

"Lucius." Lumiath did not take his eyes off the tome.

"Yes?"

"Tell Theodore to give you a bottle of *bywydur*. You and your brother will need it."

"What is *bywydur*?"

"Siegfried will know." Lumiath turned a page and said nothing more.

Lucius waited for any further instruction from the seer, but when he received none, he promptly walked down the hall to the stairs. Siegfried was nowhere to be seen downstairs. Theodore Greimane stood behind the counter again with his back turned to Lucius. The crotchety shopkeeper was rearranging his numerous elixirs and unguents on the shelves. Lucius slowly walked up to him, not wishing to startle the man and see him turn red again.

"Excuse me, Mr. Greimane?" Lucius spoke softly.

Theodore turned his head to the side, unsure if he had heard someone or not, but he soon noticed Lucius standing at the counter. "You again. Well, what do you want?"

"Did you happen to see my brother come through here?"

"Yes, I did. He stormed out like he heard a tale he didn't like," Theodore grunted. "Happens often when people visit the recluse upstairs."

"I see," Lucius said. An awkward silence followed, and he eventually found the courage to speak again. "Mr. Greimane—"

"Theodore," the shopkeeper corrected.

"Right, Theodore. Lumiath told me to ask you for a bottle of *bywydur*."

Theodore's eyes widened and his nostrils flared. "Oh did he now? And how do you plan on paying for the most expensive elixir stocked in my shop?"

"He didn't say anything about payment," Lucius replied, bracing for the inevitable outburst building up in Theodore.

"Of course he didn't. That elf is going to run my business into the ground!" Theodore yelled, his eyes were bulging and his turban was slightly askew.

Three loud knocks from Lumiath's staff above only worsened the vicious scowl on his face. The shopkeeper muttered something under his breath then crouched behind the counter. The sound of clinking glass could be heard as Theodore rummaged through his stock and finally set a bottle no larger than a tinderbox on the counter in front of Lucius. The green liquid within the bottle had a faint glow that mesmerized Lucius.

"Here it is. Now off with you!" Theodore barked, turning his back on him and focusing on reorganizing his shelves again.

Lucius grabbed the *bywydur* and stuffed it inside a pocket on his tunic. He bid the shopkeeper farewell, but Theodore only grunted in return.

Outside on the main street, Siegfried leaned against the brick wall of Greimane's shop scrutinizing a long piece of parchment.

"Are you alright?" Lucius asked, stepping up beside his brother.

"I am fine, Lucius." Siegfried replied, looking up at Lucius with forlorn eyes.

He refrained from asking anything further and opted to change the subject. "Theodore gave me a bottle of something called *bywydur*. Lumiath said you would know what it is," he said, pulling out the vial for his brother to see.

Siegfried's morose demeanor completely changed once he saw the bottle. "*Bywydur?* This is an incredible gift, Lucius."

"Really? Well, I have no idea what it's for."

"*Bywydur* means 'water of life' in the elven tongue. It is an elixir that revitalizes the body more than any food or drink ever could," Siegfried explained in an unfamiliar and animated voice.

"So, is it like drinking a hearty mead? I don't quite understand."

"No, no. It is greater than mere mead, brother."

"If that's the case, I wish the bottle were bigger. This is less than a pint and it won't suffice for both of us." Lucius held up the bottle to inspect it in the daylight.

"You do not consume the entire bottle," Siegfried snapped, snatching the bottle from Lucius' hand. "One drop of *bywydur* is more than enough for the elixir to work."

Siegfried continued to explain the benefits of using the *bywydur* as they strolled out of the Scarlet Quarter and back to the inn. Lucius reluctantly listened to his brother expound on the alchemical properties of *bywydur* and its origins over five thousand years ago. He did not share his brother's vibrant enthusiasm for the elixir, but he was contented to see Siegfried in better spirits than before. Lumiath's revelations about D'arya deeply troubled his brother, but he hoped Siegfried would come to believe the seer's words. Accepting a truth that upended one's entire view of the world was not simple—Lucius faced an identical situation in Helmer's study a few nights ago. But Lucius was less stubborn than his older brother, and he believed both his father and Lumiath with minimal hesitance.

He desired to know about his past and his place in the world, which largely influenced his tendency to believe the word of others without skepticism. But seeking truth made it difficult to choose between the two roads Lumiath had presented to him. Lucius longed to find his true family, but he equally desired to fulfill his role as the *Ellyllei*. Perhaps there was a means to achieve both? He earnestly hoped so.

TEN

The Shores of the Dulan

P lease wake, my lord." The soft sound of Violet's voice beckoned, awakening Silas from his deep slumber in the forest near the Dulan River. He opened his eyes and saw the beautiful red-haired woman standing over him holding a plate in one hand.

"I presume you're famished since you slept through the noon meal," Violet said, lowering the plate down to him. "I hope you don't mind that the fish is a bit cold."

Silas sat up—feeling a twinge of pain from his shoulder and head as he did so—and grabbed the plate. "Any food will do at the moment, my lady."

Silas examined the contents of the plate: a half-charred piece of salmon, several berries, and a small lump of what looked like cheese. Ignoring any sense of propriety, he began to shovel the food into his mouth with his bare hands. Violet sat down between him and the campfire, untroubled by his lack of table manners.

"How long have I been asleep?" Silas asked with a mouth full of fish and berries.

"A few hours; it is nearly dusk." Violet replied.

Silas glanced up at the sky through the dense foliage of the forest and saw the purple hue of the sun's fading light reflecting on the clouds above.

"I don't know your name, sir," Violet said, tilting her head to the side.

"My name is—" Silas hesitated, not wishing to reveal his true identity to a complete stranger. "Cutter. Call me Cutter."

"Cutter?" Violet raised an eyebrow. "That is a unique name. I don't believe I've heard it before."

"It's what my friends call me," Silas replied quickly as he chewed on the last piece of salmon on the plate.

"I see. Well, Cutter, what happened to you? You look as though you've been in quite a fight." Violet's eyes focused on his injured shoulder and the scrapes on his arms.

"Yes, it was quite a fight," Silas said, recalling Asher's bloodied face as he died. "My brethren and I faced a legion of Draknoir in Ithileo. There were hundreds of the king's men lying in wait to attack the fiends while the soldiers under my command acted as bait, but the Draknoir ambushed us. Somehow they knew our plan. We fought hard, but none of them survived save for me."

Violet stared at him, unblinking and mouth opened. "I ... I am so sorry, Cutter."

Silas looked at the ground and nodded. He set his empty plate down and did not speak for a while, his thoughts on his fallen comrades.

"Are you a general or commander in the king's army, then?" Violet asked, finally breaking the awkward silence.

"A commander, yes. I led fourteen of King Dermont's Drachengarde. Now only thirty-five remain. I must go to Aldron and report to his Majesty the heavy losses we've suffered." Silas sighed, imagining his father's scowl once he hears of the defeat.

"Well, you are in no condition to travel as far as Aldron, my lord. Not to mention you lack the necessary provisions for such a journey. My home is on the northeastern corner of the Burning Woods, two days away. You would gain the supplies and rest needed to make your trip back to Aldron," Violet said, the corners of her mouth upturned as she looked at him.

"That is very kind, my lady Violet. You will be handsomely repaid for such kindness, I assure you," Silas said.

"No repayment is needed, Cutter. Some good conversation and company will do just fine though," Violet replied with a wide smile.

Cutter let out a quick laugh. "Fair enough, my lady."

After a short conversation about the amount of food they had left for their trip to Violet's home, Cutter began packing up all of their belongings while Violet fetched Homer from a nearby brook where the horse was drinking water. When she returned with Homer in tow, Violet insisted Silas ride the horse while she guided it by the reins. Her concern for his health was beginning to annoy Silas—this was not the first time he had suffered wounds in combat. Nevertheless, he obliged her concerns and climbed up onto Homer's saddle.

It was just past the twilight hour when they set out and darkness was beginning to engulf the forest. Violet lit an oil lantern hanging from Homer's saddle and carried it in front of her as she guided the horse through the dense underbrush. Slowly, they waded through the woods and into a grassy meadow where the shining stars could be seen overhead. They stopped for a moment as the young alchemist's apprentice examined the stars for the correct direction toward her home. Silas looked up into the night sky as well, but he could not discern which stars were used for navigation—they all looked the same to his eyes. Violet effortlessly found the guiding star and they turned westward to the Dulan River.

Crossing the deep river proved to be a challenge, especially for Homer. The horse whinnied in protest several times when the cold, rushing water reached the base of his neck. Despite the horse's displeasure at the situation, Violet managed to calm the horse and hold tightly to the reins while treading water. Silas gave his best effort to soothe Homer by lightly stroking the horse's nose, but he constantly tried to nip the soldier's fingers in return; Silas was convinced the horse despised him. Once they finally arrived at the western bank of the Dulan, Homer whinnied appreciatively and clopped the rocks of the shore with his front hooves, which evoked a giggle from Violet and a grin from Silas.

The moon was in full view from the bank of the Dulan and its light cascaded on the dancing waves of the Dulan River. Silas guessed it was probably nearing the midnight hour, and he could tell the nightly travel had taken its toll on both Violet and her horse. She was completely drenched from the neck down, and in the soft lantern light, Silas perceived the weariness in her eyes. He felt tired and weak as well, despite little exertion on his part. A strong headache and pain in his joints had flared up just before they had crossed the river. There was no need to continue their journey exhausted.

"Perhaps we should make camp for the night," Silas said, his voice strained.

Violet set her lantern down and sighed. "I am relieved to hear you say it, my lord."

"I'll start a fire. You'll need warmth before you catch a fever in this chill air."

"Indeed," Violet replied as she rung some water out from her skirt.

Silas climbed down from Homer, and as his feet hit the ground, a sharp pain shot out from his injured shoulder. He groaned loudly as a wave of pain rippled throughout his body, causing him to grip Homer's saddle to keep steady on his feet.

"Cutter, what's wrong?" Violet asked, running quickly to his side.

"Pain ... from my shoulder," Silas grunted. "... and all over my body as well."

"Come on, sit down while I start a fire," Violet insisted, grabbing him by his elbow and leading him to a grassy area near the river bank.

Silas sat down and rested his aching head on his knees. Violet quickly gathered her flint stones and some tinder from her pack. Once the fire was started and sufficiently blazing, Violet sat down beside him and removed the linen bandage on his shoulder. She grabbed her lantern and inspected Silas' wound in the orange glow. Violet let out a quick gasp and her eyes bulged.

"What is it? What's wrong?" Silas asked, but did not wait for Violet's reply. He looked down at his right shoulder and saw the puncture wound where the Draknoir arrow had pierced him was swelled into a purplish-blue lump. Pus was oozing out of the wound and the skin surrounding it was a dark pink color.

"This isn't right," Violet said, rubbing her forehead. "I cleaned your wound thoroughly and applied salve, it shouldn't be infected."

Silas swallowed hard. "It's poison. The Draknoir arrows must have been poisoned. A slow death, they relish that."

"No, you're not going to die," Violet said, her jaw tightened. "I know how to create an antidote for poisons like this. We need a Potma weed and coriander oil."

"Potma weed?" Silas asked.

"Yes—but it doesn't grow here," Violet said, sighing heavily. "We must get to my cottage immediately. Your shoulder looks grievous, but the salve may have given us more time. How do you feel currently?"

"My head aches and so do my limbs. I feel quite tired, even though I've done nothing to help you today." Silas shot her a smirk.

"I'm not the one who needs help, Cutter," Violet said, a bemused smile on her face. "We should rest a bit, but then be on our way. I'll try to guide us through easy territory to ease your pain."

"Thank you, Violet." Silas placed his head on his knees again and closed his eyes, trying to block out the increasing pain in his body.

As he rested, Violet retrieved her salves and applied them to the wound after cleaning it again. Silas bit his lip hard as Violet treated his shoulder and wrapped it tightly in a fresh linen bandage. Once she was finished, he lay down with his back on the damp grass and surveyed the stars above. He tried to relax despite the pain, but he found himself watching Violet busy herself with the fire instead.

She collected a few more twigs and fallen branches from the trees nearby to throw into the small hearth she had created near Silas. The fire crackled loudly as the fresh wood was consumed by the flames; Violet stood close with her arms outstretched to warm her body and dry her wet clothes. In the dancing light of the fire, Silas gazed at Violet's face and saw her beauty for the first time. Her face was heart-shaped with a slightly upturned nose that perfectly complimented her high cheekbones and full, bow-shaped lips. Violet's gaze moved from watching the fire toward his direction and Silas immediately closed his eyes, feigning sleep to avoid her detection. When he slowly reopened his eyes a few seconds later, Violet had moved over by Homer and she was talking to the horse in a soft voice. Silas could not make out her words, and as he attempted to listen closer, he felt a sudden drowsiness overtake him. His eyes closed once more and he slipped into a peaceful sleep on the grass near the Dulan.

ELEVEN

The Blacksmith's Cottage

Are you ready?" Siegfried asked, securing the contents of his pack before slinging it onto his back.

Lucius nodded and slung his own heavy pack over his shoulders as they exited the doors of Griffin's Head. The previous night they had visited the Crimson Eagle and picked up the wineskins and supplies Eldred had been holding for them. Siegfried's smile was wide and his eyes gleamed when Eldred handed him their wineskins, but Lucius could not figure out why and the elf was an expert at keeping his thoughts to himself. He had not spoken to Lucius at all about Lumiath or the seer's allegations concerning D'arya. Their conversations frequently centered on their imminent departure to see the blacksmith or the bottle of *bywydur* that had enthralled Siegfried. Lucius asked his brother when they were actually going to use the elixir, hoping to get Siegfried to stop talking about it. The elf grinned at the question and told him to be patient.

After walking down the sloping hill where Griffin's Head stood, they soon reached the center square and walked past the towering statues of the man and elf. Near the statues stood the town well where an old man and his wife were drawing water into clay jars. Siegfried unhooked the wineskin hanging from his belt and walked toward the well, motioning for Lucius to follow. Once the elderly couple had finished filling their pots, the old man handed the wooden drawing bucket to Siegfried. The elf tossed the bucket into the dark mouth of the well and a faint splash followed from below. Siegfried grabbed the rope dangling from a pulley on the wooden bar above the well and pulled laboriously until the bucket appeared into view. Siegfried placed the full bucket on the lip of the stone well and dunked his empty wineskin into the water. He instructed Lucius to do the same, and after both wineskins were filled, Siegfried pulled out the vial of *bywydur* for his brother to see.

"Now you shall see the significance of this centuries-old elixir, Lucius," Siegfried said as he pulled off the cork stopper from the bottle. He gently let a drop of the shimmering liquid fall into his wineskin.

"If this will finally keep you from talking about this infernal elixir, then I'm anxious to oblige you," Lucius replied, allowing his brother to place a drop of *bywydur* in his wineskin.

"Now take a sip, brother." Siegfried leaned his head back and drank a small amount of the mixture.

Lucius raised an eyebrow and sniffed the drink, but did not smell anything questionable. He squared his shoulders and took a sip from his wineskin. He immediately felt a strong tingling sensation surge through his body, starting in his belly and extending to his fingertips and toes. The muscles in his arms and legs became taut and stronger than before. He felt as though he could fight a thousand enemies and strike them down without growing tired.

"This is ... an amazing feeling," Lucius said with a quick laugh and eyes beaming.

"I told you it would not disappoint," Siegfried replied, a wide smile forming on his face. "It will prove to be useful to us on the long days of travel ahead."

Lucius nodded quickly and fidgeted with his wineskin. "Shall we go, then?"

"Yes, let us leave Sylvania behind."

Lucius led the way toward the entrance of the city through the winding and narrow streets. The *bywydur's* effects gave him a newfound spring in his step and he barely noticed the weight of his pack, which was heavier now due to the extra supplies

Siegfried had obtained. They soon passed the Crimson Eagle on their way out, and Lucius' thoughts centered on Eldred for a moment. He thought of the elf's plight as a refugee in Sylvania, separated from his kin due to civil war. He could not fathom the elves of Evingrad ever fighting each other despite differences between clans. Peace and harmony were paramount among the elves of Lucius' homeland; he had naturally assumed every elf in Azuleah shared such ideals. He hoped the warring princes and elf king of Numa would come to a resolution sooner than not since their quarrels were petty in comparison to the looming threat of Kraegyn.

Lucius and Siegfried finally reached the city gate and departed Sylvania. Lucius bid farewell to Clay and Ruel, who sat unamused and stone-faced at their posts as the two brothers walked out toward the Barren Road. The road was crowded with travelers heading to and from Sylvania, many rode on horseback while others walked or steered wagons led by beasts of burden. Once Lucius and Siegfried reached a fork in the road and turned northward, the crowds thinned considerably. The few travelers they encountered on the northern stretch of the Barren Road were headed in the opposite direction. Lucius occasionally looked behind him, expecting to see a traveler or caravan headed in their direction, but none ever appeared.

Three hours of walking passed without Lucius noticing or experiencing weariness. Thank Yéwa for *bywydur*, he thought.

The sun was slowly setting below the tree line of Verdania to the west. He glanced at *Breninmaur* in the distance—a lone giant among the forest—and he felt very far from his home. Meanwhile, Siegfried kept himself busy watching the road, searching carefully for the deer trail Castor had instructed they follow to find the blacksmith's house. No worries of missing the trail entered Lucius' mind; he knew not to underestimate the eyes of an elf—least of all Siegfried. As a boy, Lucius used his spyglass to watch colorful songbirds nest in the branches of the Great Tree, and he often asked Siegfried which bird he was watching. His brother always spotted the correct bird without the need for a spyglass. Lucius missed those days of childhood in light of the responsibilities and burdens of their present task.

Their long trek on the Barren Road continued into the night without halting for food or rest. The lively sound of crickets, hooting owls, and distant wolf howls kept Lucius alert in the darkness. A full moon overhead provided just enough light to see the road ahead without the need for a torch. After another mile on the desolate road, Siegfried announced he had found the deer trail near a fallen elm tree. The two clambered onto the trail and descended a steep hill into a forest filled with conifers, beeches, and overgrown shrubs. They traveled through the forest for several feet before Siegfried stopped and suggested they make camp for the night. The rejuvenating effects of the *bywydur* had worn off hours ago, and Lucius now felt the soreness in his legs from their long walk. Naturally, he agreed with his brother's decision, and he dropped his pack on the ground.

Siegfried found a tall beech tree to climb and nestled his body between two branches—the perfect spot for an elf to sleep. Lucius rolled out a wool blanket they had purchased in Sylvania and lay down; a heavy sigh escaped his mouth as he watched the branches sway overhead from a light breeze blowing through the forest. Above him, Siegfried shifted in the nook of the tree and kept a watchful eye on their surroundings. The elf would only need a few hours of rest before setting out again. Lucius hoped his brother would be gracious enough to let him sleep longer. He hated early mornings and perky elves telling him it was time to wake up. He turned his head on the soft blanket and allowed the calming sounds of the forest to lull him into a peaceful sleep.

The next morning, Lucius was awakened to the sound of birds chirping in the treetops above and the mellow notes of an elf's flute. He turned over and looked upward. A flock of birds was perched on the branches of the same tree where Siegfried sat playing his flute. The birds chirped along in delight, darting and flitting to and fro on the branches of the beech tree. The harmony of the song and the warbling, chirping, and screeching of the birds was breathtaking. Lucius closed his eyes momentarily and listened closely to the symphony playing above, losing himself in the cheerful notes. But he quickly awoke from his reverie when the song abruptly ended with fluttering wings as the birds flew into the sky. He sat up and searched the tree for Siegfried, who had vanished.

"Are you finally awake?" his brother asked from behind.

Lucius flinched and swung his body around to face Siegfried. "Why must you always do that?"

"Forgive me. Even after all these years, it is difficult for an elf to grow used to the lengthy sleeping of men," he joked.

"Right, of course," Lucius said with an accompanying yawn. He began to fold his blanket when his stomach growled. "Anything prepared for breakfast?"

"Nothing except for what we carry. There is some fresh bread and aged cheese in one of the sacks, as well as *bywydur* if you feel you need it. The house we seek is not far from here, and I suspect we shall be there before noon, if not sooner."

Lucius grabbed the bread from inside his leather pack and bit a large chunk out of it. He drank some of the *bywydur* to wash it down, and then they set out in search of the cottage. The heat of summer had increased significantly since the first day they had ventured out of Verdania. Even with the strength of the elixir coursing through him, Lucius felt weary from the humid air sticking to his skin. Siegfried did not seem affected in the least, keeping a quick pace despite the temperature. Occasionally, the elf would turn around and tell him to keep up or asked why he walked so slow, which annoyed Lucius considerably. He ignored his brother after a while and concentrated on keeping cool by finding the most shaded paths through the forest.

As they crested a hill in the woods, Lucius noticed a faint trail of smoke billowing in the distance, likely from a chimney or campfire.

"Is that coming from the cottage?" Lucius said, wiping the sweat from his forehead.

"Yes, I believe so," Siegfried said.

They strolled down from the hill and finally exited the dense forest into a large glade rife with brambles, coneflowers, and several plants Lucius did not recognize. There were a few instances where Siegfried stopped him from stepping on poisonous weeds littering their path. When they climbed to the top of a large hill, Lucius spotted the aged cottage. The humble structure stood nearly hidden next to a large forest stretching for miles from north to south. He knew little about the Burning Woods except that Siegfried ventured inside decades before Lucius was born. The leaves of all the trees in the forest were arrayed in red, orange, and brown hues, never changing despite the passing seasons. The Burning Woods were in a state of perpetual autumn, brought about by the mysterious magic of the wood faeries who resided inside. Siegfried once told Lucius the faeries were guardians of the forest and did not take kindly to wandering travelers. They are nocturnal creatures who fly wildly around the treetops like overgrown fireflies. The bright glow of the faeries' bodies in the night also contributed to the forest's namesake. The few tales Lucius had heard concerning travelers entering the Burning Woods were not comforting. Even his brother refused to share any details about his past expedition into the magical realm. He hoped their journey would not lead them there.

When noon arrived, Lucius and Siegfried reached the end of the glade and stood near the doorstep of the cottage. The drab gray color of the cottage walls and the brown heather roof looked improperly juxtaposed with the bright, fiery colors of the Burning Woods surrounding the area. A continuous stream of smoke billowed from a hole on the roof, and Lucius' stomach growled when the faint smell of fried pork entered his nostrils. As they walked behind the cottage, they noticed a small enclosure nearby constructed of wooden pillars and a thatched roof. An anvil and a brick stove sat within the enclosure along with a large bellow and a barrel filled with water.

"The blacksmith's forge," Lucius said.

Siegfried nodded, peering back at one of the cottage windows for any sign of movement inside.

After quickly examining the forge and the outskirts of the cottage, they walked back to the door and Siegfried knocked on it loudly. They waited for a while without any response. Lucius knocked the second time, and to his surprise, a young woman opened the door.

She was a beautiful lady with dusky green eyes and a slender frame. The complexion of her face was dark, and the corners of her mouth were slightly upturned. Lucius could not see her hair since she wore a purple silk headscarf that only revealed her face. She wore a simple dress with lace flower patterns adorning her torso and matching her headscarf. Lucius stared at the woman and found himself at a loss for words, but luckily Siegfried broke the silence

"Good afternoon, my lady," Siegfried said with a smile. "I am Siegfried of the Silverhart clan, and this is my brother, Lucius."

The young woman shuffled her feet and bit her lip while eyeing them closely. "Tell me, what brings two travelers like you to the edge of the Burning Woods?"

"We are on an important errand, my lady," Lucius said in his most confident voice. "We were told that we could find a woman named Naomi in this cottage and she, in turn, could direct us to the blacksmith who works at the forge."

"I am Naomi," she replied with a bemused smile. "Please come in and take a seat. The blacksmith has been expecting you both."

The interior of the cottage was rather cramped, but very tidy and comfortable. There were two doors leading to bedrooms directly across a dining area with a table surrounded by four chairs. A small pantry near the dining area contained baskets of fruit, bread, and several preserve jars. The remaining space inside housed the hearth, where two benches sat near the hearthstone and the open flame. A cooking pan filled with strips of pork sat atop the flame creating a delicious aroma that filled the entire cottage. Lucius and Siegfried sat on one of the benches across from Naomi, retelling their journey from Verdania to Sylvania, their meeting with Lumiath, and finally their arrival at the cottage. For nearly an hour Siegfried told most of the tale while they feasted on the fried pork Naomi had prepared. Lucius sat quietly and unwittingly glanced at Naomi from time to time. Her beauty was captivating. There was an enigmatic air about her—something ethereal concealed behind her bright, almond-shaped eyes. He caught himself staring and would quickly look around the room hoping she hadn't noticed.

"That is quite a story, master elf," she said after learning of their quest. Her eyes turned to Lucius. "So, you are the last son of the Nostra line?"

"Yes ... Yes, I am, my lady," Lucius stammered.

"A great responsibility lies on your shoulders to defeat an evil so terrible as Kraegyn. I had almost lost hope that the prophecy would not come to pass. Dark days loom ahead, Master Lucius. Rumors are spreading of a campaign led by the Draknoir lord, Memnon, to eradicate men and elves from Azuleah," Naomi said, drooping her shoulders and casting a glance toward the smoldering hearth.

"Hasn't Memnon already waged this destructive campaign before and failed?" Lucius asked, recalling Helmer's tales of the continuing war between the men of Aldron and the Draknoir.

"Yes, but this is different than anything before. He is seeking to restore the old alliance between his kind and the dragons of Ghadarya."

The skin on the back of Lucius' neck tingled as he considered the combined threat of Ghadarya and Nasgothar.

He sighed heavily. "What must be done?"

"During the time of the Ancient War, there was a sword more powerful than any other. It belonged to King Yesu, the son of Yéwa, who wielded it valiantly against the enemies of men. When Yesu died, the sword was lost and somehow your ancestor, Cervantes Nostra, acquired the blade. Cervantes brandished the blade with the same fervor as his predecessor. He rode into battle with it and never lost a fight against Draknoir or dragon—gaining renown as the Dragon Slayer of

Joppa. Over time, the sword became as famous as its bearer and it was called the Requiem Sword—a holy blade capable of penetrating the combined evil of Nasgothar and Ghadarya."

"What happened to the blade? Was it lost with Cervantes?" Lucius asked, leaning forward on the edge of the bench.

"No, after the Siege of Arkadeus, the sword perished along with its bearer. When Cervantes dealt the final blow that slew the Black Dragon, the sword and Cervantes were destroyed by the unquenchable fire produced by Kraegyn's spilled blood. Fortunately for us, the ancient sword can be remade."

Naomi stood from her seat and grabbed an old scroll lying on a shelf on the wall behind her. She rolled out the scroll and turned it for them to see. A list of chemicals, metals, and other alchemical properties were written on the cracked and withered parchment.

"Lord Helmer's grandfather, Irribu Silverhart, wrote down the original instructions used to create the Requiem Sword two thousand years ago in the age historians now call the Golden Millennium. The sword was originally forged by a Numan elf whose name was unfortunately never recorded. Legend says that this elf received specific instructions from King Yesu himself to forge the sword. The unnamed elf passed on this information to Irribu. This is a copy of the original document, which the blacksmith can use to forge the holy blade of Joppa anew. Many of these materials were hard to come by, but we found most of them nonetheless. There are two more that are needed to forge the sword, and we will need your help in collecting them."

Lucius leaned back on the bench, dumbfounded by all the information Naomi had relayed to them. "Well ... what items are left?"

"One of the items lies in the north, beyond Jun-Jun Pass in the Grey Swamps. It is an alchemical powder known as *mithas*, which is needed to make the blade effective against dragon scales. The other item is camel leather, which will be used for the grip on the hilt, and it can be found in Aldron. But you will not be venturing there," she said, rolling up the scroll and placing it back on the shelf.

"If not us, then who?" Siegfried raised an eyebrow.

"Myself and the blacksmith's apprentice, Violet Pulfer. She is soon to return from the northern banks of the Feilon River," Naomi replied as she sat on the bench. "We shall retrieve the camel leather while you venture into the Grey Swamps. And perhaps in a fortnight or less, we can all meet here with everything required to forge the Requiem Sword."

"It seems you have been planning this for quite some time," Siegfried said, placing his right thumb and forefinger on the cleft of his chin.

"Yes, this is quite a meticulous process to forge a sword," Lucius interjected.

"Meticulous ... and dangerous. We will all face great peril on this errand. I have no doubt Memnon's spies will soon find out about you, Lucius, and our plan to restore the lost sword. And the dragons will not have forgotten the weapon that felled their leader." She looked at Lucius, her face grim. "We must all take great care to avoid the enemy until the blade is in your hands."

Lucius nodded. "I will do what is necessary, my lady. When do we leave for the Grey Swamps?"

"It would be wise to spend a day or two resting and planning our course to the swamps of the north. Would you allow us to stay here, Lady Naomi?" Siegfried asked.

"Yes, of course, stay as long as you need. I do not plan on leaving until Violet arrives tomorrow evening." Naomi spread her arms with palms upturned. "Please help yourselves to anything while you are here."

"Thank you very much," Siegfried bowed.

"Yes, thank you, my lady." Lucius stood up and stretched his legs. "I am curious, though. When will we be meeting this blacksmith who will be forging the great sword?"

Naomi stood up to meet his gaze and smiled. "You've already met her."

TWELVE

Nearing Death's Door

The long arduous road from the Feilon River had taken its toll on both Violet and Cutter. Two days had passed since she had found him in the wilderness, and they had spent most of their time together treading through the wilderness of Marsolas. Violet steered Homer, who bore Cutter, by the reins as she sought the way home. Cutter's condition had steadily grown worse. The poison from the Draknoir's arrow was spreading through his bloodstream, debilitating him more with each passing hour. Her salves had slowed the poison's effects, but without proper medicine, he would be dead in a day or less. He slept most of the time, feeling too ill to walk alongside her or even dismount the horse without help.

Violet had planned a different course to return to her cottage at the western edge of the Burning Woods to make traveling easier for Cutter. She usually cut through the northern section of the Burning Woods on her trips to the Feilon to save a day's worth of travel, but it wasn't wise with a wounded and diseased soldier alongside her. Though the troublesome faeries of the Burning Woods were night dwellers, she knew other mystical creatures lurked in the underbrush and could pose a threat to both her and Cutter.

Rain clouds were forming in the west, and she predicted they had an hour before the sky would be overcast above them. I better set up camp soon, she thought, and looked behind her at Homer and Cutter. The horse didn't look tired—they stopped earlier and he had grazed on some crabgrass growing near the forest. Silas, on the other hand, had not eaten since morning and it was well past the midday meal. His long, gold hair fluttered from the bobbing of his head as Homer trotted slowly. She found him attractive and wished he had been awake for more conversation. His manner seemed very refined and not as gruff as other soldiers she had met before. As she strolled along the tall grass surrounding the Burning Woods with Homer in tow, Violet wondered if Cutter had a wife or maiden waiting for him in Aldron. She sincerely hoped not. Imagine her, a mere alchemist's apprentice, winning the heart of a commander in the king's army—her friends back in Tarshish would be jealous. Silas groaned softly, and she suddenly felt foolish for having such childish fantasies while the man was clearly near death. Her eyes fixed again on the dark clouds looming above and she quickened her pace, focusing on her errand.

Before the sun set and the clouds engulfed the sky overhead, Violet found a hill nestled on the edge of the Burning Woods to set up camp for the night. The hill overlooked the faraway city of Sylvania to the south, which had lit up its wall torches just as she set down her pack and Cutter's sword on the ground. A pair of elms on the hill provided her enough cover from the impending rain to start a fire without fear of it being snuffed out.

Violet woke up Cutter, and he groggily climbed down from Homer to lay on the grass. She then tied Homer to one of the elms and dropped an apple for the horse to feed on. After starting a fire, she checked on Cutter, whose breathing was slightly labored. She put her palm on his forehead and felt the heat of his fever. He opened his eyes halfway, looking up at her in a helpless expression.

"How far from your home are we?" Cutter whispered.

"Not far; we can make it tonight if we hurry. But you need to eat and rest a bit," Violet said as she pulled out a blanket from her pack and wrapped it around him.

"Do you think ... I'll survive?" Cutter shivered.

Violet watched the fire, avoiding his eyes. "Yes. Of course you will."

She pulled out a piece of cold, salted mutton wrapped in papyrus from her bag along with her frying pan. Once it was thoroughly cooked, she handfed the meal to Silas in small bits. He washed the food down with some water from Violet's canteen and rolled on his side to rest.

Thunder rolled in the distance and small drops of water hit the floor around them intermittently. Soon the patter of light rain became a raucous downpour. Violet pulled the hood of her cloak over her head, but it did little to prevent the rain from soaking her hair and shoulders. The fire flickered about wildly as raindrops fell on it, yet it stayed lit throughout the storm.

After a few minutes, the rain slowed to a drizzle, which continued to soak the already drenched clothes of the weary travelers. Violet waited awhile longer for the clouds above to clear so she could see the stars above to aid her in finding the way home. She looked over at Cutter and her chest tightened. He was curled up holding his wet blanket tightly and shivering uncontrollably. Dark circles had formed around his eyes, and he looked paler than before. She hated to wake him so soon, but there was no time to rest now; he needed medicine. After they were all packed and ready with Cutter on horseback again, they set out to their final destination. A grim feeling swept over

Violet as she led Homer in the darkness—the realization she might be leading this poor man to a dark grave in the wilderness.

In the two days that Lucius and Siegfried had spent in Naomi's cottage, the Evingrad exiles had plotted their course to the Grey Swamps to retrieve the mithras powder needed for the Requiem Sword. While studying a map of Azuleah, the brothers decided the quickest path to the Grey Swamps required traversing through the northern tip of the Burning Woods in order to reach the marshland beyond Jun-Jun Pass in the north. Of course, the quickest way was not the safest way, and Lucius had reservations about entering the mysterious woodland. The hostile faeries inside the forest could prove to be dangerous, but the alternative route—the northern stretch of the Barren Road leading to Jun-Jun Pass—held greater perils to their journey. Draknoir spies and highwaymen were common on the northern roads. And if Memnon or his minions discovered an heir of Cervantes sought to reforge the Requiem Sword, their entire mission would be for naught. Besides the obvious threat the northern road posed, Lucius also suspected Siegfried had other reasons for entering the Burning

Woods. He questioned his brother about it several times over the last two days, but the stubborn elf merely told him he had unfinished business in the forest.

Aside from planning the trip to the Grey Swamps, Lucius spent some of his time helping Naomi prepare for her journey to Joppa. He wished to learn more about the attractive young woman, but his efforts at casual conversation had fallen flat. She seemed to avoid questions about her past and often changed the subject to talk about their present duties. Eventually, he gave up and resigned to speaking with her about the Requiem Sword or metallurgy, which Naomi was all too eager to discuss. Unlike Lucius, Siegfried did not seem interested in idle chatter. When he wasn't devoting his attention to examining maps of Azuleah, Siegfried took short strolls outside in the glade near the cottage, either to play the telyn or shoot arrows into tree stumps. Lucius wondered if Lumiath's words were still weighing heavily on his brother's mind. He wanted to ask Siegfried about it, but an opportune moment had yet to present itself.

On the dawn of the second day, both he and Siegfried were ready to set out for the Grey Swamps, but Naomi persuaded them to stay a day longer. She was very worried about her friend, Violet, since she had not returned the previous night as expected. Naomi feared something serious might have delayed her friend, and she did not want to assume the worst before waiting one more day. She hoped they would accompany her if Violet had run into danger on her trek and needed their help. Naomi also did not wish to travel alone to Joppa without a horse, and Violet rode the only steed available to them. Lucius knew Siegfried desired to leave, but the elf could not deny offering aid to someone in need, whether stranger or friend. Naomi pressed her palm to her heart and her face brightened when they agreed to stay.

The rest of the day passed uneventfully and slowly for each of them as they waited anxiously for Violet's return. Siegfried traversed the hills to the east of the cottage, examining different forms of plant life, while Lucius read the passages of the red scroll he had skipped or skimmed back in Sylvania. Naomi busied herself with the preparation of meals throughout the day, and occasionally, Lucius noticed her peering out of the kitchen window, searching for any sign of her friend. Soon the sun's brilliant glow faded to darkness and the dim light of the moon illuminated the woods and glade surrounding the cottage.

When Naomi had grown tired of waiting and busying herself in the kitchen, she bid Lucius goodnight and retired to her room. Siegfried walked through the front door of the cottage a few minutes later and looked around expectantly.

"No sign of Violet?" the elf asked.

"Afraid not," Lucius said as he sat on the bench near the hearth.

Siegfried sighed and pulled out the telyn from his pack on the floor.

"Don't play too loudly; Naomi has gone to bed," Lucius said.

"Do not worry yourself, brother," Siegfried replied, a half-smile formed on his face. "My music will not cause a mouse to stir."

Lucius clamped his lips together and shook his head. "No, but the birds will surely flock and sing along to your tune."

Siegfried ignored the remark and blew into the instrument before playing. Lucius turned to face the fire and watched the flames dance about wildly. Siegfried played a few notes softly on the telyn while leaning against a wall near a window. Lucius sat silently for an hour, contented to watch the fire and listen to the calm music of the telyn as they both waited for Naomi's friend to arrive. He wasn't sure when he closed his eyes or how long he dozed before the neighing of a horse in the distance stirred him awake. He straightened and gazed over at Siegfried, who stared intently out the window. Lucius stood up and marched swiftly to the door with Siegfried following close behind.

"Naomi!" Lucius called loudly. A few seconds later, the woman stepped out of her room wearing a silk gown with her headscarf still on.

She said nothing and immediately followed them out of the cottage. The clouds outside had hidden the moon and left a veil of darkness impenetrable to Lucius' eyes. He heard the sound of hooves walking on the grass a few feet away from the cottage. Lucius peered along the tree line of the Burning Woods for any signs of movement. He waited for his sight to adjust to the darkness, but his brother's eyes did not need such an adjustment.

"There!" Siegfried cried, pointing toward the northern edge of the forest.

Lucius saw nothing at first, but after a few seconds, the approaching silhouette of a horse and a rider became visible. He also noticed a second silhouette walking directly in front.

"It's Violet," Naomi said. She ran barefoot on the damp grass toward her friend like a child running to meet her parents.

"I'll fetch an oil lantern inside." Siegfried raced back to the cottage.

Lucius ran after Naomi in the darkness, hoping Violet wasn't in any trouble. When he reached Violet, Lucius realized she was leading the horse and its rider. His attention quickly turned to the rider on the horse—a man wearing armor who looked to be on the verge of death.

"Naomi!" Violet caught the other woman in a tight embrace then held her at arm's length. "This man has been poisoned and could die at any moment."

"What?" Naomi glanced at the man. "What's happened—"

"There's no time," she cried. "Go boil some water and prepare a place for him to lie down. I need to make an antidote for Draknoir poison."

Naomi nodded and ran back to the cottage.

"You," Violet said, turning to Lucius, "do you have any knowledge of shrubbery or weeds?"

"He does not." Siegfried surprised them as he walked up with a lantern illuminating his face. "But I am familiar with the plants in the area."

"Please find a Potma weed. It is the only thing that will help counteract his illness."

Siegfried nodded and ran off into night toward the glade.

"Will you help me steer Homer to the cottage?" she asked.

"Yes, of course." He grabbed the reins, and they both trotted to the cottage.

Lucius helped her carry the man down from the saddle once they were near the open doorway. The man was drenched in sweat and trembled viciously in their hands. They carried him inside by hands and feet, making sure not to drag him on the ground. Naomi placed some wool blankets on the hardwood floor where they laid him down. A black pot filled with water hung over the hearth, and when the water came to a boil, Naomi grabbed it and poured the hot water into a basin next to the man's head.

Siegfried returned to the cottage carrying the Potma weed by its stem. The weed's dirty roots dangled like long, scraggly fingers. Siegfried handed the plant to Violet, who frantically searched the small pantry for something. She finally pulled out a jar filled with a dark liquid and ran back to the hearth to set it down next to the basin. She pulled the jagged leaves off the head of the Potma weed and tore them into small pieces. Lucius watched carefully as she mixed the leaves into the hot water along with a few drops of the dark liquid. They all watched her on their knees beside the man as she let the contents of the mixture dissolve in the boiling water. A pungent aroma filled the room, which smelled like cooked broccoli to Lucius.

"Can you please lift his head?" Violet asked Lucius, who was nearest to her.

"Yes," he replied, lifting the back of the man's head and holding it up.

Violet poured some of the mixture into a small cup that Naomi held out for her. Violet then grabbed the man's chin, opened his mouth, and poured the liquid inside. After half of it entered his mouth, she set the cup down and used her free hand to pinch his nostrils, forcing the ailing man to swallow. He coughed and sputtered some of the liquid from his mouth, but Violet gave him more until he drank without issue.

Lucius gently put the man's head back on the ground and stood back, waiting for some amazing recovery to take place before his eyes. But it never came. Violet grabbed a rag hanging from one of the benches and dipped it in the bowl to soak up the rest of the mixture. She asked both Lucius and Siegfried to take off the man's plate mail from his chest. When the man was bare-chested and his bandages were removed, she swabbed the festering wound on the man's shoulder. The wound looked horrid to Lucius—blackened and completely swelled around the edges. Violet was careful to dab the rag on the wound while Naomi fetched some pieces of linen to wrap around the shoulder. When the man was fully clothed again, they placed a wool blanket over him and let him rest by the fire, hoping their efforts had not been in vain.

THIRTEEN

Machinations

L ord Memnon watched the sunrise from the west tower of the citadel inside Nasgothar. He had no need for sleep, though nocturnal in nature, his hunger for war kept him awake in the daylight hours, and there were important matters at hand requiring his attention. The dragons of Ghadarya had finally agreed to a gathering at his behest. A day prior, an envoy from the Kroshen Wasteland had returned with tidings from Albekanar, the appointed leader of the six dragon clans and the younger cousin of the Black Dragon, Kraegyn. According to the envoy—a smaller female dragon named Seeth—the dragons had been in hibernation for the past decade underneath the Maguna Mountains in the northeast. They intended to sleep until Nergoth awakened them from the abyss and their hellish leader rose from the ashes once more. Something had awakened them earlier than expected. Memnon believed their awakening to be a gracious omen from Nergoth himself. Memnon's summoning rituals and pagan sacrifices on Nergoth's altar had awakened the dragons' slumber and perhaps won him favor in the eyes of the dark god. The dragons are awake and ready to retake the western lands at last; he relished the thought. An alliance between dragons and Draknoir would greatly aid his campaign to annihilate mankind and conquer the peoples of Azuleah. The army at Nasgothar was a hundred thousand strong—enough to trample Aldron, but not obliterate it. The dragons are the key. It is time.

Once the sunlight had penetrated the dark sky, he climbed down the circular steps from the citadel's tower to a short hallway leading into the Chamber of Deliberation. Nasgothar standards and grotesque statues adorned the walls of the dim room. On a daily basis, Lord Memnon, General Genghis, and the highest ranking Draknoir commanders met in the Chamber to plan the war against Joppa. The priests of Nasgothar also visited regularly for advice from their lord on how to better serve Nergoth and hasten the campaign.

A single table carved from onyx sat at the center of the chamber where Genghis and six Draknoir commanders hovered over it examining a large map of Azuleah as they awaited their lord's presence. Memnon approached the table with his head held high, running the claws of his right hand across his left breast in a mock slash signifying the Draknoir salute. His subordinates mimicked the motion, but with their heads bowed to him.

"What news from the outpost at Feilon, Gramme?" Memnon hissed as he addressed the shorter Draknoir with multiple spikes protruding from his jawline.

"The Aldronian prince has not been captured yet, my lord," Gramme replied, fidgeting with his hands. "But one of our spies saw a woman crossing the Dulan River a few days past traveling with a man on horseback."

"And where is the woman now?" Memnon asked incredulously.

"We are not yet certain, your Eminence. I have sent warriors to trail her and find out if she is harboring the Dragon Slayer."

"Keep me posted, Gramme," Memnon said. He drew close to Gramme and glared into his eyes. "You know what failure will cost you."

"Yes, my lord. The woman will be found, and the prince shall be captured." Gramme bowed his head and slammed his claws into his chest, allowing droplets of blood to ooze out. "By Nergoth's blood!"

"By Nergoth's blood, indeed." Memnon shifted his attention to the other Draknoir, who met his gaze. He saw faces conveying both fear and reverence. It pleased him. "Many of you are well aware the dragons of Ghadarya have agreed to a gathering near Lake Ein. In centuries past, our ancestors aligned themselves with the Black Dragon and ruled their lands with an iron claw. The elves—those insipid followers of D'arya—exiled themselves to the West from the terror brought forth by Ghadarya and Nasgothar. We were mighty and prosperous in those days."

Genghis and the commanders all shook their heads in agreement. Memnon knew how much they all longed for the glory days. A new era for the Draknoir was on the horizon; he felt sure of it.

"In their quest for power, our ancestors and the dragon clans built the fortress of Arkadeus," Memnon said, clasping his hands behind him. "But the stronghold of Scipio and Kraegyn could not withstand the rise of a lesser, insignificant race in this world. The combined power of Ghadarya and Nasgothar was usurped by men—by a defiler well known to us as Cervantes Nostra. He tore down the foundations our lords created and banished the Black Dragon from this world into the Abode of Shadows."

Memnon pulled a dagger from his cloak. The eyes of all the Draknoir in the room grew wide and some shifted uncomfortably on their feet. He often made object lessons of commanders and warriors in similar assemblies to motivate the Draknoir to victory and punish failure. Sadism and torture were effective tools in spurring his soldiers to such ends, but he resisted the urge to shed any of their blood. For now least.

"My loyal Draknoir, the time has come to rebuild the empire Scipio created for our kind," Memnon said, reopening the last cut on his palm with the dagger. He walked to the onyx table and slammed his bloody palm on the map over the region of Joppa. "Our time is now! We will forge a new alliance with the dragons, and by Nergoth's blood, I shall summon Kraegyn from the Abode into Azuleah again!"

"By Nergoth's blood!" his Draknoir underlings all screamed in unison, stabbing their chests with their claws.

Lord Memnon lifted his hand and licked the warm blood from his palm, smiling delightfully. "Tonight we march to meet the dragons. Make provisions for our journey and amass a great host of Draknoir. We have a campaign to finish."

The soft breeze and warm rays of sunshine entered the open window of the room where Silas slept, waking him from the disturbing images of Draknoir and clashing swords haunting his dreams. He felt a slight stiffness in his shoulder and his head ached terribly, but the pain was the last thing on his mind. He did not know whose bed he lay on or where in Azuleah he might be. He threw the bedsheets aside and struggled to stand on his feet. A stinging sensation emanated from his shoulder and caused him to grab the bedpost to steady himself. He noticed the bandages around the wound for the first time and he gently removed them, curious to see the condition of the wound. The swelling had reduced considerably and the color of the wound had turned light pink, no longer a disgusting dark purple hue. The sight of the wound reminded him of the last few days in the wilderness with Violet, which were a haze of pain and weariness in his mind. Soreness and minor aches plagued various parts of his body—probably unhealed bruises from his wild ride in the river. Nevertheless, his present condition felt immensely better than before. Death would have surely taken him if he spent one more day on that blasted horse. Violet had kept her promise to restore him, and he owed her a great debt for her kindness. Now if he only knew her whereabouts.

Silas searched the small room for any of his armor, but only found the mud-stained undershirt he wore beneath his chain mail and breastplate. He slipped on the shirt and stepped out of the bedroom into a central room where two benches sat beside a smoldering hearth. A tall elf with silver hair sat with his legs crossed on one of the benches. His eyes were closed and he seemed to be meditating. Silas could not remember the last time he had seen an elf, perhaps when he first visited Sylvania with his mother and sister many years past. He walked up slowly to the elf, unsure whether he was a friend or foe.

"I see that you have healed considerably since last night," the elf said placidly, his eyes still shut.

"Yes, most of my wounds have healed. But I do not know where I am," Silas responded "or who you are."

"You are in a cottage near the Burning Woods in Sylvania, the home of Naomi and Violet." The elf opened his eyes. "My name is Siegfried Silverhart, and I have journeyed here from the city of Evingrad."

"From the *Breninmaur?*" Silas asked.

"Yes, have you traveled there?" Siegfried asked, tilting his head to the side.

"No, but my father ventured there long ago," Silas replied.

Siegfried's eyes narrowed slightly. "I noticed your armor is a different design than the Aldronian standard. Are you a commander or something of the like?"

"Something of the like," Silas answered, unsure whether or not to reveal his royal position. "I am a member of the Drachengarde of Aldron. My company was slaughtered by a horde of Draknoir in the forests of Ithileo."

"A dragon slayer ... not what I expected at all. There has not been an attack from a dragon for over ten years. Why has the King decided to resurrect a forgotten order like the Drachengarde?"

"Forgotten? No man in Joppa has forgotten what the sword of the first dragon slayer did for our kingdom," he said in a louder voice than he intended. "The dragons still live in their hellish mountains, and they must be killed before the Draknoir seek them out."

Siegfried pressed a thumb to his lips. "Yes, I see your reasoning. Perhaps you would be of great use to us."

Silas arched an eyebrow. "All right. Where am I? Where's Violet? I need to speak with her, and I need my belongings. I had a sword and armor; where is it?"

"Calm yourself, my friend," Siegfried said, rising from the bench. "Violet has gone with my brother, Lucius, to hunt some wild rabbits for the noon meal—I'm sure you are quite starved. And as for your belongings, they are out back in the blacksmith's forge. Naomi is sharpening your sword and repairing any damage to your armor."

He hunched his shoulders and looked at the ground. "I'm sorry. I'm not accustomed to such kindness from strangers."

"It is quite all right. We are here to help you," Siegfried walked up to him and put a hand on his uninjured shoulder. "Now I only ask that you trust us. There is crucial information

I must impart to you in hopes you might help us on an important errand."

"I'm not sure how I can be of much help."

"Believe me, there is much you can do to help our plight."

FOURTEEN

Friends and allies

Lucius sat at the dining table next to Siegfried in Naomi's kitchen across from Cutter, speaking for hours in the morning about their separate adventures in Azuleah. Naomi prepared venison stew for them in the kitchen, chopping celery and carrots while Violet sliced the meat and heated the broth in the hearth. The delicious aroma filled the cottage and roused Lucius' appetite. He couldn't recall the last time he had venison, but the smell made his mouth water. He tried hard to stay focused on the conversation between Siegfried and Cutter. They became well-acquainted with the Aldronian warrior in the past day, despite his hesitance to discuss his mission or the resurgence of the Drachengarde. But after Siegfried revealed their own intentions to forge the Requiem Sword, Cutter's demeanor changed. He listened to them intently and seemed genuinely interested in knowing more about their plans. Siegfried had left out one minor detail in his disclosure with the veteran swordsman; he hadn't spoken a word about Lucius' lineage as an heir to the Aldronian throne. Siegfried only said the holy blade of Joppa needed to be restored for the sake of the kingdom. Cutter said nothing for a while after the elf finished speaking. He hunched his shoulders and stroked his beard thoughtfully before he finally spoke.

"If it must be done, then let it be Yéwa's will."

"The sword is our only hope in defeating Kraegyn, if he should rise from the ashes," Siegfried said.

"He will rise if Lord Memnon is not stopped or the host dragon killed," Cutter said, resting his elbows on the table.

"The host dragon?" Lucius asked.

Cutter turned to face him; his eyes looked tired and somewhat forlorn. "Memnon is a necromancer just like his ancestor Scipio. He has the power to resurrect any of his minions that have fallen on the battlefield. But their lost spirits need a body to inhabit when he returns them from the Abode of Shadows. He often uses the carcasses as the host, creating an undead abomination more vile than the Draknoir themselves. But the same cannot be done with regard to the Black Dragon—there is no dead body to possess."

"It is believed that Memnon will use a dragon of equal size and stature as Kraegyn to hold the fiend's wayward spirit. The host's spirit will fade from this world into the Abode of Shadows and Kraegyn will be resurrected into a new body, which will likely change to his former, grotesque appearance before he was slain by Cervantes."

"Was your order remade for this very reason? To thwart Memnon's plan to use a dragon host?" Siegfried crossed his arms.

"Yes. Five years after the last dragon attack in Joppa, the King restored the order that defeated the dragons in Cervantes' day—the Drachengarde. We have studied the same tactics our forefathers used decades ago to defeat the mighty beasts, but we have not had the chance to prove ourselves in combat," Cutter said as he stared down at the bruises on his arms. "My men never had the opportunity."

"I see," Siegfried said, casting a quick glance at Lucius. "Is there anyone left in your order who has fought a dragon?"

Cutter sighed. "No, the dragons have been quiet for years. No man has fought them since the old days. I have trained for years, and yet, I do not know how I'd fare against a dragon alone."

"I suppose we will soon find out, Cutter," Violet interrupted, placing a hot bowl of stew in front of him. "But I think we should not worry about it just yet. The forging of the

Requiem Sword should be our main concern, as well as avoiding detection from our enemies."

Naomi stepped up to the table, holding two bowls of the stew which she placed by Lucius and Siegfried. "Violet, I don't think our guest wants to get involved with our mission. I'm sure he would rather be back in Aldron to report the tragedy in Ithileo."

"To be honest, I'm not eager to return to Aldron bearing ill tidings," Cutter replied, placing a spoonful of stew in his mouth. "I must report to the king, of course, but perhaps there is something I could do to help—at least, as recompense for all of your hospitality."

"I told you no repayment was necessary," Violet said with a lopsided grin.

Lucius noticed a quick smirk from Cutter directed at Violet.

"Well, repayment or not, Violet and Naomi are heading to Joppa to find a necessary component of the sword, perhaps you could escort them there?" Lucius suggested.

"I can't speak for Violet, but I would be delighted to have a trained soldier escort us to Aldron," Naomi smiled at Cutter and Lucius grimaced.

"I would be honored to escort you both. Women should not travel alone on the Barren Road; there are too many evil folk about. But I'm curious, where are you two headed?" Cutter exchanged glances with Lucius and Siegfried.

"Our quest will take us inside the Burning Woods and beyond Jun-Jun Pass to the Grey Swamps," Siegfried replied, dipping his spoon into the hot stew.

"Be careful, friends. I've heard terrible tales of that enchanted wood, and the Grey Swamps can be perilous as well."

"We can handle ourselves, Cutter," Lucius said, pushing his shoulders back. "We've come this far, and a mystical forest won't deter us."

Siegfried raised an eyebrow at him, but Lucius just cleared his throat and smirked.

"What do you think the King's response to the Draknoir ambush will be?" Violet asked, changing the subject.

"I'm not sure, but at any rate we must retaliate. Memnon has slaughtered too many men and escaped too many times unscathed. Perhaps it's time our armies marched through the Black Gorge and attacked Nasgothar."

"Nasgothar is teeming with Draknoir and all manner of dark beasts. It would be unwise to lead so many men to such an ill fate," Siegfried said, placing his spoon on the table.

"You may be right, but something must be done. The Draknoir have proven to be more of a threat to Joppa than the dragons, and I am tired of losing family and friends to them!"

Cutter slammed his fist onto the table. Everyone stopped eating, awkwardly silent and watching Cutter nervously.

Cutter ran a hand over his face and shook his head. "I ... I'm sorry. This war has strained me for so long. I've known nothing more than fighting and I long for it to end. Yéwa has abandoned us these past few years."

Lucius wanted to say something to console the man, but he couldn't think of any comforting words. He also felt abandoned by Yéwa. He thought back to the red scroll and Yesu's death, a violent end to a humble man with no aid from a God who claimed to be present at all times.

"Do not worry, friend; I believe this war will soon near its end," Siegfried said. "We can have a decisive advantage over the Draknoir with the blade of Cervantes—a weapon blessed by Yéwa. Evil cannot prevail forever; eventually good overcomes all."

The elf stood up from his seat and looked at each of them solemnly. "Let us go now and speed the hammer's fall on Nasgothar and Ghadarya."

The gates of Gilead Palace closed tightly shut with a resounding boom as Captain Baron Stendahl walked up the marble stairs to enter the great hall of the king. On his way he passed statuesque guards and gossiping courtiers, who instantly recognized him by his red, short hair and the high rank he bore on his armor—a golden chain looped around his shoulder. Some of the slightly inebriated loiterers in the king's hall tried to approach him, but he merely glared at them when they neared him or called his name. After climbing up another short flight of stairs, he stepped into an arched hallway with Aldronian standards hanging on either side and walked up to the double doors that led into the King's throne room. He announced his name and rank to the two guards on each side of the iron doors, and they quickly grabbed the ring-shaped handles to pull the doors open.

Once inside, Baron glanced at the large blue and white standard hung above the throne, which depicted an image of a falcon in flight at its center. His Majesty's standard filled him with hope, even in these dark days, and he occasionally pictured himself as a falcon flying far above Joppa, far from the present troubles they faced. Fading sunlight seeped in from the windows cut into the stone walls illuminating the room in a golden aura. Baron marched down the red velvet carpet to the white throne where King Alfryd Dermont sat with his head bowed and eyes closed. Baron slowed his pace as he neared the foot of the throne. He heard unintelligible whispers coming from the king's mouth and realized his Majesty was praying to Yéwa.

After a few seconds, the King opened his dull blue eyes and looked up at him. Lines covered the man's face along with silver tresses dangling from beneath his gilded crown. A prominent nose and wide jaw gave him the physical appearance of nobility characteristic of the Dermont line. He wore a green velvet overcoat with fur sewn on the collar and at the ends of his sleeves. A dark blue tunic sewn in the finest linen and by the best tailors of Joppa adorned his body beneath the robe. But for all the guise of royalty Baron recognized in King Dermont, he also saw a distressed man hunched over on his throne, weakened by old age and a decades-long war with the Draknoir.

"My lord," Baron said, kneeling before him, "there is news from our scouts on the fringes of the Ithileo forest."

The King's face brightened for a moment. "Tell me, Baron, what has occurred?"

"The mutilated bodies of three thousand soldiers from Aldron's army have been discovered in the forest along with dead Draknoir who also fell in the battle," Baron said with a strained voice.

Dermont stood up from his throne, placing a hand on his forehead. "So many dead ... what of the Drachengarde?"

"The bodies of the Slayers were found a few feet from the forest, your Highness. Asher Bowen is dead, along with the rest of his company ... save for one."

The King turned to face him with an eagerness in his eyes. "Who?"

"Captain Silas, my lord. His body was not found among the others."

King Dermont sighed with relief. He walked over to the western window of the throne room, placing his hands on the stone sill. "Can a search be arranged for him?"

"Sir, I do believe it would be best now to mobilize your—"

"Can it be done or not, Baron?"

Baron swallowed hard. "Yes, it can, my lord. But what hope do we have that the Prince still lives? Ithileo and the Dulan are swarming with Draknoir; our scouts barely escaped alive."

"You must always hope, Baron. In my old age, hope is all that a man has left." King Alfryd turned to face him. "Mobilize our soldiers to ride for Ithileo and send advance scouts to the lands surrounding the Dulan. We must act swiftly to find Silas and clear Ithileo of Draknoir."

"By your command, your Majesty." Baron bowed his head and turned on his heel toward the doors.

"Baron," Dermont called.

"Yes, my lord?" he spun around to face him.

"You are my most trusted advisor and friend; I would entrust this errand to no one else but you," King Alfryd said as he slowly walked up to him. "Please find Silas. Please find my son, Baron."

"I will do everything in my power to find the Prince, my lord. You have my word."

King Alfryd nodded, but said nothing. Baron bowed again and walked out of the throne room. As the door closed, he felt his heart beat faster as he grew anxious about the imminent battle in Ithileo. He had led numerous battles in the past and killed countless Draknoir, but this felt different. He needed to recover Prince Silas, wherever he might be, and he feared what the outcome might be. The Prince could be lying wounded somewhere in the wilderness or captured by the enemy, or even dead. Baron dismissed the grim possibility and tried to stay hopeful. He could neither bear the thought of another Dermont dead nor deliver such ill news to his Sovereign. The grief would be insurmountable for King Alfryd and all of Aldron. Baron needed to find the Prince, and he needed to be alive. He must be alive.

FIFTEEN

Dark Alliance

Numerous ranks of the Draknoir host marched through the inhospitable marshland of the Black Gorge where the fortress of Nasgothar loomed as a large spire piercing the landscape. The darkening twilight sky led many of the feral warriors to light torches as they continued on their long walk to Lake Ein. Behind the marching horde of Draknoir, Lord Memnon and General Genghis rode on the backs of their Onyx lizards. The large, four-legged lizards dwell in the caves of the Onyx Mountains where Draknoir trappers capture them and train them for war. Their long, spiked tails and talons are well-suited for combat, and they have an insatiable appetite for human flesh, which greatly pleased Memnon. The lizards' tongues flicked in and out of their mouths incessantly as they searched the terrain for rodents to devour. The lizard Memnon rode, known as Redjaw, wore a bronze helmet with a long metal horn between his eyes. Silver hooks pierced into folds of skin on Redjaw's nape where leather reins were tied through loops on the hooks. Black markings adorned the green scales of the Onyx lizard's forelegs, commemorating its victories and kills on the battlefield. Redjaw had a reputation for ruthlessness in battle. He often used his jaws to snap the necks of the enemy's horses and gored Aldronian soldiers with his horn. Memnon could hardly wait to use the lizard in the approaching battle with Aldron and indulge their mutual bloodlust.

When all traces of light vanished from the night sky except for the shimmering stars, the Draknoir horde finally reached the shore of Lake Ein, a black void on the dark landscape bordering Nasgothar. Lord Memnon dismounted Redjaw and advanced through his legions of warriors. The Draknoir made a path for him and bowed their heads as their leader strode past them. When Memnon reached the lake's edge, he looked up to the skies, searching in the darkness for a familiar shadow, but he saw none. He sighed impatiently, but suddenly a thunderous beating of wings emerged from the north. Many of the Draknoir behind him hissed—frightened or anxious perhaps. Memnon ignored them, his attention focused on the large shadowy figures approaching the lake from above.

Three dragons swiftly descended into the shallow water of the lake; their scaly bodies shone in the flickering light of the torches the Draknoir carried. A wind swept over the host from the great wing beats of the dragons as they landed. They stood tall and majestic, eyes glowing from the reflection of the torchlight. Each dragon appeared altogether different from the next. A prominent pair of horns adorned the head of the tallest dragon, whose deep purple skin shimmered as it moved about. A large dragon with green scales and golden underbelly stood next to the horned dragon displaying an iridescent fin, which began at the base of its neck and ended at the tip of its tail. Finally, a smaller, orange-scaled dragon flanked the others, and Memnon noticed three long spikes jutting from each of its temples and a long tail studded with similar protrusions. Lord Memnon could not help but smile at their majestic appearances; they were fearsome creatures who would bring glory to Nasgothar and misery to men.

"Good evening, my venerable guests. Many a night I have thought of this day, when the magnificent dragons of Ghadarya would honor me with their presence at the threshold of Nasgothar," Memnon said, spreading his arms wide in a welcoming gesture.

The dragons did not speak or acknowledge him; they only exchanging glances among each other as if deciding who should speak first. Finally, the horned dragon with purple scales stepped forward, creating large ripples in the water of Lake Ein. The dragon stood at a height three times taller than Memnon, who marveled at the beast. The warriors beside him became apprehensive at the sight of the dragon, drawing their swords and standing defensively beside their master. Memnon commanded the Draknoir to sheathe their swords and stand behind him as before. The horned dragon did not seem anxious in the least by the thousands of warriors standing around Memnon. The dragon merely stared at Memnon and released puffs of smoke from his nostrils between breaths.

"We have come by the will of Nergoth to restore our alliance with the Draknoir," the horned dragon's voice hissed.

"And we accept the restoration of such a mighty alliance," Memnon said with a grin.

"I am Albekanar, chieftain of the Amethyst tribe of Ghadarya and eldest cousin of Kraegyn, Nergoth's Chosen. Two other chieftains stand behind me as witnesses of our accord." The dragons all bowed their heads slightly. "Tell me, are you the sorcerer who calls himself Memnon?"

"Yes," Memnon replied, placing his palms together and bowing. "I am the blood descendant of Scipio, the Draknoir sorcerer who allied himself with your kin and reigned as second only to Kraegyn in Arkadeus."

"I sense that you are very powerful, Lord Memnon," Albekanar said, studying him with his serpentine eyes. "But are you as powerful as your ancestor, I wonder?"

Memnon rose to the dragon's challenge and threw his hands in the air, reciting an incantation in *shak'teph*. A black cloud encircled the Draknoir host and lightning crackled within it. Memnon's eyes opened wide and turned stark white as he continued to speak erratically, commanding the maelstrom of lightning to strike the left flank of the Draknoir army. Agonized cries filled the air as a bolt of blue lightning sent warriors flying in all directions. Memnon lowered his hands and the yellow in his eyes returned as the black cloud dissipated from the night sky.

Memnon turned around and marched through the demoralized ranks of soldiers, who cowered at the sight of him. He approached the charred and smoking bodies of the warriors who were killed from the bolt of lightning. He raised his scaly arms and uttered another incantation over the foul-smelling corpses at his feet. In a few seconds, hundreds of wispy specters emerged from the air and descended individually into the bodies of the dead Draknoir. At his command, the Draknoir rose from the ground, disfigured and hobbling, but ready to fight despite their lapse in death. Lord Memnon grinned pleasantly and turned to face Albekanar, who growled in delight at the impressive display of necromancy.

"Nergoth has shown you favor in granting such power," Albekanar said. "Do you think you are powerful enough to usher my elder cousin from the Abode of Shadows into a dragon host?"

"The power lies within me to do so," Memnon responded confidently. "I need a host for the summoning. Is there one among you whose body is strong enough to hold a powerful spirit like Kraegyn's?"

"There is one," Albekanar faced his dragon mates, who had previously been watching over them like stone sentries. The green dragon with the fin on its back met his gaze and stepped into Lake Ein to approach them. As the dragon neared them, Memnon realized the green dragon's girth was greater than Albekanar's, despite the latter's taller stature.

"This is Gerudos, chieftain of the Emerald tribe and the only dragon whose size is almost equal to that of Kraegyn," Albekanar said, shifting his tail in the water as he spoke.

"Gerudos," Memnon stared into the fierce eyes of the dragon, "are you willing to sacrifice your life so that the Black Dragon of Ghadarya may live and breathe again in your body?"

Gerudos straightened his neck to its full height. "Yes. May Nergoth take me to the Abode of Shadows in Kraegyn's stead."

"Excellent. I believe we have an accord, then, Albekanar. Let us seal this union in blood."

Memnon snapped his fingers, and in moments, three Draknoir priests came forward carrying a makeshift brazier he utilized while on his travels. One of the hooded acolytes handed their master a dagger and he immediately swiped a gash on his scarred forearm. Memnon pressed his forearm with his thumb, squeezing drops of blood into a small bowl in the center of the brazier. Albekanar honored the necromancer's request and used one of his talons to cut into his foreleg. The dragon then raised his foreleg over the altar and flexed the muscles around the cut, pushing the crimson blood into the bowl. Memnon raised an open palm over the altar and summoned a burning flame in his evil speech. The ensuing fire consumed the mixed blood and left a putrid stench, which Memnon breathed in with delight.

"It is finished, then," Albekanar said. "Our races shall conquer the lesser creatures of Azuleah; they shall be consumed by dragon's fire and conquered by the Draknoir horde."

"Yes. But there is still a small matter we must address," Memnon said.

Albekanar narrowed his eyes and puffed out smoke from his nostrils. "What matter, necromancer?"

"There is a prophecy I have been most concerned with regarding the Aldronian defilers and the elves. You see, my efforts from Nasgothar have recently given us an advantage in Ithileo and the eastern shores of Lagrimas, where thousands of

Draknoir hold fast against the Aldronian armies. But Joppa is the true target of my campaign and the place where this prophecy is most vexing."

"What is this prophecy?" Albekanar growled.

"You will know soon enough. But first," Lord Memnon glanced quickly at each of the dragons, "which of you is willing to take flight to Aldron?"

SIXTEEN

In the Realm of Faeries

I think that's the last of it," Cutter said as he attached the final leather pack filled with supplies onto Homer's saddle.

Lucius could not believe how quickly time had passed since he and Siegfried arrived at the cottage bordering the Burning Woods. Only a few days ago they had shared a meal together with Naomi and found a new ally on this perilous adventure. Now he stood outside the small cottage with Siegfried waiting to say goodbye to Silas, Violet, and Naomi as they embarked on their long journey to Aldron. He sincerely hoped no danger would befall any of them, but he was especially concerned for Naomi. Her role in forging the Requiem Sword was paramount, and should she be caught by the enemy, their journey would be for naught. He worried about the young woman's ability to fight if the trio ran into trouble on the Barren Road. She can make weapons, but can she use them? Naomi seemed a delicate lady to him, smaller in stature than Violet and very graceful in her movements—not the qualities Lucius envisioned in a warrior maiden. He wished she could travel along with them to the Grey Swamps so he could protect her and know her better, but he knew their task was more important than his growing affections.

"Do you both have everything you need?" Naomi asked as she slightly adjusted her blue headscarf.

"I believe we do, Lady Naomi," Siegfried replied, slinging his heavy pack around his shoulders.

"Thank you for all of your generosity, Naomi," Lucius said. "Please take extra care on your journey."

"I will, Lucius," she said. She reached out and gently squeezed Lucius' forearm. "Be careful in the forest, all right?"

Lucius' heart pounded against his chest and he loudly cleared his throat. "Yes ... yes, we will be careful, my lady."

Naomi smiled then turned to Silas and Violet, who both walked up.

"Keep a watchful eye in the forest, friends," Silas said. "It is a perilous place, but you will endure it if you stay close together."

"We'll do just that," Siegfried replied.

"I'm sorry we could not all be together. I've quite enjoyed the company of new friends," Violet said, smiling warmly. "It can be lonesome in the wilderness of Marsolas."

"I am certain our paths will cross again, Lady Violet. Hopefully, our next meeting will be soon and during less tumultuous times," Lucius said.

"Indeed." Cutter grinned and slapped Lucius' shoulder unexpectedly. "Yéwa lead you and sustain you, brother."

"Thanks." Lucius forced a smile as he lightly rubbed his shoulder.

After exchanging farewells with Siegfried, Cutter and Violet joined Naomi at the edge of the glade where Homer was grazing. Cutter grabbed the horse's reins and the trio walked into the glade toward the direction of the Barren Road beyond a cluster of trees. Lucius and Siegfried watched them disappear into the distance before entering into the Burning Woods behind the cottage.

The woods were unnaturally quiet, no singing birds or scampering squirrels could be heard as they roamed the forest's interior. Lucius marveled at the bright colors of the autumn leaves overhead despite the summer season. A cool breeze from the east rustled the leaves, creating a soothing sound amid the serenity of the enchanted woodland. Lucius wondered if the stories of faeries dwelling in the woods were true, since he saw little evidence of any living creatures as they walked several yards without spotting a single animal. The stillness and silence of the forest soon became unsettling to Lucius and even the occasional sound of leaves rustling could not quell the eerie ambiance.

"Is it always so quiet?" Lucius asked, darting his head around searching for any movement among the trees.

"I'm afraid so," Siegfried replied, undeterred by the lack of sounds.

Lucius frowned. "Fantastic."

He tried not to think of their silent surroundings, and his mind eventually drifted to Naomi. He hoped she reached Sylvania before sunset, fearing the dangers she might face on the Barren Road in the night. Fortunately, Lucius and Siegfried had not encountered trouble on the road a few nights past, but safe travel was not guaranteed for Naomi and the others.

"Do you think Naomi will be safe on the Barren Road, Siegfried?"

"Cutter is an experienced swordsman; he will keep Naomi and Violet secure," Siegfried said, pushing aside a low branch from his path.

"Yes, of course, Cutter." Lucius tightened his jaw, recalling Naomi's joy when Cutter agreed to be her escort.

"Do not worry yourself, Lucius. I doubt Cutter is as fond of Naomi as you are," Siegfried said, suppressing a laugh.

"What? I don't know what you mean," Lucius said, a flushed sensation spread around his neck and ears.

"It's very obvious you have feelings for Naomi. There is no shame in that; she is an attractive and kind woman."

Lucius pinched his lips together. "Oh, it's very obvious, is it?"

"You were stammering when she touched your arm," Siegfried laughed.

"Well, what about your obstinance? That's very obvious to me!"

"Whatever are you talking about?"

"Your stubbornness over Lumiath's words concerning Father and D'arya. You've said nothing about it since we left Sylvania," Lucius said. Siegfried stopped walking and faced him. Lucius hated to bring this up now, but he could not resist.

"That has nothing to do with the subject at hand."

"I don't want to discuss my supposed feelings for Naomi with you, but I do want to know why you don't believe Lumiath."

"Father is a worshipper of D'arya, and I refuse to believe anything different!" Siegfried yelled. "I care not if a rebellious seer thinks otherwise."

"If he is so rebellious, why did Father send us to him?" Lucius asked, lowering his brow. "Why did he risk his reputation with the Cyngorell by suggesting Lumiath was the seer in Zebulun's prophecy?"

Siegfried inhaled and slowly released his breath. He averted his eyes and gazed at the tree branches overhead for a moment. Lucius fought the impulse to speak, knowing his brother needed time to reflect on the matter, but the awkward silence was excruciating.

"I do not know why Father sent us to Lumiath," Siegfried finally replied. "I can only surmise that the meeting was for your benefit—to know your responsibility as the *Ellyllei* and learn more about Yéwa. Father has been very deliberate in fostering a desire in you to seek the God of men, but that does not mean he has abandoned the worship of D'arya or aligns himself with a heretic."

"But Siegfried—"

"No, Lucius," Siegfried interjected, lifting a palm up at him. "I do not want to talk about this any further. We need to keep moving."

Lucius sagged his shoulders and nodded reluctantly. Siegfried turned around and walked through the thicket and underbrush surrounding the area. Lucius followed resignedly, wondering if his brother would ever agree with him. He believed Lumiath spoke the truth about Helmer's beliefs. Perhaps the only way Siegfried would also believe was if their father acknowledged the seer's revelation. But what if Helmer denied Lumiath's words? Could Siegfried be right and Lumiath be wrong?

Lucius shook his head—he trusted Lumiath and his father trusted the seer too. *My Father is not a heretic; he just knows the truth every elf denies. D'arya is not a god.* But Lucius still didn't understand Yesu's needless death, which kept him from fully trusting Yéwa.

The bright sun peeking through the treetops above moved steadily downward as the late afternoon waned and their trek through the Burning Woods carried on into twilight. Lucius grew bored of seeing the same kinds of trees, fallen leaves, and bushes along their march to the northland. His patience also teetered on edge in the deafening silence of the woods. Crunching leaves underfoot or swaying branches in the breeze were the only sounds heard among the stillness around them. Siegfried had not spoken since their argument, and Lucius wasn't about to open his mouth anytime soon. He rejoiced inwardly when they came upon a new sight in a small clearing, a solitary boulder next to a decaying log. Large white mushrooms adorned the log, and Lucius wondered if they were edible. Hours had passed since their last meal at the cottage, and his stomach growled at the thought of the mushroom pastries Peniel prepared for them back in Evingrad.

"Can we stop for a moment? I'm famished and those mushrooms look delicious," Lucius said, kneeling next to the log.

"You will be disappointed then to know they are Death Caps and quite poisonous," Siegfried said.

Lucius curled his lips and backed away from the log. "What else is there to eat?"

Siegfried smiled and placed his pack on the ground beside the boulder. He opened the pack and pulled out two raw salmon fillets wrapped in paper.

"If you can start a fire, we can try the salmon Violet caught in the Dulan River. I'm sure it will taste better than a Death Cap," Siegfried said.

"I'll gather some wood," Lucius said. He darted around the clearing collecting twigs and fallen branches. Siegfried arranged some rocks in a circle on the ground to prepare for the campfire. In mere minutes, they both enjoyed the warmth of a roaring fire and the smell of salmon grilling on a wrought iron pan. Lucius cleared the log beside the boulder of all the Dead Caps and dragged it by the fire to sit on. Siegfried sat on the ground cross-legged staring vapidly into the flames. Lucius desired to break the silence between them, but no words came. He caught a glimpse of the darkening clouds moving quickly through the reddish sky and wondered how far they were from Jun-Jun Pass.

"We will not escape the woods before nightfall," Siegfried said, still looking into the dancing firelight.

"But we must," Lucius said, feeling his heart beat faster. "Who knows what evils lie in this woodland, brother. You know the tales of the abominable faeries here."

"I know more than tales, Lucius." Siegfried looked into his eyes and Lucius saw weariness he had never seen before. "We cannot leave this place before I make amends for my crime."

"Crime? What crime?" Lucius asked incredulously.

Siegfried sighed. "When I was but twenty years of age, I came to the Burning Woods with a friend—someone I would now consider a rival. His name was Abelard, eldest son of the Windsong family. We traveled to the woods in search of large game to hunt, like griffins or forest trolls. Being foolish young elves, we wandered into the Burning Woods under the cover of darkness and encountered a band of faeries. The faeries did not see us at first, and Abelard dared me to shoot one from the air with an arrow. At first, I was reluctant, since I knew nothing about faerie folk and did not wish to inflict harm on what I perceived as intelligent beings, but Abelard convinced me they were devilish creatures with inferior minds. He goaded me until my temper flared and I let an arrow loose."

Siegfried shifted his eyes towards the fire once more and his shoulders drooped.

"The arrow found its mark, and one of the faeries fell to the ground. Tinny shrieks erupted among the other faeries, and I distinctly heard them cry, 'our king! Our King Blik has fallen.' From behind our hiding spot in the bushes, I saw the tiny king pinned to the ground by the arrow. The bright light of his body slowly faded until darkness surrounded him. Abelard laughed at the scene while immediate remorse consumed me. The faeries found us and chased us out of the forest. I have not forgotten their vengeful cries nor the sheer horror on King Blik's face as he died in the grass. I killed their king."

"But as you said, Siegfried, you were young and foolish," Lucius said, attempting to console him. "This happened over sixty years ago; surely the faeries will not remember this crime?"

"You are wrong, brother. They do remember, and they know I have come. Faeries hold deep grudges against those who have wronged them, and they have every right to do so in this case."

Lucius swallowed hard and ran a hand through his hair. "How can you be certain they know you are here or that you were the elf who killed Blik?"

Siegfried smiled briefly, an expression that caused Lucius' nape to prickle uncomfortably.

"Why do you think the forest is so quiet, Lucius?" Siegfried asked. "They're watching our every move and keeping the other creatures at bay. When the night comes, they will come for me."

"Then we must get out of here, Siegfried. I will not allow you to be taken by some meddlesome faeries."

"No, Lucius. I am prepared to die to pay for my crime. Please do not interfere with the judgment to come. You must go on to the Grey Swamps alone and find the mithras then meet up with the others."

"This is madness. I am not leaving you here—"

"The fish is cooked," Siegfried said abruptly.

"What?"

"Let us eat now and we will speak of this later," Siegfried said, extending the frying pan with the sizzling salmon to Lucius.

Lucius squinted his eyes and snatched the fish from the pan. "You are impossible."

They both ate in silence while the sky above the clearing slowly grew darker. Lucius occasionally scanned the perimeter of the clearing, searching for any lights or signs of faeries moving in the forest. When Siegfried finished eating, he played a melancholy tune on his telyn and watched the wood burning in the fire. Lucius could not sit idly while his brother resigned himself to whatever punishment might come from the faeries. He stood up and gathered more wood for the fire, including the dead log he'd been sitting on. The gloomy notes of the telyn continued as he strapped on his quiver and grabbed his bow. Lucius stood with his back to the boulder in the clearing and held the bow next to his hip with an arrow nocked. He watched the woods around him, preparing for any attack from faeries or other creatures.

A full moon shone in the night sky above the clearing, providing ample light in the darkness. Siegfried stopped playing his telyn and tried to convince Lucius to leave for the Grey Swamps. He refused, remaining fixed to his post beside the boulder. With a heavy sigh, Siegfried laid down on the grass and closed his eyes. The fire slowly burned until it became a smoldering heap of ash. Lucius leaned his back against the boulder and relaxed his grip on the bow. His arms and legs felt numb from holding the same position for so long, but he remained planted to his spot, focusing on the trees around the clearing. For hours he saw only the branches swaying softly and their subtle shadows on the tree trunks. No lights or sounds from the fabled faeries. In the stillness and darkness, his eyes grew weary and his posture slacked. Several times he jerked himself awake after dosing off for a few seconds. Eventually, his head drooped to his chest and he let sleep overtake him.

SEVENTEEN

Siegfried's Trial

L ucius woke with a start and gripped his bow tight. Darkness surrounded him in the clearing; the moonlight became obscured by clouds. He wasn't certain how long he had slept, but his neck and back felt stiff from leaning against the boulder. A few quick stretches helped the stiffness in his muscles and reduced his drowsiness, but he wondered how much longer he could stay awake and alert. He immediately remembered the *bywydur*. The vial was likely in Siegfried's pack. He walked towards the smoldering campfire to retrieve it and gasped. Siegfried was gone. Lucius quickly turned in every direction, searching for any sign of his brother in the clearing and nearby woods.

Nothing in sight except the swaying tree branches. His heart pounded incessantly as questions flooded his mind.

Where is he? Did the faeries capture him? Is he still alive?

Lucius stood motionless, unable to decide on a course of action. He didn't know where to look for Siegfried, trees stretched for miles all around—his brother could be anywhere. Lucius dropped his bow and grabbed Siegfried's abandoned pack on the ground. Inside the pack, he found the vial of *bywydur* and quickly removed the stopper to add a drop of the elixir in his canteen. He placed the vial back in the pack and grabbed one of the extra jerkins Siegfried had purchased in Sylvania. Lucius tore off strips of the jerkin and wrapped them around a thick piece of wood nearby. After strapping on his sword and lighting the torch with the remaining embers of the campfire, Lucius searched the clearing for any visible tracks. His tracking skills were quite modest in comparison to Siegfried's. Frustration easily mounted when he couldn't find any noticeable imprints in the grass near Siegfried's resting spot. He nearly quit looking until he noticed a faint sparkle on the ground next to the boulder. With the torch held low, Lucius discovered a thin layer of glittery powder sprinkled all around the grass below the boulder. Faerie dust. The sparkling dust formed a trail that led from the boulder into the forest. Lucius held the torch low enough to illuminate the faerie trail, following it into the Burning Woods.

He walked in the forest for over a mile along the erratic path the faeries created. As he traversed the woods, several faerie dust trails converged onto the main path. The more he walked, the more he saw converging trails. Lucius was convinced the trails all connected onto a central route used by the faeries to travel in the forest. He swallowed hard and continued onward, hoping the main path would lead him straight to Siegfried and the faeries' dwelling. The mysterious magic used by the faeries to keep the forest quiet was no longer in effect. Lucius heard hooting owls, chirping crickets, and an unknown creature bellowing softly in the distance. He instinctively clutched the hilt of his sword whenever something rustled in the underbrush, but he ignored the sounds and kept moving.

When he crossed over a fallen tree along the path, he caught a spectacular sight. Thousands of multicolored specks shone brightly in the darkness a few yards ahead of him. He slowed his pace and unsheathed his sword. The torchlight would likely reveal his position to the faeries, but they probably already knew he was coming and he didn't care to hide. The brilliant glow of the faeries intensified as he drew closer. They all seemed to be gathered in a large clearing where they huddled around a large mass, but their intense light obscured the object. Several of the tiny beings flitted around rapidly like hummingbirds as he approached the clearing with his torch and sword held high. When he entered the clearing, the faeries flew around him quickly like a cloud of gnats. Lucius swung his sword and torch at them, but did not land any hits on the faeries. They giggled at his failed attempts and eventually withdrew to perch on the trees encircling the clearing. Lucius scowled at the flying devils, whose glowing bodies illuminated the faerie dust covering every inch of their woodland home.

"Lucius!" Siegfried called out from his left.

Lucius quickly turned and saw his brother standing beside a cluster of tall mushrooms—presumably, the large mass the faeries gathered around earlier. A faerie sat atop the tallest mushroom on what looked to be a wooden throne. A handful of faeries hovered near the mushrooms and next to Siegfried, who stood on a tree stump with his hands tied. He clenched his jaw and glowered when Lucius approached.

"What are you doing here? I told you to leave me!"

"A pleasure to see you too, brother," Lucius replied.

"Stop right there, ground-treader," a faerie brandishing a sword yelled. He flew in front of Lucius' face and pointed his tiny blade at the bridge of his nose. Ten other faeries holding swords and wearing breastplates surrounded his head.

"Let my brother go, you pest!" Lucius remained still, locking eyes with the faerie directly in front of him.

"You will be silent in King Klik's court, ground-treader," the faerie replied.

"At ease, Brom," the faerie sitting on the throne commanded. "Tell your guardians to stand down."

Brom frowned, but followed orders and sheathed his sword. The other faeries followed suit and flew back to the glittering mushrooms.

Klik studied Lucius with his glowing silver eyes. "So, you are a kinsman to this murderous elf? You appear human to me."

"He is my adoptive brother. He is no murderer and I demand that you release him!"

"Demand?" Klik chuckled softly and quickly frowned. "You have intruded my court and trespassed into the faeries' forest realm, ground-treader. I will make demands, not you."

"Excuse his ignorance, your Majesty. He is unlearned in the customs or culture of faeries," Siegfried said.

"Be silent!" Klik said with lips pulled back, baring miniature fluorescent teeth. "Was it not enough that you murdered my father? Must you also display your arrogance in my presence, Silverhart?"

Siegfried's shoulders hunched slightly and he stared at the ground. His deferential demeanor surprised Lucius. The confident, stubborn elf he knew was nowhere to be seen.

"You don't seem to understand the reason your brother is standing before me, ground-treader," Klik said.

"I am aware of my brother's crime," Lucius said. "He made a mistake long ago when he killed your father, Blik. He was foolish in his youth, like many tend to be, and he is genuinely remorseful for his deed. Please have mercy on Siegfried, your Majesty. If you knew him as I do, you would know this crime was not borne of hate or ill will, but of folly and ignorance."

"Folly and ignorance?" Klik said, pursing his lips. "Yes, I suppose folly plays a significant role in the killing of innocent life. Ignorance must also be prevalent in one's mind when the consequences of murder are wholly ignored—when a royal family and kingdom is torn apart by the death of their king."

"Your Majesty, I did not mean—"

"Silence, ground-treader!" Klik lifted a finger at him. "Siegfried Silverhart has been judged here tonight. He is guilty, and he will die for his crime."

Siegfried remained silent, his gaze concentrated on the sparkling faerie dust littered on the ground.

"As for you, outlander," Klik said, glaring at Lucius. "I have no quarrel with you, despite your insolence. Leave now and my guardians will not cut you to ribbons."

Lucius suppressed a laugh, unconvinced the faerie warriors could do much damage. "I will not leave without my brother, your Highness—even if I must fight you all to free him."

He lifted his sword in a defensive stance prompting Brom and his guardians to unsheathe their blades. King Klik gritted his teeth and clenched his fists. Brom eagerly awaited the king's command to attack, but it never came.

"Wait, your Majesty! Please wait a moment!" a yellow faerie shouted and descended from the multitudes perched on the trees. The male faerie flew toward Klik's throne, close enough where Lucius could discern the small creature's appearance. The faerie did not wear armor like Brom or the other guardians, but only a simple tunic made of hemp and leaves sewn together. His hair glowed an intense yellow, which matched the color of his eyes and near-translucent skin.

"What do you want, Syl?" Klik said, tapping his fingers on the throne's armrest.

"Your Majesty, as your chief royal advisor, I must protest against any course of action that might create needless bloodshed," Syl replied.

Klik rolled his eyes. "And what alternate course of action would you advise?"

"Well, my lord, it is evident that this outlander wishes to free his kinsman—"

"Obviously!" Klik roared.

"Erm, yes," Syl said, clearing his throat. "Might I advise that we exonerate the criminal, Siegfried Silverhart, in exchange for a favor from the ground-treader?"

Klik stood up from his throne and crossed his arms. "And what favor could possibly atone for my father's murder?"

"The loss of King Blik was grievous, your Highness," Syl said, flapping his wings quicker than before. "But as you know, our kingdom is in great peril ever since we lost our fiercest warrior—the golem, Tok. The banshees are taking more of our precious woodland, and many faerie-folk have died battling the Screech Sisters and their kind these past six years."

"I am well aware of the troubles posed by those wretched banshees, Syl. What is your point?"

"My point, your Excellency, is that we must retrieve our golem champion—who defended us against those shrieking wretches," Syl said. He spread his arms wide, motioning to the thousands of faeries in the trees. "The will of your people is to see Tok restored to life and freed from the banshees' control."

"Free Tok!" One of the faeries in the crowd yelled, inciting a chant that reverberated throughout the clearing.

Klik listened to his subjects' chants with bemused annoyance then raised his hands to silence them. The faeries did not hesitate to obey the motion, and Lucius noticed Syl's wings flapping quicker again—anxious to hear Klik's reaction no doubt.

"I know our kingdom has suffered greatly these last few years," Klik said, pacing slowly on the mushroom's surface. "Tok's absence has created an irreplaceable hole in our defenses, and I do wish for his return. So it is with severe reluctance that I will acquiesce to an accord with you, ground-treader."

"I'm listening," Lucius said. He glanced at Siegfried, who now looked on with renewed interest in his fate.

"Just as a faerie's inner light burns, so does my hatred for Siegfried Silverhart. Nothing would give me greater pleasure than to bring forth his demise." Klik's nostrils flared, and he sneered when he glanced at the elf. "Be that as it may, the prosperity of my kinsfolk and kingdom must come before my vengeance. I will allow your brother to be released if you retrieve Tok from those screeching specters in the South Passage. What say you, ground-treader?"

"I do not know the way to the South Passage. And how will I retrieve this golem of yours? Surely, you don't expect me to carry him back here?"

"Tok must be revived with the Bezalel sigil, which you can write on his head," Syl said with a wide grin. He turned to his king, who grimaced at his advisor. The yellow faerie slumped his shoulders and hovered lower in the air.

"The South Passage is not far from here, but do not worry about finding it. Syl will guide you there," Klik said.

Syl's eyes widened, turning to Lucius with terror visible on his luminous face. Klik crossed his arms and waited for any protests from his advisor, but Syl merely nodded his head in resignation.

"What assurance do I have that you will let Siegfried go free once I have completed this task?" Lucius asked.

"You have my word as a sovereign ruler. Unlike your vile kinsman, I am no criminal and worthy of your trust," Klik replied, jutting his chin. "Now, do we have an accord or shall I execute this filth you call a brother?"

Lucius clenched the hilt of his sword. He grew tired of the king's arrogance and self-importance. Part of him longed to plunge his sword into Klik's minuscule chest and rid Azuleah of the ruler forever, but his Father would never condone such an act, and neither would Siegfried. The faeries also proved to be quicker than his fastest strokes with the sword. Freeing Siegfried and escaping Klik's forces would likely be a futile attempt. He bit his lower lip and exhaled slowly—he had no choice. Going to the Southern Passage and retrieving the golem is the only way to restore his brother's freedom.

"We have an accord," Lucius said, sheathing his sword.

"Excellent," Klik said, smirking. "I hope you realize that if you die on this errand, ground-treader, our accord is nullified and your brother's life is forfeited."

"I'm sure you won't be disappointed once I return alive with your golem, your Highness."

Klik's eyes disappeared beneath a harsh squint, but Lucius ignored him and turned to Syl.

"Shall we go?" Lucius asked.

"Oh my, no! Not in the middle of the night," Syl said, flapping his wings faster than ever. "Banshees are more powerful in the darkness. Let us wait until morning to set out and face them."

"Fine. May I speak to my brother?" Lucius asked turning to Klik, whose scowl persisted.

"Yes, you may speak with the condemned."

Lucius walked up to the Siegfried, who held a stony expression on his face.

"You should have left these woods, Lucius. You are risking your life on a fool's errand! Your focus should be on the Requiem Sword, not on my life," Siegfried said.

"I'm not going to leave you here to die, Siegfried. We need each other to finish what Father entrusted us to do. You may have given up on your life, but I haven't."

Lucius stuck his torch in the ground and hopped onto the stump, surprising Siegfried with a tight embrace. As Lucius loosened his grip on his brother, he deftly placed a hand in his brother's belt pouch.

"What are you—"

"Diaphanousphere," Lucius whispered, retrieving the translucent object and tucking it into his belt.

"Brom, take the prisoner away now. I tire of seeing him," Klik commanded.

Brom bowed and flew toward Lucius with his entourage. He watched as the faeries drew their swords and motioned for Siegfried to follow Brom into the Burning Woods. Siegfried complied without question. When they reached the tree line, Siegfried glanced at Lucius and mouthed, "be careful", before disappearing into the darkness of the forest.

Lucius felt a sudden loneliness for the first time since leaving Evingrad. He let out a long breath and bent down to pull his torch from the ground. Klik watched him from his mushroom throne, saying nothing, but conveying contempt through his icy stare. Lucius ignored the monarch and called out to Syl. The yellow faerie flew over to him, but abruptly stopped a few feet away from his face.

"What do you want?" Syl asked, raising a brow.

"I'm not going to hurt you. I just wanted to ask a favor," Lucius said.

"Oh?"

"Could you please come find me in the morning? I'm going back to my campground to rest before our little excursion."

"Oh, yes, I suppose I could do that," Syl said, shrugging his shoulders. "But surely you can sleep here?"

"On the sparkling ground with lights flying all around me?" Lucius frowned. "No, thank you. Come find me in the morning, Syl."

Syl nodded and then flew away into the mass of faeries now hovering above the clearing. The faeries conversed in hushed whispers, watching Lucius all the while—their disdain evident in their grimacing looks. He marched out of the faeries' haven without looking back and felt relieved to be in the darkness of the woods again. With his torch, Lucius searched the ground for the main path to his campground. He followed a narrow trail of faerie dust until it joined with the larger path. The night sky had cleared and streaks of moonlight fell through the forest canopy onto Lucius' path. When arrived at the campground, his head hurt from lack of sleep. He put out his torch and settled on the ground for the night, hoping to rest for a few hours before the dawn.

EIGHTEEN

The Southern Passage

Sleep did not come easy to Lucius. He tossed and turned on the grass throughout the night—his thoughts centering on Siegfried and the banshees in the Southern Passage. The reddish dawn pierced the sky above the clearing, prompting him to surrender the futile attempt at a pleasant slumber. He roused his groggy body from the ground and started a fire to warm himself from the chill morning air. Rummaging through his sack, he pulled out a loaf of bread and chomped into it. He washed down the doughy morsel with some *bywydur*, which counteracted his exhaustion.

Lucius watched the sun rise slowly into the clearing, glad to see its light dispel the cold and dark of the woods, but also dreading the errand he was expected to complete. His last attempt at slaying a banshee in the Evingrad tournament had been a pitiful showing. The banshee's screeches interrupted his concentration too much and his aim with a bow suffered incredibly. He hoped the diaphanousphere would remedy the problem. If he infiltrated the Southern Passage invisibly, he might be able to kill a few of the specters before they knew what was happening. Of course, he wasn't sure how many banshees guarded the area. Syl mentioned the Screech Sisters, which meant there were at least two, but Lucius anticipated more.

After finishing breakfast, Lucius packed up all of his and Siegfried's belongings. He grunted when he picked up Siegfried's pack, underestimating its weight. How did Siegfried carry all of this and not collapse? Carrying two packs would certainly slow him down in combat against the banshees, so he chose to leave the packs behind and carry only his weapons. Lucius hacked off a few branches from a nearby tree and arranged them around the bags, hoping to camouflage them from any wandering travelers or animals. The finished work looked like a dilapidated bush, but it was convincing enough. He spent the rest of the early morning practicing his archery skills in the clearing by loosing arrows onto tree trunks. A bright speck of light entered the clearing when he nocked his final arrow.

"Are you ready to venture to the Southern Passage, ground-treader?" Syl asked, hovering over Lucius.

"Yes, I am ready. But before we go, there is something you must know," Lucius said. He retrieved his arrows from the trees while Syl watched with head tilted to the side.

"Oh? What is that?"

"My name is not ground-treader," Lucius said, tugging an arrow out of the tree bark. "You may call me Lucius."

"Lucius? What a peculiar name." Syl placed a finger to his lips. "Well, Lucius, it is a pleasure to formally meet you despite our current circumstances. I say, have you ever fought banshees before?"

"Yes," Lucius replied. "Although I did not fare well against her.

"Her? You mean a single banshee? You've only fought one?" Syl asked, his voice rising with each question.

"That is correct, my little friend. I don't make a habit of searching for banshees to fight. Now, let's go." Lucius placed the last retrieved arrow in his quiver and strapped on his sword.

"Oh dear me, I cannot believe I mistook you for some competent banshee warrior. We're going to die in the Southern Passage. The banshees will peel off our skins with their claws for sure," Syl said. He incessantly flapped his wings and flitted in circles.

"Will you stop being so dramatic? I have a plan, you know. Just lead the way and everything will be fine."

Syl wrinkled his nose. "What plan?"

"Nevermind. Come, lead the way, Syl," Lucius said, walking towards the southern end of the clearing.

"All right, all right, just wait a moment!" Syl chased after Lucius and popped up a few inches from his face.

"What now?"

"I must show you how to inscribe the Bezalel sigil—you'll need to know it to revive Tok."

Lucius sighed. "Fine, show me."

Syl flew down to the ground and landed on a patch of dirt in the clearing. The little fairy used his diminutive feet to draw a circle in the dirt. Lucius watched closely as Syl hovered over the dirt and drew several curved lines that eventually formed a triquetra. The sigil looked nearly identical to the symbol on Lumiath's necklace.

"You must inscribe this sigil on Tok's head and say the word, 'Loew'," Syl instructed. "The sigil's power will then revive the golem."

"What does this sigil mean, or represent?" Lucius asked, eyes fixed on the triquetra in the center of the symbol.

"The sigil is ancient, and among the faerie folk of the Burning Woods it represents life. I'm afraid I do not know more about it than that."

Lucius scratched his temple. "All right, well, we should be off, then."

Syl nodded and flew toward the trees. "This way."

Lucius followed the faerie into the woods, and they traveled south for over an hour's time. During the walk, Syl explained the last few years of enmity between the faeries and the banshees. The animated royal advisor recounted the steady migration of banshees from the cairns near Neroterra, where an ancient gateway to the Abode of Shadows resides. None of the faeries knew why the banshees left the cairns and settled in the Burning Woods, but Syl believed some powerful magic or evil frightened them off, which seemed impossible to Lucius. Banshees were terrifying creatures on their own, and he couldn't fathom what might scare them away from their haunting places. Once the first wave of banshees infiltrated the faeries' realm, Klik summoned Tok to repel them, and the golem struck down many of the banshees in the forest. But the banshee numbers increased in a second migration led by the Screech Sisters—Siobhan, Lilith, and Fiona.

The three banshee sisters were unlike any banshees the faeries had faced previously. They were more intelligent and devious than the other banshees. Siobhan, the leader of the trio, organized calculated attacks against Klik's faerie guardians. And in one of the skirmishes, Fiona and Lilith managed to screech loud enough to kill half the faerie army. In retaliation for the deaths, Klik sent Tok and a host of faeries into the Southern Passage to clear the banshee haunting ground. The Screech Sisters were prepared for the invasion, and unbeknown to the faeries, a trap was set for the lumbering golem. An ancient cistern in the Southern Passage had been hidden from sight by a dense fog created by the banshees. During the heat of battle, Lilith and Fiona diverted Tok to the cistern and the large golem easily fell into the watery pit. The water washed away the Bezalel sigil inscribed on Tok's head, and the golem sat lifeless in the cistern, which gave the Screech Sisters a significant advantage against the faeries.

"We didn't stand a chance without Tok," Syl said, staring off into the dense cluster of trees and bushes ahead of them. "The king ordered a retreat, and the banshees continue to grow in number within the Southern Passage. If the Screech Sisters become more brazen, they might try to invade the King's court and the faerie haven. I'm not confident our kind would survive such an attack."

"Is the golem the only weapon you possess? You have swords and magic, don't you?" Lucius asked.

Syl scoffed. "Our magic is a mischievous sort, Lucius— useful for concealing ourselves and confounding interlopers who enter our woods. But such trickery is useless against cursed spirits like banshees. Most magic has little effect on them."

"All right, what about the petite sword hanging from your hip? Is it made from *efydd*?"

"*Efydd* and iron—and it is not petite! It's proportionate to my size, ground-treader," Syl replied, turning his nose up at Lucius. "While our swords are useful in killing banshees, getting close enough to do so is another matter entirely."

"I imagine one of their screams is enough to cause serious injury," Lucius said, ducking under a low branch.

"Or simply kill us. A faerie's body cannot withstand the force of a banshee's scream, which is why we need Tok."

"How is it the golem can hurt the banshees?" Lucius asked.

Syl flashed a smile. "His body is made of orichalcum ore, a mystical metal like *efydd*. The banshees are vulnerable to it. They cannot pass through Tok like other objects, and they cannot hurt him."

"All the more reason to wake him up, then."

"Aye," Syl said with a quick nod.

They crossed a shallow stream in the woods, and beyond it the ground sloped down into a deep glen. A light mist enveloped the glen, masking the vibrant hues of the autumn leaves in a drab gray. They had entered Southern Passage. Syl grew deathly quiet save for the faint beating of his wings. Lucius nocked an arrow and scanned the area ahead of them. Thick tree trunks and bushes along the ground were all he could see in the mist. As he walked further south, the mist thickened into a dense fog and he could barely discern his surroundings. Syl hovered lower than before and did not stray far from Lucius.

The sound of rustling leaves in the branches overhead caused Syl to swoop down behind a tree where he drew his sword and waited to attack. Lucius aimed his bow at the foggy sky above, searching for a clear target. He reluctantly loosed an arrow, hoping to draw out whatever lurked in the trees. A pair of crows cawed loudly above and flew from their perches when the arrow whizzed by. Lucius chuckled and relaxed his grip on the bow. Syl's chin jutted beneath a frown as he fluttered up to Lucius, who could not help smirking at the faerie's skittishness. He turned to walk when a woman's voice suddenly called out, "Who enters our domain?"

Lucius drew another arrow and whirled to his left where the voice originated. Syl flitted to and fro until he finally landed on Lucius' shoulder, pointing his sword in the same direction as Lucius' arrow.

"Who goes there?" Lucius asked.

A slight breeze parted the fog in front of him and the thin silhouette of a feminine figure approached through the haze. The woman's features became visible as she drew closer. Her face was pale and slightly sunken with dark circles around her eyes. Dark wispy hair adorned her crown and shoulders. The woman's white gown gleamed, despite the lack of direct sunlight around her, and she walked with a graceful gait. Lucius held his bow steady, meeting the odd woman's steely gaze.

"Do not step any closer! Who are you?" Lucius asked.

The woman stopped and cocked her head to the side, observing him from head to foot.

"Shoot her," Syl said, his voice shaky. "She's one of them."

Lucius gripped the arrow's shaft tighter in his fingers.

"Please, my lord. Have mercy on a humble maiden of the wood," the woman said, bowing her head to him.

"I'll ask once more: who are you?"

"Have you seen my sisters, kind sir?" She asked with her head still bowed.

"Shoot her!" Syl cried.

Lucius released the arrow and it flew directly at the woman's head. With unnatural speed, the woman caught the arrow a few inches from her face and snapped it in two. She bared her jagged teeth in a crooked smile and watched them with bright red eyes.

"I am Siobhan and you are no more," she said.

Loud screams erupted on both sides of Lucius, knocking him to the ground. He covered his ears as the banshee's cries increased all around him. Five banshees flew out from the fog and hovered near Siobhan, who cackled at her prey. Syl fluttered wildly over Lucius' head in a panic, but Lucius ignored the faerie and watched as the banshees hovered closer to his position. While still prone, Lucius slowly grabbed Siegfried's diaphanousphere from his belt.

"I cannot fight these monsters alone while you sleep, Lucius! Get up!" Syl shrieked.

"I just need you to distract them, Syl. Fly into the fog and let them chase you," Lucius whispered.

"What?"

"Tear their flesh apart, sisters," Siobhan growled.

"On my mark," Lucius said, lifting himself into a crouching position.

"Curse you, ground-treader!"

"Now!"

Lucius popped the diaphanousphere in his mouth and sprinted behind some overgrown bushes with bow in hand. The tingling sensation on his tongue spread quickly throughout his body and in a few seconds, his body disappeared from sight. Lucius ran for a few yards, sensing banshees were on his trail. He ducked behind a large oak and waited for them to pass by. Two banshees flew slowly past him in plain sight, searching the area for their quarry. In the distance, Syl's shrill cries echoed in the forest along with the screeches of his pursuers. Lucius quietly pulled an arrow from his invisible quiver and nocked it. The two banshees roamed around the underbrush around him, floating a few feet from his position. He aimed his bow at the closest one and let the arrow fly. The *efydd* tip pierced the banshee's temple and she fell to the ground in an explosion of dust, leaving no trace of her carcass. The remaining banshee whirled around and screamed at the death of her comrade. Lucius slowly walked between the trees, watching the banshee's movements as he prepared for his next shot.

The banshee darted quickly throughout the area, searching for Lucius in the dense fog. Her face was contorted into a twisted snarl and she yelled at random, perhaps hoping to catch him off-guard. But Lucius had the upper hand. And despite the banshee's erratic movement, he managed to land an arrow in her chest where presumably her black heart resided. When the banshee's remains dissipated, Lucius fetched his arrow from the ground and listened for Syl. He hoped the faerie's size and speed had served him well in escaping the banshees, but Lucius no longer heard any sounds in the Southern Passage. Although he wished to find and aid Syl, finding Tok was more important right now.

Endless fog enveloped the forest and every direction looked identical—trees and thick underbrush. He stumbled around the glen, searching for the ancient cistern Syl had spoken about. A faint banshee scream to his right caused him to flinch. Several screams followed the first, getting closer and louder. He leaned his back against the thick trunk of an elm and readied his bow. A small light pierced the thick mist ahead of him and descended to the ground—it was Syl. The yellow faerie panted breathlessly and tensed his shoulders when another scream filled the air.

"Syl?" Lucius whispered, moving the diaphanousphere with his tongue to speak clearly. "Are you all right?"

"Lucius? Where are you?" Syl asked.

"I'm next to the elm tree directly in front of you."

"There are lots of trees in front of me, ground-treader!" Syl shouted.

"Hush! Look." Lucius grabbed a low branch and shook it. "I'm right here."

"Oh. That is a neat trick; you'll have to teach it to me sometime—if we make it out of here alive!"

"How many are coming?" Lucius asked. A series of screams followed in rapid succession a few yards to his left.

"More than before," Syl said, still catching his breath. "I think Siobhan called out to the rest of her hags and they're on their way now."

"Yeah, they're encircling the area, trying to trap us here. We have to find Tok. Do you remember where the cistern is?"

"I think east of here, but I cannot be sure. Everything looks the same in this blasted fog!" Syl cried.

Lucius bit his lip. The banshees' cries were coming from the east, and he didn't want to venture there if Syl wasn't certain about the location. A bloodcurdling scream cut the air around them, nearly knocking Lucius to the ground. Siobhan flew out of the fog and swiped her claws at Syl. The faerie dodged the strike and sped into the air, flying inside the leafy canopy above. Four banshees quickly appeared at their leader's side, waiting for her to chase the faerie, but Siobhan did not move. She sniffed the air and gazed around the trees until her crimson eyes met Lucius'.

He stood frozen in place as Siobhan squinted and scrutinized the elm's trunk. She floated slowly towards the elm, sniffing incessantly with her cronies following her. Despite holding his muscles taut, he could not slow his thumping heart. The banshees crept closer, and he knew Siobhan would scream at any moment. He took a deep breath and ran at full speed toward the east. The leaves snapping of twigs and crunching leaves beneath his feet alerted the banshees immediately. Siobhan shrieked incessantly, chasing him with ferocious intensity. He could feel the banshee leader's cold breath behind him, and he tried to gain some distance by running in a zigzag pattern between trees and bushes. His pace slowed considerably when the terrain sloped upward into a steep hill. More screams filled the air from the base of the hill, and Siobhan's raspy laughter taunted him from behind. Once he crested the hill, Lucius turned and fired an arrow at the banshee leader. She dodged the arrow with ease, flying through multiple trees in her intangible form. Lucius nocked another arrow while finding cover within some overgrown buckthorn bushes. He cautiously peered from behind the leaves as a band of banshees flew overhead, rabidly searching for their prey. Three arrows shot from his bow made quick work of three stragglers in the band without alerting the others.

After the fallen banshees dissipated, Lucius stepped out from the buckthorn, looking and listening for more banshees, but no more passed by on the hill. He sighed heavily, examining his surroundings. Yellow and orange buckthorn bushes surrounded the autumn-colored beech trees on the hill and the fog seemed less pervasive here. Lucius walked around the hill aimlessly, savoring the respite before a sharp pain tore through his upper back and left side. The familiar laughter of Siobhan greeted him as he fell to his knees.

"You cannot run from me now that your blood is spilled," Siobhan said, waving her long, bloodstained fingernails.

Lucius stood up and tried to pull an arrow from his quiver, but the searing pain from the gashes caused him to recoil. Warm blood ran down his back and dripped onto the ground, completely visible unlike the rest of his body.

"Lilith! Fiona! I have found our scampering rat!" Siobhan yelled. She flew with amazing speed and screamed at Lucius.

Her shrill and powerful voice knocked him back several feet. Intense pain erupted from his left ear and back. The forest was completely quiet except for a faint ringing noise. He tried to stand, but his legs felt incapable of holding his weight and he stumbled uncontrollably like a heavy drunk. The last stumble proved to be the worst when he tripped on an exposed tree root and fell headlong down the side of the steep hill into the thick fog.

NINETEEN

Golem

Lucius crashed through multiple shrubs and jutting rocks before his tumbling stopped at the base of the hill. The agony coursing through his body discombobulated him, but somehow he managed to stand up again. He shuffled listlessly until the ground beneath his feet ended and he fell once more. The chilling sensation of water slapped his face and arms, waking him from his painful daze as he plunged into the abyss. He kicked wildly toward the surface and gasped for air when his head rose from the freezing water. Heavy fog hovered over the water, obscuring most of his view, but he quickly realized where he had fallen—the ancient cistern.

The retaining wall of the cistern rose to a considerable height, and Lucius doubted he could easily climb out. He tread the dark water searching for Tok, but stopped when he saw his reflection in the water. He was no longer invisible. The diaphanousphere had probably fallen out of his mouth during the fall from the hill. His bow was also missing, but the quiver and arrows remained strapped to his back. Besides the arrows, the only weapon he still possessed was his sword, but the iron blade would be useless against banshees.

A sharp pain coursed through his back and ribs as he swam to the center of the cistern. The sound of banshees screaming nearby startled him, and he quickly realized the hopelessness of the situation. He was defenseless and injured inside a pit. The banshees would make quick work of him unless he found and revived Tok. He propelled himself in the water with long strokes, frantically scouring the water for the golem despite the foggy surroundings.

"Lucius!" a familiar faerie cried. "They're coming! Where are you?"

"Syl! I'm here, in the cistern!" Lucius yelled, scanning the fog overhead until a pinprick of yellow light emerged.

"The Screech Sisters are coming!" Syl said, landing on some driftwood floating near Lucius. "I cannot continue this chase; my wings are giving out."

"Syl, we're in the cistern. Tok is here somewhere; you need to find him. I can't see anything in this fog," Lucius said.

"Of course, the golem!" Syl said, bounding off the driftwood and into the center of the cistern.

"Syl, wait!" Lucius called, but the faerie did not stop. Lucius followed Syl, but fatigue began to set in due to his wounds. He took a break from swimming, treading water and waiting for Syl to reappear. It was impossible to know the full diameter of the cistern in the gray haze surrounding him, but Lucius guessed the pit to be the same size as a small lake.

A quick flicker of movement to his right followed by a gust of air alarmed him. He turned and saw three banshees hovering above the water to his right with at least two dozen more floating behind them.

"Can I tear his flesh, sister?" A balding banshee with a jutting nose asked.

"No, Lilith! I want to peel his skin with a scream," the second banshee urged. She was equally as hideous with deep scars cut across her shriveled face.

"Fiona, Lilith, this one belongs to me. I've already tagged him; don't you see?" Siobhan said, motioning to the cuts on Lucius' back. She smiled devilishly. "But I shall allow you both to rip out his eyes and leave the rest to me."

"Syl!" Lucius screamed as he plunged forward in the water. He swam hard, using wide strokes to propel forward.

Lilith was the first to attack. She darted beside him with her clawed hands, taking a swipe at his face, but he dodged it by diving underwater. Her disappointed scream filled the air as he resurfaced and saw her swoop into the fog above.

Fiona came at him next. She flew faster than an arrow and stretched her arm back, ready to gouge his eyes. There was no time to dodge and he braced himself for the pain by closing his eyes. But the pain did not come, only the agonized scream of Fiona. Lucius opened his eyes and saw a new cut on the banshee's face courtesy of Syl's sword.

"You'll get more than that, you odious hag!" Syl huffed, brandishing his sword confidently.

"Did you find Tok?" Lucius asked.

"Yes, he's a few feet ahead of you beyond the fog," Syl replied, his eyes fixed on the banshees. "Go, Lucius. Revive Tok; I'll hold them off."

Siobhan cackled and her sisters followed suit. "You will both die in this pit, and the water shall be your grave."

"Syl—" Lucius began.

"Go!" Syl shouted. He flew straight at the Screech Sisters, parrying their swiping claws and managing to slash their arms before ascending into the sky.

"Kill the firefly!" Siobhan ordered. The banshees chased Syl once more, screeching with all their might.

Lucius submerged into the water and kicked the water savagely. Some of the banshees were likely following him, but he kept focused on reaching Tok. He rose out of the water to take a breath and felt claws graze the back of his head. Fiona screeched hysterically as she turned wildly in the air to face him, ready to strike once more. Lucius tried to mask his pain by scowling at Fiona and taunting her by saying, "come finish it, then." The banshee curled her lips and launched herself at him. When she was at arm's length, Lucius quickly pulled an arrow from his quiver and thrust the shaft upward into the banshee's neck. Fiona arched backwards, gurgling as she clutched her mortal wound. She slowly evaporated into the fog and was no more.

More screams came from the fog as Lucius swam rapidly. A large shadowy outline appeared before him in the water. It looked like a small island inside the cistern. When the golem came into view, Lucius was slightly terrified at its hulking size—the lifeless pile of gray rock could easily be taller than the Tower of Evingrad! Tok's body was on its side, half-submerged in the water and covered in muck and grime from the cistern. Lucius swam toward the golem's head, checking the sky for banshees. A cluster of them were quickly approaching toward him led by Lilith. He heard Syl's battle cries along with Siobhan's wicked laughter and feared his little friend might not survive their ordeal.

The golem's head was a faceless boulder, distinct only by the iridescent streaks of orichalcum ore peeking through the pitted surface. Lucius dipped his forefinger in the blood dripping on the back of his head and hurriedly inscribed the Bezalel sigil onto Tok's head. Before he completed the overlapping circle of the sigil, a deafening yell pushed him forward against the rock.

"You killed my sister!" Lilith screamed. A dozen banshees around her screamed in unison.

Lucius covered his ears, but he could not block out their penetrating voices. The noise reverberated within his skull and he let out an agonized scream easily muffled by the cacophony. To his surprise, the collective screaming abruptly ended when he felt certain death would take him. He glanced up, hands still over his ears, and saw Lilith clutching her right arm. A blackened stump had replaced her clawed hand, and Syl desperately weaved through the onslaught of attacks by Lilith's companions.

The yellow faerie yelled something to Lucius in the frenzy, but he could only hear the loud ringing in his ears. He felt sick and disoriented, struggling to stay afloat in the water. Lucius gripped the rock to steady himself and noticed the nearly complete sigil on Tok's head.

"Lucius, hurry up!" Syl cried, his voice very faint.

Lucius frantically inscribed the circle with his bloody finger and said the word, "Loew". The sigil erupted into a bright orange light that blinded him for a moment. He heard a sound like rocks grating against each other and slowly, Tok's head rose from the water. The banshees immediately focused their attacks on the golem as he raised his body from the water. Lilith and her band clawed at Tok's rocky exterior and screamed in their highest pitch to no avail—the golem did not flinch or move.

Syl dove down from the fog onto Lucius' shoulder, and they watched with awe as Tok suddenly swiped his arm at the banshees. Lilith and half a dozen banshees exploded into an ethereal mist, unable to thwart the orichalcum's power over their spectral bodies.

"No!" Siobhan screamed, tugging at her black hair. She hovered over the water and witnessed Tok destroy six more of her subjects with ease.

Lucius could not help but smile at the banshee leader's misfortune. "Time to take your leave, Siobhan."

"Come to me, sisters!" Siobhan commanded. The remaining banshees ceased their futile attacks on Tok and retreated to Siobhan's side. She scowled at Lucius. "This is not over," she growled.

"It is today," Syl chimed in.

With a final scream of rage, Siobhan and rest of the banshees shot into the sky and disappeared into the surrounding wood. The dense fog began to clear around them, allowing the noontime sun to illuminate the cistern. Exhaustion from the battle and the constant swimming overwhelmed Lucius.

"I really would like to rest for a moment," Lucius said. "Do you see any way out of this cistern?"

"There are earthen stairs over there," Syl replied, pointing to stone steps hewn into a section of the cistern's circular wall.

"Well, that's further than I desire to swim," Lucius said with a slight frown, his arms and legs aching terribly just from treading water. The stairs were at least a hundred feet away.

"Who said you had to swim?" Syl said, his mouth curving into a smile. "Tok, would you carry our friend to the stairs?"

Tok stood like a giant obelisk rising from the water, unmoving and ominous. He slowly bent down on one knee, extending his large craggy arm toward Lucius and spreading his fingers to create an open palm.

"This will be an interesting tale," Lucius said, hoisting himself onto the golem's hand. He sat cross-legged and held onto Tok's stony fingers as the golem rose to his full height.

Syl flew up to Tok's face and whispered something to the golem. Tok immediately began stomping through the water and burst into a full gallop toward the stairs.

"Not so fast! You'll run right into the wall!" Lucius cried, clutching Tok's fingers tightly.

Syl laughed for the first time since Lucius had known the faerie. "It's quite alright, Lucius. No need for fear now."

Tok neared the inner cistern wall at an impressive speed for his size and did not stop when they were a stone's throw from the steps. Instead the golem bounded over the embankment, landing in the forest surrounding the cistern with a thunderous boom. Lucius nearly vomited from the unexpected leap and rough landing while Syl simply giggled at the whole affair.

"All right, let me down," Lucius said, struggling to contain his breakfast inside his stomach.

"No, no. You are quite injured, my friend, and we have a ways to go before we reach King Klik's court. Rest on Tok's hand, and I promise ... no more long jumps," Syl said, raising his hand as if making an oath.

Lucius raised an eyebrow, but did not have the strength or willingness to protest the idea. He reclined on one elbow on Tok's palm as Syl ordered the golem to head north in a slower pace than before. Syl floated near Tok's head for most of the journey back home, leaving Lucius to rest in the golem's hand. The throbbing pain from the gashes in Lucius' back and head tired him, and he felt drowsiness come upon him as they traversed through the forest. Despite the rough surface of Tok's hand, Lucius fell asleep easily to the rocking motion of

Tok's lumbering gait. His dreams were dark, and visions of the Black Dragon plagued him once more.

TWENTY

Hidden Royalty

The Barren Road is a foul lane to travel at night, mostly due to bandits who lie hidden along the path waiting to throttle unsuspecting travelers. Wandering coyotes and trolls were also notorious for seeking out a fresh meal on the road, or so the local bards will lead others to believe. Silas could handle wild animals, trolls, and even bandits on his own without worry, but with two women accompanying him, an urgency to shield them from such dangers was ever present on his mind. He let Naomi and Violet walk in front where he could keep a close eye on them, and also scan the area every so often for movement.

A nearly full moon shone in a cloudless black sky and chilly gusts of wind swept through the wide road, whipping

Silas' cloak wildly. The trio walked in silence; Homer's hooves clopping on the pebbled ground were the only sound heard besides the howling wind. Before dusk, they had managed to arrive in Sylvania and purchase a few necessary items for their long journey. Besides the food and mead Silas acquired, Violet bought an extra lantern from an elderly beggar when she learned the man's son had died from consumption. Although two lanterns would be useful on their nightly travels, Silas insisted they kept them unlit on the Barren Road; lanterns would make them easy prey for bandits watching the road from a distance.

When Homer's pace on the road began slowing down, Naomi suggested they should make camp for the night. The travelers veered off the road and found a secluded copse a half-mile away. Violet prepared a fire while Silas gathered wood in the moonlight. The satisfying warmth of the fire put the women at ease as they sat near the flame and chatted about the day, but Silas stood guarding the perimeter of the camp, just like the nights in Ithileo before the ambush.

"Cutter, won't you join us by the fire?" Violet asked.

"I will in a little while, my lady," Silas replied, pacing near the tree line of the copse.

"Are you still worried about bandits?" Naomi asked, her brows wrinkled. "We're far enough from the road now."

"We are fairly secluded here save for the fire, of course," Silas admitted.

"But?" Violet said with a teasing smile.

"When you've traveled as often as I have, you'll find there is no fault in being extra cautious, especially at night where evil lurks."

The ladies both agreed and allowed him to continue his watch, but Silas sensed a pang of disappointment from Violet and he regretted not joining her by the fire. After an hour of talking—including several questions directed at Silas about their travel plans—the two women turned in for the night. Silas sat close to the fire, but kept his back to it and faced the Barren Road. He continued his watch diligently, but every so often peered above at the myriad of stars. He pulled out his mother's ring and twirled it between his fingers as he gazed at the beauty above.

"Do you fancy the stars?" Violet asked quietly from behind, startling him.

"I thought you were sleeping, Violet," He sighed with relief and quickly tucked his necklace under his chainmail.

"Forgive me, I did not intend to startle you," she said with a slight curve to her mouth.

"You didn't," he lied, clearing his throat. "Having trouble sleeping?"

"Yes. Sleep escapes me in the wilderness it seems." Violet walked over and sat down next to him.

They sat quietly for a moment, staring up at the starry sky together.

"They're beautiful, aren't they?" Violet said.

"Aye. My mother once told me the heavenly lights were our ancestors looking down upon us from Yéwa's Hall. As a boy, I longed to go there and see the ivory palace of Caelum and the throne seat of Yesu, but now—" Silas hesitated and looked down, unsure if he should confide in Violet.

"But now?" Violet asked, searching for his eyes.

"Now I wish to go there to see my mother and sister again," he said, meeting her gaze.

"Oh, I'm sorry Cutter," Violet said, tucking her hair behind her ear. "What happened to them?"

Silas sighed. "We were traveling to Tarshish for a holiday when I was just a boy. My mother and sister rode in the carriage while my father and I followed them on horseback. There was a bend in the road around a bluff, and on the other side, the Draknoir were waiting for us. My father and I fought them fiercely. Our carriage driver was killed immediately, so my mother took the reins and charged out of the battle at my father's insistence. We didn't see the dragon until it was too late. It breathed fire down on us and the Draknoir, but my father and I managed to escape the flames unscathed. When the fires subsided and the dragon had left, we raced up the road to find my mother and sister. All we found was a heap of ash and melted iron bolts from the carriage."

Violet held a hand to her mouth as he recounted the story, her eyes glossy with tears. "Yéwa have mercy on you and your father," she said.

"Mercy eluded us that day, but I am confident we shall all be reunited again. Until that day comes, I fight to avenge the death of my mother and sister, even if it leads to my own demise."

"That is a noble purpose, Cutter," Violet said, wiping the corners of her eyes. "But don't become consumed by death and vengeance—such things will blind you and you'll overlook the many blessings of life."

"And what blessings might those be?" Silas said, glancing up at the stars again. He could not imagine anything in his life presently to be a blessing. The Draknoir continued to ravage his father's kingdom, and now dragons might rise up once more to torment the world. The future looked altogether bleak, and blessings were in short supply.

"Friendship is a blessing, Cutter. I think you are rather blessed to have a friend to talk to under the stars who also happened to save you from certain death," Violet said, her lips curving again.

Silas chuckled. "I suppose you will never let me forget that deed."

"Not ever," Violet replied, playfully crossing her arms.

"I am very grateful for your friendship, Violet," he said, glancing down at her blue eyes. She forced a smile, but it quickly faded as he held her gaze. He drew closer to her and their lips met. Violet's shoulders and neck tensed up initially, but she did not withdraw from his affections.

The tender moment in the moonlight was cut short by the snapping of a twig nearby. Silas reached for his blade and rose from the ground to guard Violet from the unknown prowler. An arrow whizzed by Silas' ear and pierced the ground near Naomi's head, rousing her from a peaceful slumber. A familiar battle cry from Draknoir warriors filled the chill night air followed by more arrows.

"Violet, find cover!" Silas shouted as he sidestepped between the trees in the copse.

Violet ran to the nearest tree and pressed her back against the trunk, seconds before multiple arrows sunk into the bark. Naomi ducked behind a pair of bushes as another volley of arrows flew through the copse. Four Draknoir ran into the campground with swords drawn, and Silas immediately lunged his sword at the closest one. The blade sunk deep into the reptilian warrior's ribs causing the shocked Draknoir to tumble forward. Silas pulled the blade out and quickly decapitated the downed warrior, then swiped wildly at the next Draknoir who parried his advance with a serrated blade.

As he exchanged blows with the Draknoir warrior, the other brutes targeted the women. Silas blocked several of his attacker's swings and waited for the Draknoir to provide an opening through an ill-judged thrust. With a quick jab of his blade in the creature's exposed thigh, Silas sent the Draknoir reeling and used the opportunity to plunge his sword through the warrior's back.

He quickly turned at the sound of Violet shrieking and saw her fall on the ground at the feet of a Draknoir warrior wielding an ax. Silas sprinted toward the Draknoir, tackling him before the brute swung his weapon down. They both hit the ground hard, but the dark creature scrambled to his feet instantly and thrust the elongated tip of the ax at Silas' back. He rolled to his side, avoiding the sharp tip of the ax as it poked the dirt.

Before the Draknoir pulled the ax out of the ground, Silas swung his sword upward and severed the warrior's scaly forearm. The Draknoir roared in pain, holding his bloody stump. Silas stood up and thrust his sword, but the wounded Draknoir dodged the attack and raked Silas' face with his claws. Silas fell to one knee, reeling in pain from the gashes on his cheek. The warrior lunged at Silas with jaws open, ready to bite his face. Silas blocked the beast's bite with his gauntleted forearm and slipped his blade beneath the Draknoir's armor and into his belly. The attacked made a gurgling noise and grew limp.

Silas pushed the dead Draknoir off and spun around to face Violet; she was laying on her back, crying softly as she clutched her bloody arm. Silas ran to her side and tried to examine the wound, but Violet clutched his wrist tightly.

"I'm fine, go help Naomi!" she yelled, pointing toward her friend.

The last Draknoir warrior was attempting to slice Naomi in half with an enormous scimitar, but the petite young woman was surprisingly agile and managed to parry her attacker's every move. As Silas approached the skirmish, he saw Naomi wielding an unusual weapon in her hands. Upon closer inspection, he realized the weapon was an elvish glaive with blades on each end. Naomi twirled the glaive skillfully and swiped at her opponent, but her attack missed and left her vulnerable. The Draknoir grabbed the top of Naomi's head and jerked it backwards, preparing to slit her throat with the scimitar.

Silas pushed his sword between the Draknoir's shoulder blades, feeling it pierce through the attacker's chest. The Draknoir shoved Naomi to the ground and whirled around to face Silas with the blade still stuck in his chest. With a wide sweep of the scimitar, the warrior attempted to cut him in two, but Silas ducked beneath the strike and charged the Draknoir.

His advance was thwarted by the attacker's well-timed kick to his chest. Silas crashed to the floor, unable to catch his breath before the Draknoir towered over him. The beast held the scimitar high for the final blow, but Naomi jumped onto his back and drove a curved dagger into the Draknoir's jugular. Silas watched as their attacker sunk to his knees and muttered curses at them before collapsing on the ground.

Naomi retrieved Silas' sword from the Draknoir's body and handed the blade to him. He glanced up at her and realized her head was no longer covered by the headscarf. Naomi's hair was dark and long, flowing down beyond her shoulders, but the most striking feature of her uncovered head were the pair of pointed ears clearly visible in the moonlight.

"You're an elf?" Silas said, standing up.

"Yes ... I am," Naomi said, looking away. She turned around and pulled her headscarf from the dead Draknoir's claws.

Violet walked up to them slowly, holding a rag to the deep cut on her left arm and looking rather pale.

"Are you all right? Let me see that," Silas said, reaching for her arm.

"I'm fine, Cutter, really. I've already added some salve to the cut," Violet insisted, grabbing hold of his hand before he could examine her wound again. She squeezed his hand gently and smiled momentarily before she saw the cuts on his face.

"Those look awful, Cutter! Here let me get some salve and wrappings."

"It's just a few scratches, Violet. I've dealt with worse—I'm more concerned about you and Naomi right now," he said, looking over to Naomi. The elf had reapplied her headscarf and busied herself with packing her weapons away.

"Why didn't you tell us you were an elf?" Silas asked.

"I didn't see how it mattered on our present errand," Naomi replied while tying her leather sack tight.

"It doesn't, but I'm curious as to why it needed to be a secret. What do you have to hide?"

"Cutter, please—" Violet interrupted.

"Did you know she was an elf?" Silas turned to Violet.

Violet sighed and averted her eyes, "Yes, I did."

Silas frowned. "I don't understand the secrecy. Am I missing something here?"

"I'm not the only one here with a secret, Cutter," Naomi suggested, shooting an accusatory glance at him.

She was right. He had not told them about his royal parentage, which was likely the reason for the Draknoir attack tonight. But did Naomi know he was the prince of Aldron? And if so, what else did she know? He was unsure if he could trust her, but he could not hope to keep his secret much longer with each passing day bringing them closer to Aldron.

"You're right, Naomi. I have also been hiding something," Silas said, swallowing hard. "My true name is Silas Dermont, son of King Alfryd Dermont of Aldron."

Violet's eyes widened and she stepped back, staring at him as though he were a strange creature to behold. "You're the ... prince of Aldron?"

"I am," Silas replied. He turned to Naomi, who did not seem the least bit surprised at the revelation. "How did you know?"

"You and your father visited my homeland several years ago. We met briefly, but you seemed preoccupied and uninterested in idle conversation at the time."

"I'm sorry, I do not recall this meeting. Where is your homeland?"

"Numa," Naomi said, lifting her chin slightly.

Hearing the name of the last elven kingdom in Azuleah brought back a flood of memories for Silas. Two years past, King Sikahr had invited his father and him to visit Numa in order to negotiate a trade agreement between their kingdoms, but the whole affair turned out to be a ruse. Sikahr was a paranoid monarch. He suspected an imminent threat to his rule from those in his inner circle and desired Aldron's military aid if an insurrection occurred. The false pretense of a trade agreement was concocted to divert attention from the Numan king's supposed rivals, but it only succeeded in further straining the weak relationship between Numa and Aldron. King Alfryd was furious at Sikahr for the deception, and their heated exchanges were often mediated by Silas, which proved to be an exhausting chore. The only bright spot of the entire trip was seeing the ancient elf city with all of its regal trappings and splendor. He never ventured beyond the walls of Sikahr's palace during his stay, and he could not remember meeting any elves besides Sikahr and his immediate family: Queen Vilina, twin Princes Alamgir and Balbir, and ... Princess Avani.

Silas scrutinized Naomi's face and suddenly remembered her. "You're the missing princess—Avani Rubiwind!"

"Yes," Avani replied. "I was wondering when you would remember me, Silas."

"We only met briefly, and as you said, I was preoccupied. Our fathers were having petty disputes at the time, and I was tasked with keeping the peace."

"As was I," Avani said firmly. "My father couldn't fathom why King Alfryd would not agree to a military alliance after being duped by the false hope of a trade agreement. He never looks beyond his own self-importance."

"My father is equally guilty of that," Silas admitted. "Kings tend to view themselves with higher regard than they should, especially in the company of other royals."

"I suppose that's true," Avani said, looking down at her packed belongings.

An awkward silence passed between them and Violet finally spoke. "We should go. More Draknoir could be headed this way."

"You're right, Violet. We cannot stay here tonight," Silas replied, glancing at the rag on her arm, which was now thoroughly soaked in blood. "Forgive me; this is all my fault. The Draknoir must have been trailing me from Ithileo. I should have been more vigilant to keep you both safe."

"You could not have known they were following you," Violet replied. She briefly met his gaze, but turned away to check on Homer.

He felt a pang of regret for keeping his secret from Violet. She had saved his life, and yet he still hid his identity from her.

"We should move deeper into the woods to a more secluded area. I can guard the camp for the rest of the night," Avani offered.

"All right," Silas agreed.

Avani picked up her sack and started for the dense forest beyond the copse at the foot of a ridge.

"Wait," he said. "Why have you left your home and disguised yourself as a lowly blacksmith in the middle of nowhere?"

Avani did not face him. "I was called to be a blacksmith, and my father did not agree. That is all I will say on the matter." She continued toward the forest without looking back.

Silas crossed over a dead Draknoir and approached Violet, who was rubbing Homer's nose gently. "I'm sorry, Violet," Silas said.

"Sorry for what, my lord?" Violet said, her back stiffened a bit and she squared her shoulders.

"I am sorry for all this," he replied, gesturing at the mess of bodies and weapons around them. Silas grabbed her hand and held it gently. "I'm sorry for not telling you who I really was. I owe you a great debt, and I should have trusted you."

Violet pulled her hand away and glared at him. "You lied to me, Cutter...or Silas—whatever your name is!"

Silas rubbed the back of his neck. "Violet, I—"

"I don't want your apologies," she interrupted. Her furrowed brow softened briefly and she opened her mouth to speak, but stopped herself. "It's late and we need to rest, my lord," she finally said. Violet grabbed Homer's reins and led the horse out of the copse toward the forest, leaving Silas to himself.

Silas watched both women fade into the darkness as he grabbed his belongings and trailed behind them. He couldn't believe the unexpected turn of events this night had taken. His amiable relationship with Violet had changed drastically in the course of an hour and timid Naomi turned out to be Numan elf princess. Their journey to Aldron had also become more perilous now with the Draknoir pursuing him. But how far would the Draknoir be willing to chase him? They were nearing the borders of Joppa, and surely Memnon would not be foolish enough to send his warriors so deep into hostile territory. The Draknoir leader was becoming more brazen, and Silas feared the worst if Aldron did not mount a massive attack on Nasgothar.

Despite his growing concerns, Silas found himself more preoccupied with Violet. The single kiss they shared had revealed a longing in his heart he did not know was there. War had torn at his life since his youth, and he knew little else, but he longed for something beyond the battlefield—he longed to love. Violet had awakened him from a long slumber, and he'd hurt her in return. Somehow he needed to make things right and become worthy of her love again.

TWENTY-ONE

A Dark Errand

Two days had passed since Rebecca Ravenmane had arrived in the port city of Tarshish from her long trek through the Onyx Mountains, Ithileo Forest, and the great Dulan River. The journey had exhausted her, but she did not have the luxury of time to rest. Her old tutor, Rekk, had always said, "Rest is for the weary, and a weary spy is better off dead." Old Rekk always had a way with words, and under his tutelage, Rebecca had become a very competent spy and assassin. She was closer than ever to avenging her mother's death. Rebecca could still hear her screams.

Rebecca and her mother were traveling by wagon on the Barren Road, heading to their cottage in the Golden Plains when three hooded men walked out in front of them. Rebecca's mother refused to give up their belongings to the bandits and tried to fend them off, but she was stabbed to death before Rebecca's eyes. She fled into the woods near the road when the men turned to kill her next. After running for what seemed like an eternity, her pursuers lost her in the underbrush, and eventually they turned back to the wagon. Wishing to see her mother one last time, Rebecca sneaked back toward the road and waited for the thieves to gather their plunder before she walked out from the cover of the trees. From a distance she witnessed something she would never forget. The three hooded thieves took off their dark cloaks and revealed their vivid blue and white uniforms underneath—the standard colors of Aldronian soldiers.

She remembered crying there in the forest alone for hours as the corrupt soldiers packed all of their clothes, jewelry, and food in sacks. They scurried off with her mother's horse carrying the spoils, laughing at their victim's misfortune. The lifeless eyes of her mother were forever burned into Rebecca's memory that day. Grief-stricken, frightened, and alone, her only recourse was to run. She ran far to the east—far away from the cold corpse that used to be her mother. The way back home was unknown to her as a child, and even if she knew it, no one was waiting for her to return.

During those first few days of running, she learned many things about survival. She learned how to forage for food: eating insects that dwelled inside logs in the forest or catching rodents that disturbed her sleep at night. Looking back, she recalled how primitive her efforts were, but as time passed she became more proficient in her methods. While searching for food along the banks of the Feilon River one morning, Rebecca came upon a Draknoir encampment teeming with warriors. She thought the end of her life had surely come when the lizard-like beings surrounded her, but she was surprised to find another human was among their company—an older man with graying hair and a hooked nose. He told her she was safe and no harm would come to her.

The man's name was Rekk, a spy employed by the Draknoir. He expressed more kindness to her than anyone she'd ever known, treating her as a father would his own daughter. Rekk had once been an illegal trader on the Sea of Lagrimas, importing Draknoir goods to spies and black market merchants in the cities of Aldron, Tarshish, and Haran. When the war with Aldron began to escalate, Rekk gained a promotion as a spy for his loyalty to the Draknoir horde. He always told her the money was good and that the Draknoir offered the one thing no man could ever give him—vengeance. Rekk's family were once nobles in the Court of Gilead, but they were exiled when Rekk's father was charged with treason for actively pursuing a peace accord with the Draknoir. Rekk's father hung for the crime, and his mother was left impoverished to care for four children in the foreign province of Ragnara. Rekk despised the royals of Aldron since— convinced that his father's dream of peace with the misunderstood Draknoir was the right course.

Rebecca came to share this dream since she equally despised the Aldronians for murdering her mother and destroying her life. As an adolescent, she embraced the Draknoir's customs and traditions from her surrogate father and eventually became a spy herself. She was taught how to gather information from the towns and cities she infiltrated, concealing her identity and searching for secrets in the most detestable of places. Rekk taught her most of his trade, but after he died, she learned much more from the best tutor among the Draknoir—Lord Memnon.

After losing Rekk, Memnon recognized the talents of his elite spy's adopted child. The charismatic Nasgothar leader trained her in concealment and the arcane arts, making her a vicious threat against the Aldronians. He nurtured her hatred and desire for vengeance, teaching her to wield her anger as a powerful weapon. In time she became more than a spy for the Draknoir, but also a formidable assassin—the best in Memnon's employ. It was the primary reason for her appointment to Tarshish. She was uniquely gifted to assassinate a high-ranking official like Baron Stendahl.

Rebecca had spent the past two days gathering information in Tarshish, and her findings were quite interesting. Rumors of a military retaliation by King Dermont were running rampant in many circles. A few unscrupulous Aldronian soldiers were keen to share information with her informants for the right amount of coin. Apparently, the King believed his son had escaped the attack in Ithileo and had sent scouts to the areas near the Dulan to find him. The same soldiers believed a massive offensive led by Baron Stendahl was likely to follow. Trusting her intuition, Rebecca would relay the information quickly to Lord Memnon, but first, she needed to know Stendahl's whereabouts. Only one person in the city knew the answer, and luckily, she had enough solidi in her coin purse to pay the greedy rat known as Durgan.

After grabbing a meal at a local tavern in the evening, Rebecca made her way to the docks on the eastern shore. Tarshish's streets were rank with homeless beggars and urchins looking for charity. The night air reeked of rotting fish from the wharf nearby, forcing her to hold her breath. It was just past the ninth hour of the night, an inconvenient time for a woman to be wandering the streets. She caught a few stares from both drunken and sober men that revealed more of their intentions than she wished to know, but she was no simple village girl. She knew what they wanted and desired to take by force if the opportunity arose.

Come and get it.

To her dismay, no one did, but she recalled with amusement the few instances when men had tried to take advantage of her. Imagine their surprise when the seemingly frail woman didn't cower when they threatened her or tried to pin her against a wall. Instead, they found themselves thrown to the ground beneath her boot heel, regretting ever laying eyes on her. Yes, those moments always gave her a bit of pleasure.

Rebecca walked past a row of squalid tenements and arrived at the townhouse next to the docks where her informant hid. Patches of mold covered the wooden door of the house and the daub walls were cracked, revealing the wattle underneath. A small rectangular panel on the door slid open and a pair of dark, beady eyes stared back at her inquisitively.

"Why does the gull nest on the dock?" the voice behind the door mumbled.

"A nest on the dock is better than a nest in the wolves' den," Rebecca recited.

The small panel slid shut, and she heard the bolts on the door unlock. A heavyset man with a ruffled mop of hair and stained clothing stood behind the door, waving her inside.

Rebecca walked down a dark, narrow corridor with the man following closely behind. They entered a large room with a circular table in the center, and the man asked her to sit in one of the two chairs beside the table. She sat down as the man disappeared into a connecting room. Overturned mugs and chopped tobacco leaves littered the tabletop. The entire room was cluttered with soiled clothes, fishing rods, and rotting bait in buckets. She coughed at the stench of it all. Voices came from the adjacent room and diverted her attention from the squalor around her. It sounded like arguing: one man shouting at another and then the sound of a fist smacking the side of someone's face. Seconds later, the man who had escorted her inside rounded the corner. He rubbed his hand over a welt below his eye and walked out the front door without acknowledging her. Another man came around the corner, taking a seat in the other chair across from her. She quickly recognized his stubble beard, bagging eyes, and widow's peak. It was Durgan, her greedy informant.

"Well, 'ello, love. What brings you to my shanty? A kiss and a nightcap perhaps?" Durgan said. He always sought to charm, but it was a wasted effort on her.

"Why do I always come, Durgan?" She forced a smile. "Information, my friend."

Durgan scoffed. "Well, I must admit you've got the worst timin'. I was just tellin' Troy out there how I'd specifically said no more visits today."

"Well, how many solidi will it take to change your mind?" She dropped a small coin purse on the table.

Durgan snatched the pouch from the table and counted forty solidi. "I think this'll do, love," he smiled, revealing a few missing teeth.

"I need to find Baron Stendahl. Tell me everything you know," she said, crossing her arms, awaiting a quick response.

"Stendahl is at Gilead Palace, o' course. Rumor has it he's been appointed to lead a campaign against your friends, the Draknoir, very soon. The Aldronians have been on the move for the last two days, and my sources tell me they plan to move before the week's end. The Captain of the Guard is most likely marching off with the king's army."

"Where is the King's host headed?"

"Ithileo, but who knows how they plan to get there. Dermont's airships can't carry more than a thousand men, so I doubt he'll use them. That leaves three options in my mind," Durgan said, fiddling with a coin from the pouch. "The army can journey northeast through the Golden Plains and cross the Dulan into Ithileo, or Dermont could sail them over through the Sea of Lagrimas on frigates."

"What's the third option?" Rebecca asked.

"Well, he might send half his army through the Golden Plains and half through the Sea of Lagrimas, which might make a nasty fight on two fronts for yer lads, the Draknoir. I'm betting my money that's what he'll do," he said, shaking the coin purse vigorously.

Rebecca leaned back in her chair and let out a heavy sigh. If Dermont was attacking on two fronts, the Draknoir warriors guarding Ithileo would fall quickly. There was also no way for her to know which front Stendahl would be directly leading. Aldron was a day and a half's away on horseback, leaving her with little time to find the Captain among all the commotion surrounding the impending departure of troops. She bit her lower lip, "That will do, Durgan. Thank you for your time."

"Anytime, love. Just try to be a lil' more courteous next time and announce yer coming, will ye?" He gave her a lopsided grin.

She rose from the chair, narrowing her eyes at him. His smile quickly faded, and he nervously escorted her out the door where Troy sat smoking a pipe outside. The burly man glanced her way, but said nothing as she walked past him.

Rebecca traversed the empty streets again, heading southward to the city entrance where her horse was stabled. A chilling breeze from the nearby sea caused her to pull her cloak tighter around her lean frame. She thought hard about how she might find Stendahl before he left for Ithileo. She'd be a fool to think Dermont wouldn't pursue an attack on two fronts as Durgan had suggested. And it was equally foolish to think she could make the journey to Aldron in time to find Stendahl, kill him, and escape without alerting anyone. Her mission was already a failure. Lord Memnon would never show her favor again if she returned now.

No.

Her pride and desire for vengeance would not allow her to succumb to defeat. She would make swift flight to Aldron and kill the Captain—even if it needed to be done in public. The errand would undoubtedly cost her life, but her master's favor would not be taken away by any Aldronian—no matter the cost.

TWENTY-TWO

As the Crow Flies

Nightmares of the Black Dragon deprived Lucius of any sleep on his final night in the Burning Woods among the faeries. The dreams were more vivid than before. When the violent images woke him, he instinctively checked his body for burns from the dragon's fire, but the only true wounds he carried were from his encounter with the banshees who had succeeded in scarring his back and deafening his right ear. The faeries' simple herbal remedies had eased much of his pain, but no one could say with certainty if his hearing would ever return.

Despite his infirmities, he had been in good spirits— especially on the previous day, when the faeries threw a grand celebration for the triumphant return of Tok. The faeries' haven in the forest—which was called Gwyltref—lit up like the sun when Tok returned carrying Lucius in his rocky hand. Syl's kinsfolk could not stop flitting about wildly and cheering loudly, their bodies shining brightly with excitement. Faerie men sung songs in Lucius' honor, and faerie maidens served him deliciously sweet cakes made of honey. All the faerie folk were in a jovial mood except for King Klik, who watched the entire spectacle from his throne with a cold expression on his face. Once the merriment subsided, Klik decreed that Siegfried would be released in the morning and advised Lucius to take rest and comfort in the security of Gwyltref. Wounded and exhausted, Lucius lacked the strength to protest for his brother's immediate release and chose to let the matter rest. After Klik departed from his throne for the night, Lucius sat for hours listening to Syl and his eight siblings discuss faerie lore. Like Syl, the faerie's four brothers and three sisters were very animated when they spoke and constantly flitted around Lucius. He enjoyed listening to their stories, but he eventually succumbed to his exhaustion and fell asleep on a soft patch of grass in the glittery, illuminated clearing.

Now he sat wide awake in the clearing, waiting for the sun to rise in the pinkish sky. He stared at the treetops around the perimeter of clearing and saw a few fairies flying among the branches, but most of the residents of Gwyltref were still slumbering in their small huts of woven hemp. Lucius stood up and walked over to his knapsack resting against Siegfried's pack next to a tree stump. Syl and the faeries had brought the packs to Gwyltref from the pitiful makeshift bush where Lucius had hid them. How the tiny beings managed to carry Siegfried's hefty bag was beyond him.

Lucius loosed the pack's drawstring and retrieved the red scroll. He sat cross-legged on the ground and carefully scanned the scroll, reading sections he previously skimmed to search for any answers concerning Yesu's death. When the dawning sun appeared, Lucius had found no answers to the mystery. He shoved the scroll back in his bag and leaned his back on the stump, drawing a deep breath before releasing it slowly. The significance of Yesu or Yéwa on his journey continued to escape him, and he wondered if there was any significance at all. Aside from witnessing the mysterious power of the Bezalel sigil, he had seen no divine intervention from Yéwa in the trials he faced. He was half deaf, plagued by ominous visions, and far from forging Yesu's all-powerful sword. If his father and Lumiath were correct, the task of attaining the Requiem Sword would become far more difficult for him and Siegfried. So where was this almighty Yéwa who had spoken the prophecy of the *Ellyllei*? Were the affairs of men and elves too trivial for him? Or perhaps Helmer and Lumiath were wrong about Yéwa—maybe he didn't even exist. Whatever the case might be, Lucius would continue on for the sake of his family and

Evingrad, but he would not expect help from a God who remained silent and distant.

Lucius grabbed the wineskin in his pack and drank the last of the *bywydur* mixture. As the effects of the drink began to take effect, he noticed movement from the corner of his eye and looked toward the cluster of mushrooms where Klik's throne sat. Beyond the wooden throne, Brom and his legion of guardians floated slowly out of the forest and into the clearing, escorting their king to the royal seat. Following the main procession were four guardians holding ropes fastened to Siegfried's arms and legs. The elf stepped up onto the tree stump with a stoic expression and allowed his escorts to bind his wrists together. Lucius ran toward the throne, hoping to speak with his brother, but Brom and the guardians blocked his path.

"You will wait for his Majesty to address you, ground-treader," Brom ordered.

"Fine," Lucius replied, glaring at the diminutive commander.

King Klik flew up to the throne and sat down. He picked up a small staff decorated with heather and flower petals. Klik struck the side of his throne three times with the staff and everyone waited expectantly. The ground suddenly shook with the lumbering steps of Tok as he emerged from the forest and joined the gathering.

"Tok, please rouse the fair folk of Gwyltref from their slumber," Klik ordered.

The golem lifted his huge arms then smacked his hands together in a thunderous clap. Sleepy-eyed faeries exited their huts reluctantly and descended from the treetops. Very soon an enormous throng of faeries gathered around the throne, flitting about and whispering loudly to each other. Syl eventually showed up and landed on Lucius' shoulder. The yellow faerie greeted him with his familiar grin, but Lucius did not return a smile. His stomach was in knots. Klik had been slow to deliver on his promise to free Siegfried, and Lucius feared the monarch did not intend to release his brother.

"My dear kinsfolk," Klik said, raising both arms to address the crowd. "We have been shown favor by our ancestors and the forest herself. The golem, Tok, has returned to Gwyltref!"

The crowd erupted into raucous cheering and hollering. Lucius could not believe their tiny bodies were capable of producing such an uproar—he was almost happy his hearing was limited to one ear. Despite the numerous cheers, Tok did not move or acknowledge the faeries' adoration for him, seemingly content to cast his large shadow over the proceedings.

Klik raised his hands once more to quiet the crowd. "We owe a debt of gratitude to the ground-treader, Lucius, and to Syl for their heroic effort."

Lucius felt his face redden, but Syl basked in the praise from his peers.

"Syl, your willingness to serve your king by helping the ground-treader will be rewarded," Klik said with a bemused smile. He turned to Lucius and lifted his chin slightly. "As for you, Lucius ... we had an accord."

"We did," Lucius said, glancing at Siegfried. His brother straightened slightly, ready for whatever edict the king might make.

"As sovereign king of this woodland realm, I shall honor our agreement and release the prisoner, Siegfried Silverhart," Klik said, leaning back in his throne. "Brom, cut the prisoner's bonds."

Brom raised an eyebrow at the king, but immediately followed his orders when Klik scowled at him. The faerie commander cut through the ropes around Siegfried's wrists then ordered the guardians to untie the ropes fastened on the elf's arms and legs. Lucius grinned when Siegfried stepped down from the stump and approached him.

The elf smiled then turned to the king, "Thank you, my lord. Your graciousness is much—"

"Silence!" Klik yelled, slamming a fist on his throne. "You may be free from imprisonment, but I still have judgment to decree upon you, elf."

A hush fell over the entire assembly as Klik stood up from his throne and pointed his staff at Lucius.

"You may have saved this kingdom from ruin by returning Tok to us, but your association with this criminal tarnishes any favorable standing you might have with me, ground-treader," Klik said, contorting the corners of his mouth in a deep frown.

"Your Majesty—" Lucius began, but Siegfried clutched his forearm and shook his head.

"Let him speak," Siegfried whispered.

"As for you, Siegfried Silverhart," Klik said, pacing the top of the mushroom, "you killed my father and ruined my family. Blik's death brought severe grief upon my mother, leading to her premature death, and my sister fled the sanctuary of Gwyltref, leaving me to pick up the shambles of your evil."

Siegfried hunched and avoided eye contact with Klik.

"I hereby decree that you and your kin are forever banished from Gwyltref and the Burning Woods. If you should ever step foot in my realm again, then your death shall come swiftly," Klik said. He sat on the throne and narrowed his eyes. "Now get out."

Brom and the guardians drew their swords and quickly surrounded Lucius and Siegfried. The assembly of faeries in the clearing gasped and spoke in hushed voices about this unexpected development. Syl flew up from Lucius' shoulder and faced the king.

"My lord, please! Lucius and his brother are much-needed allies in our fight against the banshees. Let us not be hasty in breaking any fellowship, your Majesty. I appeal to your mercies as royal advisor."

"I have shown mercy, Syl. Banishment is a lesser punishment than death, is it not? Tok will be a sufficient ally in our war in the Southern Passage. Now, turn aside lest you wish to be exiled as well," Klik said, fiercely grimacing at his subordinate.

Syl pressed his lips tightly and clenched his fists, but bowed his head in deference. Turning to Lucius, he whispered, "I'm sorry."

"It's alright, Syl. Thank you for your help, both here and in the Southern Passage," Lucius said, feeling his chest tighten. He had grown close to Syl in the last few days and lamented the fact they might never see each other again.

"Time to go, brother," Siegfried said, placing a hand on Lucius' shoulder.

Lucius nodded and turned his back on Brom and his eager enforcers. He walked to the center of the clearing to retrieve their packs. Every fairy in Gwyltref watched them closely, some saddened to see Lucius leave while others expressed relief at the interlopers' departure. After a final farewell to Syl and his family, Lucius and Siegfried entered the forest. They headed north toward Jun-Jun Pass, hoping to reach it before midday.

The walk was unbearably quiet due to the eerie stillness of the forest, which Lucius had not experienced since he first set foot in the place. He wondered if Klik was responsible for silencing the realm—his final act of contempt before they left the Burning Woods. The silent environment visibly unsettled Siegfried, who kept walking faster to the point of sprinting. Lucius continually lost track of the elf, incapable of keeping a fast pace due to his injuries.

He was relieved when they exited the forest cover around the noon time and rested on an outcrop encircling the northern border of the woods. Lucius climbed onto a smooth boulder and pulled out a sweet honey cake he saved from the previous night. He quickly devoured it as Siegfried surveyed their location. The elf jumped onto a rock formation facing north, scanned the horizon for a moment, then sat cross-legged on the large stone.

"I'm sorry for rushing you through the forest, Lucius," Siegfried said, exhaling deeply. "The quiet ... it unsettles me greatly."

Lucius raised an eyebrow. "Why? The silence didn't bother you when we first entered the woods."

"Yes, but that was before I faced it night and day during my imprisonment," Siegfried replied. He stared at the autumn-colored trees of the Burning Woods for a moment. "Klik imprisoned me in a hole under the earth where I heard nothing

... I saw nothing. Only darkness and a haunting silence dwelled there."

Lucius swallowed hard. "I'm sorry, Siegfried."

"You need not be sorry, Lucius. You freed me from a horrible fate of my own doing. Though I assuredly deserved death, I am grateful that you did not leave me. Thank you."

"Of course, Siegfried. You would've done the same for me," Lucius said, smiling. "Besides I cannot hope to complete this errand on my own. I barely escaped the Southern Passage with my life, so your company is quite necessary if I'm to continue living."

Siegfried chuckled, but suddenly lifted his chin up thoughtfully. "I was told you lost your hearing in one ear?"

"Yes, this one," Lucius said, tapping his deaf right ear.

Siegfried hopped down from the rock formation, threw off his pack, and searched contents inside. He pulled out a small glass bottle and walked over to Lucius. "Remember this?" Siegfried held up the glowing vial of *bywydur* for Lucius to see.

"I've already drank some *bywydur* this morning. It didn't restore my hearing," Lucius said.

"Of course it didn't," Siegfried said, smirking as he removed the stopper from the vial. "Diluted *bywydur* is not suitable for healing such a wound. Undiluted *bywydur*, on the other hand, can be applied directly to a wound. The result is quite miraculous. Now lean your head to the left."

Lucius cocked his head to the side and Siegfried let a single drop of *bywydur* fall into his ear. Siegfried said something while standing on his right, but Lucius only heard a muffled rasp. "I didn't hear a word of that. It didn't work."

"Give it time. The *bywydur* will heal you," Siegfried said, returning the vial to his pack. "Now, let us move on from this place. The Grey swamps are not far from here."

Lucius picked up his knapsack, and they ventured north toward Jun-Jun Pass. They followed a game trail for a few miles, but when it veered east, they ventured off onto a range of hills. The hills bordered the cursed eastern province of Loredia where the Kroshen Waste, Ghadarya, and Arkadeus were located. The Kroshen Waste was a vast desert that had once been a beautiful jungle and the ancestral home of the druids. North of the Kroshen Waste, beyond the Maguna Mountains, resided the barren lands of Kraegyn and his kin— Ghadarya. Lucius prayed their path would never lead them to that forsaken place. However, he was keenly aware his journey would eventually take him to Arkadeus. The spectre of Kraegyn lurked within the shattered walls of the fortress ruin, haunting his dreams and unsettling his mind. Imagining what dormant evil lived in Arkadeus brought a tingling sensation to the back of Lucius' neck. The foreboding thought was interrupted as they crested the last hill of the range and Lucius caught sight of a majestic mountain in the distance. The summit towered over a misty marshland stretching for miles to the northwest.

"I didn't expect to see a mountain here," Lucius said, scrutinizing the distant peak.

"That is Raven's Peak, home to the dwarves of Úlfr's kingdom. The Eternal Mines rest beneath the mountain where dwarves have dug for metals and treasures since time immemorial. When they aren't mining, they spend their days drinking or selling their wares to travelers in Buck's Folly," Siegfried said, pointing to an indistinguishable settlement just west of the mountain.

"Will we find lodging there?" Lucius asked, longing for a warm bed to settle into for the night.

"I'm afraid we will not reach the town before the sun sets, and it is unwise to travel the Grey Swamps in the dark. There is a grove across the road; we will camp there for the night."

"Fantastic." Lucius sighed and readjusted the straps of his pack. "Let's be on our way, then."

The two travelers hiked toward the grove and crossed Jun-Jun Pass. The northern road was a simple dirt path with deep ruts where wagon wheels had worn away the earth. A hundred yards from the pass, they found a grove of walnut trees and settled in for the night. At dawn, they set out for the gray marshland. In the distance, Lucius glimpsed dozens of dead trees dotting the landscape; their gnarled, deformed shapes unnerved him.

Upon entering the ominous mire, his dread of the place increased as they sloshed through the moist, stench-filled ground. Crows watched them from the boughs of the twisted trees, cawing in protest at their presence. The annoying black birds followed them on their trek through the marsh, incessantly squawking overhead. Lucius hoped they could find the *mithas* powder soon or he planned to loose arrows on the feathered pests. Naomi told them the powder would be found within the interior of the swamp and warned them not to travel too far north, but did not explain why. Lucius was certain Siegfried knew the reason. The elf's mood had changed since they entered the swamp; he kept quiet and walked very cautiously in the bog.

"Exactly where is it that we'll find this *mithas* powder?" Lucius turned to Siegfried, whose attention was elsewhere.

"There is an old druid that lives in these swamps. He is something of an alchemist and—" Siegfried paused and listened to the crows cawing above, "—a bird charmer."

"Bird charmer?" Lucius asked, glancing at the crows. "Where do we find this druid?"

"It is likely that he has already found us," Siegfried said, watching the black birds closely.

Lucius gripped the hilt of his sword. "Can we defeat him?"

"His spells are quite powerful. We would be hexed before any strike fell," Siegfried replied plainly.

"What about the skills you displayed in Sylvania?" Lucius suggested, recalling Siegfried's swift thrashing of the two robbers. "Surely, no druid can counter that?"

"Are you so sure, my boy?" A strange voice asked from behind them.

Lucius and Siegfried both spun around to face the stranger, but they only saw endless rows of trees and dark wetland. The crows above had flown away at the sound of the voice.

"Who goes there?" Lucius asked, feeling his breath quicken.

"Tell me first who you are since you have taken it upon yourself to invade my home," the voice declared.

Lucius glanced at Siegfried, who scanned the area for any movement. "My name is Lucius. We have entered these swamps in search of a powder known as *mithas*."

"*Mithas*? ... What brings a young man and an elf to this bleak land for such a trivial item when there are so many more noble pursuits to be had?" the voice asked incredulously.

"I am on a noble pursuit, and it's no business of yours to know why we need the powder. Unless you know where we can find the powder, I suggest you show yourself or leave quickly," Lucius said, unsheathing his sword.

Siegfried shook his head disapprovingly, but Lucius did not sheathe the blade.

"Well, you're rather demanding for an interloper," the voice scoffed. "I suppose you leave me no choice then ..."

Lucius gripped his sword with both hands, preparing himself for an attack. Siegfried also readied himself by nocking an arrow to his bow. The swamps suddenly grew silent. Sweat dripped from Lucius' forehead to the tip of his nose as his eyes darted around him, searching for their would-be assailant.

A flutter of movement startled him—a magpie flew past their line of sight and landed on the ground. Lucius drew his sword backward to strike, but laughed in spite of himself when he realized it was only a bird. "Gave me quite a start, you stupid—"

"Who's stupid?" the bird yapped in a familiar voice.

"It talked!" Lucius said, pointing his sword at the magpie.

Siegfried looked at the bird curiously for a moment, then lowered his bow. "It is the druid, Lucius."

"What? I thought you said he was a bird charmer—not a bird himself!"

"To be a charmer one must know what he is charming, boy," the magpie chided. "I've found the best way to know is to be that which I charm."

"Right. Well, do you have a name, magpie?" Lucius asked.

The magpie puffed his feathers and shook his body fiercely. In a matter of seconds, the magpie's small frame began to gain more girth and stature. His small talons elongated and formed into four-toed feet while his body lengthened to more than seven feet in height. The raven's plumage became a long fur cloak with a white feathered collar. Wings stretched to become arms with four-fingered, long-nailed hands. Finally, the bird's beak became a long nose, and the feathers on his head were replaced with scraggly, silver hair. What remained after the transformation was a tall, beady-eyed druid with a grizzled beard reaching to the center of his chest.

The druid's mouth turned slightly at the ends, and the corners of his eyes wrinkled. "I am Alistair Skylark, master druid of Garoc and keeper of the birds. You need not fear me, I mean you no harm."

Lucius sheathed his sword, but remained uneasy at the sight of the tall druid. "Pleased to meet you, Master Skylark. I am Lucius of Evingrad, and this is my brother, Siegfried of the Silverhart clan."

Siegfried bowed his head and uttered an elvish greeting to the druid.

"Forgive me for startling you earlier. I needed to know you weren't enemies of the marshland or servants of ... him." Alistair's pasty face turned grim.

"Him?" Lucius' brow furrowed.

"It is best if we do not talk about that here," Siegfried said before Alistair spoke. "Tell us, Lord Skylark, do you know where we can find the *mithas* powder in this swamp?"

"Why yes, of course," the druid chuckled. "I have a plentiful supply in my home."

"Fantastic! I was hoping we wouldn't need to walk in this quagmire for much longer," Lucius said, grinning.

"Is there anything you require in return for the powder?" Siegfried asked politely.

"Some company perhaps," Alistair said, clasping his hands behind his back. "It's been a long time since I've had any visitors to my home. I would be very delighted if you would honor me with your company."

"Wait a moment," Lucius said, narrowing his eyes. "How do we know you won't cast a spell on us before we get there?"

Alistair chuckled and stroked his beard. "I suppose you'll have to trust me, my dear boy."

TWENTY-THREE

The Magpie's Roost

Alistair's home resided at the center of the Grey Swamps, near the edge of a stagnant lake covered in moss. A heavy mist hovered above the lake and crept up onto the bank where the druid's ramshackle house sat. The house looked like an overgrown plant: wild vines and moss grew on each of its sides, but its most distinguishing feature was the beech tree that sprouted from the foundation and poked out through the roof. The dwelling reminded Lucius of the *egini* on top of *Breninmaur*, but less elegant and more untamed in appearance. Crows and songbirds perched atop the beech, watching silently as they approached the front door.

Feathers, leaves, and hardened bird excrement littered the floor of the house. Alistair apologized for the mess, grabbing a broom propped on a chair and sweeping most of the refuse out the door. Lucius explored the main room of the house, marveling at the odd collection of relics the druid had amassed. Small wooden statues of various birds were displayed on shelves on every wall and decorated birdhouses were affixed to the thick trunk of the beech tree in the center of the room. A round table in a corner contained over a dozen corked bottles, jars, and flasks filled with liquids and powders of all colors. As he surveyed every corner of the cluttered house, Lucius noticed a metal rack next to a table where wooden staffs were stored. Every staff was different in adornment and length, but one of them in particular caught Lucius' eye—a white staff with a pearlescent orb attached on top. Silver whorls and runes covered the carved white surface of the staff. He reached out to hold the exquisite stave, but Alistair quickly slapped his hand.

"Don't touch that," Alistair chided.

Lucius pulled back his hand. "Sorry, I was only curious."

"This is no ordinary staff, my boy. It once belonged to a druid of great renown—a master of the winds. Unfortunately, he lost his mind and sought to overtake the world with his overwhelming power," Alistair explained in a casual tone.

"Really? What happened to this druid?" Lucius asked.

"His soul was banished to the Abode of Shadows by the Order of Celestine. This staff is all that remains of his power in this realm. It is my charge to guard it along with the other staffs that belonged to the Order," Alistair said.

"So, your part in this Order is that of a guardian?" Siegfried asked, raising an eyebrow.

"It was my part, Master Silverhart," Alistair replied. He sat down on a rickety chair next to the table and sighed. The old druid gazed up at two chirping sparrows perched on a birdhouse, and after a moment finally spoke again. "The Order of Celestine has long been disbanded. None of its members still live. I am the last of the druids."

"The last?" Siegfried said, mouth gaping. "Are you certain?"

"Yes, quite certain I'm afraid. The War of Winds decimated much of my kind, but the Siege of Arkadeus cost us greatly."

"Arkadeus? Did you fight against...Kraegyn?" Lucius asked, lowering his voice as he uttered the dragon's name.

"Not directly. Not like the elves or men with swords and shields and all that nonsense," the old druid replied, waving a hand dismissively. "King Cervantes entrusted the Order of Celestine with conjuring protective spells and enchantments for his army. But our greatest task was weakening Scipio's power."

"The Draknoir sorcerer," Lucius said.

"Yes, that foul conjurer. He had created a magical bond between himself and the Black Dragon, which increased their power twofold. We druids managed to break the bond and seal Scipio's fate at the hands of Reyeon," Alistair said, slumping back in the chair. "The Draknoir never forgot our role that day, and just like Cervantes' heirs, we were sought out."

"They hunted you?" Siegfried asked.

"Yes. We were hunted in our homes in the forests of Ithileo. The Draknoir waged war on the Order and killed our most powerful mages, alchemists, and healers. We were so few at that time, we did not expect the attack," Alistair said. He leaned forward and narrowed his eyes. "The command to massacre the druids came from a certain Nasgothar overlord."

"Memnon." Lucius sneered.

"His necromancy skills were far greater than anything we druids could conjure to defeat him. Knowing the fate of my race was quickly being extinguished, I fled to the Grey Swamps with all the knowledge, power, and wisdom the Order had collected over the ages. I've guarded the Order's weapons and secrets from the enemy," Alistair said. He glanced at the collection of staffs, and the lines on his forehead creased. "Should Memnon ever wield such power as these, the world would be in great peril."

"The world is already in great peril, Master Skylark," Siegfried said, crossing his arms. "Lord Memnon is sure to resurrect the spirit of the Black Dragon soon."

Alistair's eyebrows shot upward. "Kraegyn? No, it is impossible. A suitable host is required for a summoning to take place, and the dragons of Ghadarya still slumber in their caves."

"Memnon and his minions have slaughtered a company of the Drachengarde, and the attacks on Aldron have increased," Siegfried said, looking into Alistair's gray eyes. "The dark lord of Nasgothar is becoming more brazen. He will seek out the dragons and find a host."

Alistair cursed under his breath. The druid's face tightened, and he tapped his thumb on his lips thoughtfully. He remained quiet for a long moment before Lucius huffed impatiently. "Our time is running out; the blade that defeated Ghadarya and Nasgothar must be forged again," he said.

Alistair raised his eyes toward him, his forehead wrinkling. "You speak of the Requiem Sword? There is no one worthy of such a powerful weapon—save for King Cervantes himself."

"One worthier than Cervantes has come," Siegfried countered, his eyes motioned to Lucius, who slouched slightly.

"You?" Alistair scoffed. The old hermit studied him closely and shook his head. "The line of Cervantes is as bereft as the druids, my dear boy."

"You're wrong, Alistair," Lucius declared. He abruptly took off his pack and rifled through its contents while Alistair watched. Lucius removed the stone seal of Nostra from his bag and handed it to the druid. "I am the last heir of Cervantes, king of Aldron. It is my charge to forge the Requiem Sword and stop Kraegyn from rising again."

Alistair inspected the seal, running his four-fingered hand across the eagle carved into the stone. "The royal seal ... in my old age I never thought I'd see a living descendant of the house of Nostra," he said. The druid gazed at Lucius with misty eyes for a moment before his face grew solemn. "Dark days lie ahead for us all if Memnon resurrects the Black Dragon ... but I take heart in knowing there is hope in the coming gloom."

"Will you help us, Alistair?" Lucius asked.

Alistair handed the seal back to him and stood from the chair. "I will do what I can for you, my young Nostra."

TWENTY-FOUR

Bitter Wine

The daylight hours passed quickly in Alistair's house as the druid recounted his exploits to Lucius while searching through his collection of bottles for the precious *mithas* powder. Growing restless in the musty old house, Siegfried decided to explore the marshes, planning to return before dinner. Alistair warned the elf not to linger in the Grey Swamps after sunset. The power of the Draknoir demon, Nergoth, permeated the marshland, and darkness increased his influence on the animals of the swamp. Hostile creatures like marsh wolves, lynxes, and crocodiles were particularly susceptible to Nergoth's will, but the will-o'-the-wisps were the most dangerous. The wisps appeared at night to lure weary and unsuspecting travelers to their deaths. Alistair believed the wisps were servants of an ancient evil dwelling in the forest—an ally of Nergoth. The mere mention of this unknown evil caused Siegfried's face to grow pale, but he reassured them his foray into the swamp would not last into the dark hours. With a curt nod, the elf grabbed his quiver and bow and left the house.

While Alistair continued rummaging around the house, Lucius dwelled on the look of fear on his brother's face. What evil could possibly scare Siegfried? His brother had been willing to die at King Klik's hand a few days ago and yet Siegfried had shown no hint of fear at the possibility. Lucius' musings were interrupted by Alistair's jubilant whooping upon finding a small wooden box among his possessions. The old druid used his long, skinny fingers to pull off the lid to reveal shiny silver granules inside.

"This calls for a drink," Alistair declared, handing the box to Lucius. He walked into the hall at the rear of the main room and disappeared into a storage room. Lucius heard the druid humming to himself as glasses clinked and unknown items dropped inside the room. Seconds later, Alistair emerged with two chalices and a skinny bottle filled with some kind of mead. Lucius carefully placed the *mithas* on a disorganized shelf when the druid handed him an empty chalice.

"One of the advantages of being the last living druid in Azuleah is having a bountiful supply of the Order's wine," Alistair said, pouring the purple liquid into the two glasses.

Lucius sipped the wine and immediately spit it out. "This wine tastes terrible," he coughed.

"Your tongue hasn't acclimated to it, my dear boy," Alistair said, gulping down the wine. "Druid wine is quite strong—perhaps too strong for young men like yourself, but the mixture of honey, elderberries, and aged cod is irresistible to any druid."

"Aged cod?" Lucius grimaced. He grabbed the wineskin from his pack and guzzled down the *bywydur* inside.

"It is an acquired taste," Alistair said, smiling.

"I don't wish to acquire it, thank you."

"Well, more for me then."

Alistair refilled his chalice with more of the disgusting drink and proceeded into a lengthy explanation about the alchemical properties of the *mithas* powder. The druid used terms and formulas that were unknown to Lucius, and although he listened attentively, his eyes grew heavy many times during Alistair's enthusiastic ramblings. The elder druid told him the exotic mineral could be found in the mines of Raven's Peak. The dwarves were the first to discover the silvery rocks, which they crushed into fine powder to form *mithas*. In a powdered form, the mineral could be used to enhance the metal of any sword, armor, or shield. A weapon forged with *mithas* was a bane to creatures like trolls, orcs, and—most importantly—dragons. Dragon scales were nigh impenetrable to the weapons of civilized peoples, but a blade bonded with *mithas* could rend a dragon's hide.

Lucius looked at the small wooden box on the shelf beside him and pondered the significance of its contents. The *mithas* would be crucial to forging the Requiem Sword and defeating Kraegyn. The weight of his duty to rid Azuleah of such an evil burdened him, and his thoughts shifted to the red scroll and Yéwa. Doubts entered his mind again: could he trust Yéwa? What was his involvement in all of this? Could he slay Kraegyn as was prophesied? His thoughts spiraled into despair, and he could no longer hear Alistair speaking. Images of Kraegyn replayed in his mind from the nightmares he had experienced for weeks. He recalled every vivid detail from the blue fog to the Black Dragon's twisted smile. Not a single dream was without the same horrid imagery.

When he felt as though the despair would overtake him, a faint memory entered his thoughts. Amid the terrifying images of Kraegyn, Lucius remembered another dream of a grand palace and an enormous light. A voice had spoken inside his head, and he heard it now as clearly as before. *Lucius ... the time has not yet come for you to enter the door ... you must forge the Requiem Sword ... go and seek counsel in the swamps of the north. Ask him about the scroll.*

"My boy, are you quite all right?" Alistair asked, gazing at him inquisitively.

Lucius looked up at the druid and suddenly realized he was not dreaming. He waited for the voice to speak again, but heard nothing except for sparrows chirping inside the house.

"What's on your mind, Lucius? You look as though you've seen an apparition," Alistair said, taking another swig of wine.

"I ... I have an old parchment in my possession," Lucius said finally. "I am very confused by it, and I wonder if you could read it?"

"I would be honored, lad. Reading ancient texts is one of my favorite hobbies, in case you hadn't noticed." Alistair gestured to the numerous cluttered bookcases and shelves filled with scrolls and tomes around the room.

Lucius fetched the red scroll from his bag and handed it to Alistair, who sniffed it a few times before unrolling it. His gray eyes squinted thoughtfully, and he mumbled to himself while reading the first few passages. Lucius watched him closely for a time, waiting for some insight about Yesu, Yéwa, or his own fate.

"Dearest Celestine!" Alistair cried, eyes opening wide. "This is a copy of the first volume of the Genesian Chronicles! The Order has been in search of this text for ages."

"Wait, I don't understand," Lucius confessed. "What are the Genesian Chronicles?"

"The Genesian Chronicles are the origins of men written millennia ago. There are two volumes: *Primorus* and *Ultimum*. This red scroll is the *Primorus*—the beginning of man. The *Ultimum* is the second volume, and it chronicles the eternal reign of Yesu and the fate of mankind's future."

"The eternal reign of Yesu?" Lucius asked. "But he died. The red scroll says he was killed."

Alistair smiled. "Aye, he was killed, but he did not remain dead, my boy. According to the *Ultimum*, Yéwa lifted his son out of the grave and exalted him into a glorious state of new life. It is quite a fascinating read."

Yesu is alive? Lucius could not believe it. All this time there was another scroll—a second chapter to a story that seemed so final and hopeless.

"The second volume speaks more about the son of Yéwa and also of Ysbryd, the eternal spirit," Alistair said, rising from his seat. He began searching through one of the bookcases and eventually procured a white scroll tied with a golden ribbon. "Here it is, the Order's copy of the *Ultimum*. You are free to read it if you plan to stay, but it cannot leave here since it is the only remaining copy in existence."

"Thank you, I would very much like to read it," Lucius said, taking the scroll. He untied the ribbon and unrolled it. Gold lettering adorned the parchment, and a rich smell of myrrh emanated from the page.

"I do wish to caution you, Lucius," Alistair said, suddenly grim in expression. "You will learn more of Yesu in this scroll, but you will also learn more about his enemy."

"His enemy?" Lucius looked at him quizzically. "Do you mean Kraegyn?"

"No. Kraegyn is a foul villain to be sure—as is his master, Nergoth. But they are servants to a darker evil as old as time itself. I do not dare say his true name now, but he is come to be known as the Wretched One," Alistair whispered.

"You spoke of him before when we first met in the swamp. Is he also who you warned Siegfried about?"

"Indeed. The Wretched One roams in the shadows and dark places of the world. He is an entity of malice, exiled from Caelum in ages past. He has lingered here since the days when men first arrived in Azuleah. The elves tried to cast him out by the power of D'arya but failed in their efforts," Alistair said, stroking his long beard.

"So what does this Wretched One want?"

"Vengeance upon Yéwa. He seeks to deceive the living and lure men away from their God. The Genesian Chronicles implore men to ignore his lies and follow the light, but many in Azuleah have unknowingly succumbed to his evil by their own ignorance. Many have abandoned Yéwa and forgotten these texts."

Lucius felt a twinge of guilt at the druid's words. In his own way, he had abandoned Yéwa when he learned of Yesu's downfall. He had no faith in Yéwa's ability to help him or guide him. But Yesu was alive, and the voice of the light led him to Alistair. Doubts about Yéwa still tugged at him, but his heart longed to trust in a power greater than himself. If Alistair's words were true, the Wretched One was an evil force beyond any mortal. Lucius did not want to face such a powerful enemy without Yéwa at his side. He wondered if he had already underestimated the Wretched One's power by succumbing to doubt.

"How does the Wretched One lure men away from Yéwa?" Lucius asked.

"Why, he lies to them, of course. He promises power, wealth, and immortality to all who align with him. You can seldom find a man uninterested in such things," Alistair said, nodding his head gently. "Elves are not so easily ensnared, but he is a crafty devil. He found a way to lure thousands of elves away from D'arya to Nergoth, resulting in those fiendish abominations, the Draknoir."

"What about dwarves? Has he ensnared them too?"

"Oh yes. The dwarves of Ulfr's kingdom have often succumbed to their greed and lust for treasure. I don't doubt the Wretched One has somehow influenced their selfish pursuits and isolated existence. The same could be said of the faeries, who hide themselves from outsiders and care not for the affairs of others in Azuleah. I suppose if you really consider it, all who live for their own pursuits and neglect the plight of others fall victim to the Wretched One."

Lucius sank in his seat. What mortal could withstand the Wretched One's influence? How could he hope to overcome such evil? Perhaps Yesu was the only one capable of doing it. The *Primorus* had shown Yesu's compassion and genuine love for others countless times. Lucius wished he had the strength to be so selfless, but he had enough trouble getting along with Siegfried.

"Is there any way to stop the Wretched One's influence? Surely evil can be overcome by good?" Lucius said, thinking aloud.

Alistair laughed, which startled Lucius. "My dear boy, of course evil can be overcome by good—that is hardly the issue. The real question is whether or not you are willing to sacrifice everything to overcome evil. The Order of Celestine was willing to sacrifice their lives, and we rid Azuleah of a terrible threat. Good triumphed ... but at a very high cost," the old druid said, tears welling at the corners of his eyes.

Lucius ran a hand through his hair and sighed. "I'm sorry. I did not mean to rekindle painful memories."

"It's quite all right, Lucius," the druid said, wiping his eyes. "Come, let us forsake this ill discussion of evil and fill our bellies with salted mutton."

Lucius' stomach growled at the mention of food, forgetting he hadn't eaten for hours. "Salted mutton sounds delicious, but please tell me it tastes better than your wine."

TWENTY-FIVE

Aldron's Bane

The streets of Aldron were bustling with activity as the infantry, archers, and horse riders of King Dermont's army crowded the streets preparing for war against Nasgothar. Aldronian peasants and lords looked on as they saw their fathers, brothers, and sons file into ranks in the square outside Gilead Palace, wondering if they would see their loved ones return from the battlefield. At the height of all the commotion was the Captain of the Royal Guard, Baron Stendahl, suited in his gilded plate armor. He steered his warhorse to the front of the city square amid the entire army and people of Aldron. He felt a sudden exhilaration for battle as all eyes turned to him.

"My friends and countrymen," Baron yelled, "we stand on the threshold of a great battle that will shake the foundations of our age. Long have we fought the Draknoir hordes of Nasgothar attempting to finally be rid of our oppressors, and long have we failed at this task. Many of us have lost hope in seeing a day when our families could walk on the Barren Road or sail in the Sea of Lagrimas without worry of being attacked by the Draknoir filth. Even now many of you fear an attack on this great city, and many more have lost their faith in Yéwa, our protector, believing the glory days of men are all but spent.

"But I tell you, dear folk of Aldron and Joppa, the sun has not yet set on our time! If we must die, then let us die fighting a battle worthy of remembrance in the tales of our descendants! Our enemies will face our wrath in this war on two fronts— through land and sea. Even as I speak, twenty-thousand of the King's men march to Ithileo for battle, and those you see here will depart on ships through the Sea of Lagrimas to our enemy's door." Baron paused for a moment, feeling the tension of the crowd and his men building.

"The age of men is now. Let us fight for our children, for our families, and for our city! For Aldron!" Baron cried, unsheathing his sword and holding it high. The Aldronian army mimicked him and thrust their swords into the air with a thunderous war cry.

Baron felt a rush of excitement wash over him, and he began leading the army to the docks. But before they could exit the square, he heard a piercing scream behind him. At first, he thought someone was wailing—saddened to see a family member leave for battle, but then he noticed everyone's eyes were glued to the sky above. A trio of screams erupted from the crowd as Baron finally turned his face upward and saw a horrible sight—two dragons barreling down from the sky toward the square.

Pandemonium swept through crowd like a broom through dust. Mothers clutched their children and ran for cover while soldiers lifted their shields to defend themselves from the imminent attack. Baron was frozen in place for a moment before he finally yelled an order.

"Archers! Ready your arrows and aim!" he ordered, raising an arm in the air.

The sound of thousands of bowstrings being stretched filled the square as Baron watched the dragons in flight. The beasts descended from the clouds, and he heard the massive flap of their wings growing louder. Sweat trickled from his brow down his cheek as he waited for the opportune moment. The dragon's scaly faces and gaping jaws were distinguishable now in the distance. Baron heard the single twang of a bow as a frightened archer released an arrow early.

"Hold!" Baron yelled.

The dragons roared above, now within shooting distance of the archers. Baron dropped his arm and signaled for the men to fire. A great volley of arrows flew in the air like a flock of birds. Growls of pain escaped the mouths of the dragons as arrows forged from *mithas* became embedded in their hides. But the attack was too weak to slay a dragon, or severely injury them. The dragons continued their descent while Baron commanded the archers to prepare a second volley. It was a vain effort. In an instant both dragons were upon them, swooping low and releasing torrents of fire from their mouths.

Instinctively, Baron jumped off his horse and ran with his shield covering his face toward a nearby colonnade. The flames wrapped all around his shield and poured out behind him where his men crouched with their shields held over their heads. Screams of agony filled the square as unprotected peasants were engulfed in the fire.

When the dragons completed their fiery assault, Baron dropped his melted shield and frantically stamped out the flames still burning the unprotected parts of his body. He then looked out from the colonnade and witnessed the horrific sight before him. Many soldiers and peasants lay dead in the square, burnt husks of the living people they once were. Those still living writhed in pain from the red, seared flesh that had now replaced their healthy skin. Baron coughed at the stench of smoke and death filling the air. He could not keep his eyes away from the slain and suffering until he realized the dragons were circling the city, burning all of Aldron.

Dozens of palace guards poured out from the gates of Gilead Palace, none of them prepared for the massacre outside. Baron ordered them to man the ballistas on the second level of the palace. He ran out of the portico and toward the palace gates, cautiously watching the sky for another attack on the square. Loud cries of pain and fear echoed throughout the city along with the roars and blasts of fire coming from the dragons. Baron ordered everyone in the square, wounded or not, to enter the palace—the only place built to withstand the dragon's siege. He held the gate open, yelling for anyone nearby to hurry through the palace courtyard into the king's hall, but many perished before reaching the gate. In a split second, the dragons had made another pass in the burning square and engulfed everything in flames. Baron was forced to shut the gates to avoid the fiery onslaught, leaving many innocents to burn. He heard the dragons' wings beat loudly as they ascended once more, likely targeting another section of the city.

Hundreds of terrified Aldronians and soldiers in the courtyard ran up the stone stairs leading into the king's hall. Baron climbed up the stairs and grabbed the arm of a young commander who was ushering the people inside. "Tell King Alfryd he must seek refuge with the people below ground—in the armory," he ordered.

"Yes, my lord," the young soldier replied. He gave a quick nod before rushing into the king's hall with the rest of the frantic crowd.

Baron descended back into the courtyard and peered into the sky. The dragons were nowhere to be seen, but he could still hear screams and see smoke rising outside the perimeter of the palace walls. The large stone walls would prevent the fires from spreading into Gilead Palace, but the damage would be extensive for the rest of the city. Baron quickly walked through the empty courtyard to the smoldering gate and pushed it open. Steady fires and piles of ash filled the square accompanied by plumes of smoke in all directions. He searched the square for any signs of life, but found none.

A bellowing cry in the distance startled him. Baron looked up and saw the flying nightmares high above in the distance, raining their molten breath just south of where he stood and rapidly approaching the once regal square. Exasperation and despair gnawed at him. *So much death ... so much destruction.* The exhilaration of battle he relished was long gone in the face of this threat. Now he only prayed for Yéwa to spare Aldron from being razed.

As the dragons drew nearer, Baron gazed up at the palace walls and cursed when he saw the unmanned ballistas. All the soldiers had fled, but perhaps he could land a bolt in a dragon's neck before the day was done. He raced back to the gate, but a woman's cry for help stopped him. Searching through the embers and smoke, he found her outside of a burning inn facing the town square. The woman was pinned under some debris and Baron worked quickly to free her. Once the debris was clear, he helped the woman to her feet. She wore a black cloak matching her dark hair and looked quite distraught.

"Come, those dragons are heading back this way. Follow me," Baron said.

The woman nodded and followed him to the blackened gates. The thundering sound of dragon wings increased behind them followed by a glottal cry from one of airborne monstrosities. Baron looked behind and saw an orange dragon descending closer toward the square. He willed his legs to move faster and bounded through the gates. The stairs to the king's hall were within reach, but an unexpected jolt of pain in his lower back caused him to stumble and fall hard on the stone floor. His hands instinctively searched for the source of the pain as he clenched his teeth. Near the small of his back, where the armor failed to shield him, Baron felt the hilt of a dagger sticking out. The assassin's boots came into view beside him as he painfully removed the dagger from his back. She looked down at him with a pleased smirk as blood drained profusely from his body.

"I must admit it was a challenge to finally get close enough to kill you, Captain Stendahl," the woman said, kneeling beside him with her elbows on her knees.

Baron's sight began to blur, and he struggled to grip the dagger tightly in his right hand. He quickly used his remaining strength to thrust the dagger into the assassin's neck, but was foiled when she blocked the attempted strike effortlessly. The woman twisted his wrist in her hand—breaking it—and grabbed the dagger with her free hand. He yelled in agony and struggled to escape, but his fatally wounded body prevented any exertion. He could only lie on the floor and bleed.

The woman opened her mouth to say something, but the nearby scream of the dragons diverted her attention. Baron struggled to crawl toward the stone stairs, but his killer pushed him down with her boot as she stood up. She glared down at him for the final time, aiming the point of the dagger at him for the killing stroke.

"I don't usually let my quarry escape, but I doubt you'll avoid the dragon's fire," the assassin said, tucking the dagger in her belt. "Be comforted in knowing you did not live to see the full measure of Lord Memnon's wrath on Aldron, Captain."

The woman spit and uttered something in the Draknoir tongue before she fled out of the palace courtyard. Baron felt his body grow numb and cold, but soon felt a searing heat near his feet. He looked down and saw the most terrible sight of his life. The orange dragon had landed in the courtyard. Baron pleaded for Yéwa to take his soul as the dragon opened its jaws wide. Flames and smoke engulfed Baron's body before a curtain of darkness fell over him.

TWENTY-SIX

The Approaching Army

The walk to Aldron had taken Silas and his female companions longer than he anticipated. They were still two days from reaching the city on their current course, but if they circumvented Tarshish, Silas estimated they could cut a half a day from their trek. He really saw no need for them to stop when their supplies were not lacking yet. And he really hated visiting the filthy port city. The place reeked of rotting fish and tanned leather, but he resigned himself to go to Tarshish if either Violet or Avani needed a break from their travel.

The past few days had been rough. They stayed away from the Barren Road to avoid any encounters with Draknoir or wandering rogues looking for coin, but journeying through the wilderness delayed their progress on foot. The two ladies were also in poor spirits. Violet had not spoken more than a sentence to Silas since the night of the Draknoir attack. She kept her distance from him, walking at the rear of the company while leading Homer along. It pained him to see their budding courtship fade away. Avani's characteristic warmth had also cooled since the night her identity was revealed. She spoke more often than Violet, but only of trivial matters like the weather or their supplies. The elf princess said nothing about Numa or her warring family, and Silas chose not to inquire despite his curiosity.

The dense forest landscape began thinning as the traveling company crossed the southern border of Marsolas into the Golden Plains of Joppa. Rolling hills and tall grasses gradually replaced the thickets and glades of the Marsolan countryside, making the travel considerably easier. Even Homer seemed to prefer the open fields, whinnying delightfully and stopping abruptly to nibble on some Joppan grass.

"I'm glad he enjoys the southern country," Silas said, stroking the horse's mane. Homer snorted loudly and jerked his head away from Silas' hand. "Whoa! Easy, Homer. I guess we're still not the best of friends."

"I still can't fathom why he dislikes you so much," Violet giggled as she patted the horse's neck.

Silas enjoyed seeing her smile again, after days of hard traveling and awkward silences.

"What's that on the horizon?" Avani asked, looking toward the southwest.

Silas turned to gaze in the same direction. Beyond the grassy hills, a thin black line stood out amongst the greenery. Without a spyglass, Silas could not tell if the line was a settlement or something else.

"Let's continue onward. I'll keep an eye on whatever it might be."

Avani nodded, walking ahead at a quicker pace.

Violet tugged on Homer's reins, and the horse followed them, but let out another snort conveying displeasure at leaving the grazing grounds.

"What do you think is out there?" Violet asked, marching up beside Silas.

"I'm not sure," Silas replied, glancing at the horizon. "But we should be wary."

Silas and the ladies walked in the grassland from morning into the early afternoon, taking short breaks whenever they reached a large hill. The taller hills allowed Silas to survey the mysterious line in the distance, which approached and increased in size at a steady pace. Silas led the women and Homer cautiously along the hills, endeavoring to both keep out of sight and find vantage points to survey from. After another mile of hiking, Silas crested a steep hill and finally deciphered the unknown line. Ranks of armored men and horses marched on and along the Barren Road holding familiar standards.

"It's the king's army!" Silas shouted. Relief and worry simultaneously struck him. Why were his father's soldiers marching to the north? They had no quarrels with Marsolas.

Violet and Avani strode up to the top of the hill next to Silas and watched the hundreds of Aldronian soldiers move closer in their direction.

"I've never seen so many soldiers," Violet said, mesmerized by the sight. "Where are they going?"

"I don't know. Why don't we go ask them?" Silas replied.

"Are you sure that is wise?" Avani asked, raising a brow.

"I'm the prince of Aldron; these men are loyal to me. We need not fear them."

"That's not what I meant," Avani chided. "We have a very sensitive errand, and I do not wish it to be jeopardized."

"Are you saying you don't trust my men?" Silas said, clenching his jaw.

"I don't trust my own family, much less a mass of Aldronians. Memnon's spies are everywhere, and we must be discreet about our task."

Silas sighed. "Look, I understand your concern, but we cannot hope to overcome the greatest evil of our time without help. My men will likely have extra horses we can use to reach

Aldron faster. And once there, we can meet with my father. He will help us reforge the Requiem Sword."

"None of this was part of our agreement," Avani protested.

"Agreement? What agreement?"

"You agreed to escort us to Aldron. Nothing was spoken about meeting with the King of Aldron. I only wish to retrieve what I need for the weapon and leave."

"Is she always this stubborn?" Silas turned to Violet, attempting to keep his temper.

"Enough. Both of you," Violet said, shaking her head. "Avani, I think we should consider meeting the Aldronians, if only to procure horses for the rest of the way to Aldron."

Avani crossed her arms. "Fine, but we say nothing about the Requiem Sword or about my royal lineage."

"Of course, Naomi," Silas said smirking, which elicited a scowl from Avani.

Violet retrieved Homer from the foot of the hill where the horse was grazing, and they all set out onto the Barren Road to meet the Aldronian army. The soldiers were less than a mile from them, keeping in a lockstep march behind a cavalcade of more than a dozen riders. When Silas and his company came within a yard of the army, one of the riders shot an arrow in their direction. The arrow landed ten paces in front of Silas. The red fletching signified it was a warning shot.

"Halt! Do not step any closer!" The leader of the cavalcade shouted from afar. "Move off the road or you will incur punishment by King Alfryd's sovereign authority."

"Remind me why this was a good idea?" Avani whispered to Violet.

"I'll handle this," Silas said. He raised his arms into the air and stepped slowly forward. "Peace! It is I, Prince Silas, son of Alfryd, who comes before you!"

"This will be your final warning, citizen. Step off the road!" the cavalry leader shouted.

Silas squinted as he scrutinized the rider. The man had a thick, bushy mustache and wore a silver helmet with eagle wings emblazoned on each side, denoting his rank as the field marshal. "Rainier? Is that you?" Silas whispered to himself.

The field marshal said something to one of the riders beside him then unsheathed his sword. He commanded his horse to run at full gallop toward Silas. Violet and Avani backed away as the speeding rider raced toward them, but Silas remained still. The cavalry leader suddenly pulled the reins, and the horse whinnied in protest as they stopped just short of the arrow on the ground.

"Heavens above! Prince Silas, it is you!" Rainier exclaimed.

Silas smiled. "Were you planning on beheading me, Rainier?"

"Forgive me, my lord. I thought you were some dissident posing as the Prince."

"Ah, but I am a dissident, Rainier," Silas laughed, but received a quizzical look from the cavalry leader.

"Lord Silas, the King will be so relieved to know you are alive. We've had scouts sent out across the Dulan and around Ithileo searching for you. We feared the Draknoir had captured or killed you, sire."

"They've tried to on more than one occasion, marshal," Silas replied. "Tell me, where are you leading these men?"

"We're headed to Ithileo, my lord. Your father has ordered an attack on the Draknoir residing in that land."

Silas felt his heart flutter for a moment. The chance for a decisive campaign against Memnon had finally arrived.

"We are five thousand in number, sir. Another contingent will sail across the Sea of Lagrimas and march from the south of Ithileo."

"A two-pronged attack," Silas whispered.

"Yes, sire."

"Is Ithileo the only target? What about Nasgothar?" Avani asked, stepping up from behind Silas.

"I'm sorry, you are?" Rainier asked, squinting his eyes at her.

"This is...Naomi and her friend, Violet," Silas said, gesturing to both women. "They are responsible for my survival, Rainier, and I am repaying their kindness by escorting them to Aldron."

"Ah, I see," Rainier said with a nod. "Well, to answer the lady's question, no plans of a campaign to Nasgothar have been made. Our orders are to secure Ithileo."

"Is Baron Stendahl leading the force from the South?" Silas asked.

"Yes, sir. Two thousand of your Majesty's army."

Silas could not help but smile at the thought of seven thousand Aldronians decimating the Draknoir horde situated along the Feilon. Although the amount of troops his Father sent were a bit excessive for anything less than invading Nasgothar, it seemed fitting to drop the full weight of Aldron's army on the fiends who killed his Drachengarde brethren. Perhaps a successful campaign in Ithileo might be the perfect opportunity to persuade his Father to cross the Black Gorge—a prospect that never ceased to create tension among the royals and nobility. But Silas knew the time to strike was upon them. If Nasgothar could be sacked, then Ghadarya would be without allies and severely weakened. The dragons could finally be eradicated, and the memory of Kraegyn would fade from Azuleah.

"I'm coming with you, Rainier," Silas declared.

"What?" Violet said, mouth agape.

"It would be an honor to fight with you again, my lord," Rainier replied, bowing his head slightly.

"Cutter—I mean, your Majesty," Violet stammered. "You are not fully healed from your injuries in Ithileo, and we still need an escort to Aldron."

Violet's eyes softened as she waited for his response. Silas saw the longing in her expression, and he immediately recalled their kissfrom a few nights ago. He desperately wanted to kiss her again and hold her in his arms, but duty to his countrymen tore apart his newfound romanticism. Abandoning his Father's army before battle was not an option, no matter how much he desired to be with Violet. His mother and sister also deserved to be avenged. Destroying the Draknoir had to come first before any hope of love.

"I'm sorry, Violet, but as the Prince of Aldron, I must accompany my men to battle," Silas finally said.

Violet's shoulders drooped, and she averted her eyes. "Yes, of course, my lord."

"But I will do what I can to help you get to Aldron with as little trouble as possible," Silas said, forcing a smile. He then turned to Rainier, who sat on his horse awaiting orders. "Rainier, do you have horses to spare for these ladies?"

"I believe so, my lord. I'll check with the auxiliaries and bring whatever mares can be spared." The field marshal tipped his head at Silas then rode back to the front line.

Avani folded her arms across her chest and sighed. "It is very bold to engage the Draknoir in such close proximity to Nasgothar. D'arya be with you, Prince Silas."

"I believe we can make a successful assault on Memnon's forces—weaken his resolve and possibly turn the tide in this war," Silas replied. "It's worth a try anyway."

He glanced at Violet, who had occupied herself with feeding Homer an apple. Silas stepped up beside her and patted the horse's neck. "I will miss our adventures together, Homer."

"He will not miss them in the least," Violet said, grinning slightly.

"I suppose not," Silas chuckled. He let an awkward silence fall between them before his face grew stern. "I need you meet with my Father, Violet."

"Absolutely not—we already discussed this—" Avani interjected.

"I know, just hear me. You needn't say anything about who you truly are. My father can help us if he knows what is at stake. If the Draknoir find out about the Requiem Sword, all of Nasgothar will be hunting you both as well as Lucius and Siegfried."

"We risk being hunted by revealing our errand to a Sovereign," Avani argued. "I do not trust anyone in a royal court to keep quiet."

"Not even me?" Silas asked.

Avani opened her mouth to speak, but only a heavy sigh came out.

"Look, I am on your side. I want to help, and you can trust me. My Father will provide aid for this task. I ask you only to consider it when you reach Aldron."

"Silas, why would King Alfryd even consider an audience when you won't be there to vouch for us?" Violet asked.

Silas bit his lower lip then reached inside his chainmail shirt. He pulled off the silver necklace with his mother's ring attached and placed it in Violet's hand. "This ring belongs to my mother. It is precious to me, and my Father will recognize it. Take it to Gilead Palace, and you will gain an audience with the King."

"Silas ... I can't take this. Not when I know how much it means to you," Violet said, swallowing hard.

"It is not a gift. I'm only entrusting you to keep it safe for me while I'm away," Silas said. "Will you take it?"

Violet hesitated for a moment before she nodded then put the necklace around her neck.

Clopping hooves nearby signaled Rainier's return from the front line. The field marshal held the reins of two horses galloping alongside his own steed. "Two mares as requested, my lord," Rainier said, gesturing toward the two brown horses.

"Thank you, Rainier. Here you are, Naomi," Silas said, offering the reins to the elf princess.

Avani took the reins and climbed up on the saddle of the mare. Silas turned to hand the other mare's reins to Violet, but she had already mounted Homer.

"Don't worry, he'll be able to bear me and our supplies," Violet said with a bemused smile. "I think Homer might also get jealous if I rode another horse in his presence."

"Fair enough, my lady," Silas said. "I'll take the other mare, marshal. Go wait with the men while I bid my farewell."

"Very well, sire," Rainier said, tipping his head before galloping back to the waiting army.

When Rainier was out of earshot, Silas turned to both women. "Please be wary on the road to Aldron. I doubt you'll encounter any bandits this far south, but the Draknoir still lurk about."

"We will be cautious," Avani said. "You should leave now before your men grow restless without their leader."

Silas nodded. "I bid you farewell, ladies. I do hope to see you in Aldron before long. And I hope my Father is helpful to you."

"Yéwa be with you, Silas. Come back to us safely," Violet said softly. She did not look at him, but he heard her sniffing and knew she fought back tears. Violet dreaded this parting as much as he did.

The two women steered their horses southward, and with a final farewell, Silas watched them ride off past the scores of soldiers and into the horizon. He climbed the saddle of his mare and rode toward the men, preparing his mind for the great battle to come.

TWENTY-SEVEN

The Wretched One

Darkness and a heavy fog settled onto the Grey Swamps as the midnight hour approached. Marsh lizards skittered through twigs and weeds, frantically searching for insects to devour. Lucius watched the lizards closely before an owl swooped down to snatch them up in its talons. He scanned the gloomy landscape while pacing on the porch of Alistair's cabin, longing to be in the bright greenery of Evingrad again. Sleep had eluded him inside the cramped bedroom Alistair offered to him, but not due to the usual nightmares.

The revelation of Yesu's resurrection had kept him awake. He pored over the Ultimum for hours, learning more of King Yesu and his immortal reign to come. An unexpected feeling of comfort entered his mind when he learned Yesu saved the descendants of the Terrín—the Aldronians— from the wrath of Nergoth by forging the Requiem Sword. The blade was used by Yesu to cut down the demon and end his terror in the province of Ragnara. But Nergoth endured in a spiritual form granted by the Wretched One, and the demon became a powerful deity to the Draknoir.

Alistair had revealed the origins of the Wretched One, but much about the demon lord was shrouded in mystery. Lucius managed to find a few passages in the Ultimum that provided more details. Yesu had called the demon lord, the Accuser, and the sole reason for the suffering of mankind. The Wretched One had been responsible for the Terrín's betrayal of Yéwa and the death of Yesu. Lucius grew more unnerved with each passing reference to the Wretched One, and dread filled his heart when he realized the Accuser now resided in the Grey Swamps. Despite his fear, Lucius also felt an inexplicable urge to face the tormentor of men. Whether this was mere curiosity or utter folly, he was not sure, but the desire to challenge the dark creature kept Lucius awake and searching for any signs of the Wretched One outside the cabin.

While he paced the damp mossy ground, he noticed a strange light emanating beyond the eastern shore of the lake. He stared at the soft gray light for a minute, wondering if it was a will-o'-the-wisp, but he couldn't be sure in the dense fog.

Against better judgment, Lucius pulled his sword from its scabbard and approached the light. Frogs croaked along the stagnant shoreline as Lucius trudged through the swampland and into a glade of dead trees. The gray light shone bright beyond the trees, and when Lucius approached, it shifted further away from him. Caution and sense pleaded with him to turn back, but he could not will himself to do so. Lucius called out to the light, hoping it was merely the glowing lantern of a lost traveler. But no reply came. The light moved faster with every step he took, and he jogged through the haze to keep up. Excitement and dread pulsed through him as he wandered past gnarled trees in the ethereal ambiance of the marsh. The rush of adrenaline slowed considerably when he lost sight of the light after entering a glade. Lucius searched the glade for any sign of the gray light, but he saw nothing.

Without any knowledge of the terrain, Lucius found it was an insufferable chore to make his way back to the cabin. The density of the fog also prevented him from navigating successfully through the darkness and mire. The futility of his efforts became clear when he entered the same glade after traversing the swampland. He thrust his sword into the ground in exasperation and sat down beside it. Hushed voices in the dark forced him to look up and around the glade. Lucius saw no one, but the voices grew closer. He stood up quickly, pulling the sword from the mud and taking a defensive stance.

"Who's there?" Lucius yelled into the misty night.

No one answered, but after a moment, the gray light reappeared and entered the clearing. Lucius put a hand up to shield himself from the intensity of the nearby light. When his eyes grew accustomed to it, he peered within the light and saw a beautiful maiden clothed in a white gown. Lowering his sword, Lucius became instantly mesmerized when she spoke. Her voice was like a rushing waterfall and a bubbling brook all at once.

"Lucius, my heart is glad to see you," the lady said with a smile.

"Who ... Who are you?" he stammered, feeling weightless.

"I am the light of Azuleah. I have come to help you on your quest," the lady replied, extending an open hand toward him. "Come to me, Lucius. It is in my power to grant your desires."

Lucius faltered briefly. "My desires?"

"You are the heir to Cervantes' throne and a great dynasty. Come to me and your ascent to royalty will see fruition." Her voice tugged at him with unexpected force.

His thoughts raced to the dream of the ball of light hovering in the heavens and the gilded archway door inside a beautiful palace.

Lucius ... the time has not yet come for you to enter the door ...

"Is it time for me to enter the door?" Lucius asked out loud, more to himself than the maiden.

"Yes, Lucius ... come and enter the door ..." Her eyes glowed strangely, and he noticed a shadow pass over them.

"I ... I'm not sure if I'm ready," he said, stepping back with all his strength.

The woman's eyes lost their allure and warmth, but she persisted. "It would be unwise for you to deny the inheritance prepared for you, *Ellyllei.*"

"I will secure it in time," Lucius said with confidence. "As Yéwa wills."

"Yéwa?" she scoffed. "His power does not exceed my own."

"I think it does, my lady," Lucius said. He held up his sword, comprehending the threat before him. "Or would you prefer to be called Wretched One?"

The mention of the unflattering title stung the maiden, and her shining light began to fade. The maiden's golden hair turned jet black and her bright eyes a silvery gray. The silky gown contorted to a tunic textured in purple scales, which glimmered in the moonlight. The thin, tall figure standing before Lucius watched him curiously for a minute before flashing a sharp-toothed grin.

"So it seems you are privy to my countenance, Lucius Nostra. I am indeed the Wretched One, the Accuser, and a host of similar disparaging titles, but I prefer my true name. You may call me Sêrhalon," the creature said. His voice held an indescribable allure despite his mysterious appearance. It was like listening to a beautiful elven ballad with a grim note playing faintly in the background.

"You are unlike anything I have ever seen or heard of," Lucius uttered aloud. His eyes were fixed on the creature's silver irises, which seem to pulse with an indescribable energy.

"I have that effect on man. They find me both beautiful and despicable." Sêrhalon's face changed to that of a beautiful red-headed woman then back again. "You should not fear me, Lucius ... I can offer you a great many things."

Lucius felt a sudden longing in his heart. "What kind of things?"

"Power, wealth, and prestige," Sêrhalon said, the corners of his mouth upturned. "With my help, you could wield a power greater than Memnon or Kraegyn. Your kingdom would be unmatched in all of Azuleah."

Lucius grit his teeth, fighting the temptations in the deepest recesses of his mind. He looked up at the simpering demon and gripped his sword tighter. "You're a wretched liar! I know Yéwa is more powerful than you!"

Sêrhalon frowned. "I am not as wretched as some would have you believe, Lucius. It would behoove you to consider me an ally in your quest. After all, hasn't Yéwa failed you time and time again? Are you not doubting his power even now?"

"Silence! I do not wish to hear anymore!" Lucius felt a sharp pain on his temples like a vice tightening around his head.

"My dear boy, don't be a fool. Without my help, Kraegyn and Memnon will destroy you and everything you hold dear," Sêrhalon said, clasping his hands behind his back.

"Your help?" Lucius scoffed. "You're the one who gave them power! No one can trust you except demons and filth."

Sêrhalon smirked. "You've got this all wrong, Lucius. I'm not the one responsible for the actions of Kraegyn or Memnon. Weren't you told that Yéwa is all-powerful? All wise? All encompassing?"

"Yes, but what does that—"

"Weren't you told you could trust him?" Sêrhalon pressed.

"Yes," Lucius replied.

"And yet, the all-powerful, trustworthy Deity of men has done nothing for you. Why hasn't he vanquished Kraegyn or Memnon? Why did he allow Yesu to die so unjustly?"

"No, you're wrong; Yesu is alive," Lucius said, feeling anxious all of a sudden.

"Is he? Is that what the druid told you?" Sêrhalon asked, raising a brow. "What makes you think you can trust him? After all, he killed all the druids whose staffs he so proudly displays in his home."

"What?" Lucius whispered. His stomach churned at the idea of Alistair committing genocide. He knew little about the druid and couldn't completely dismiss the accusation. But it had to be a lie. It had to be.

The Wretched One paced slowly in front of him for a moment, saying nothing.

"You're lying," Lucius said, unconvincingly.

"No, I'm afraid not, Lucius. I'm not lying about your new friend, just as I'm not lying about Yéwa," Sêrhalon said in a compassionate tone. "Heed my words, I beg you. Yéwa has never been there for you. Think of the Southern Passage."

"What of it?" Lucius barked.

"You fought bravely against those banshees, but you barely left the Burning Woods with your life. You're scarred and unable to hear. Where was Yéwa?"

"I came out alive, that's all that matters."

"Really? Will you come out alive when a host of Draknoir assail you? Can you survive a flight of dragons breathing fire from the heavens?"

Lucius shivered as Kraegyn's fire erupted into his mind. He could feel the searing heat and the agony immediately. He dropped his sword and fell onto his knees, clutching his torso as the flames spread all over his skin. He screamed as his body spasmed from the pain. Without any warning, the flames vanished and the torturous ordeal ended. Lucius looked around frantically for Kraegyn, but only saw the clearing and Sêrhalon standing over him with a worried expression on his face.

"You need not suffer like this, Lucius," the Wretched One said.

Lucius sighed heavily and fought the temptation to weep. The fire and pain had been so real.

"Please let me help you," Sêrhalon insisted. "I can end your suffering. You can return to Evingrad and forget this foolish quest."

"Why? Why would you help me?" Lucius asked, genuinely curious.

Sêrhalon smiled and reached out a hand to help Lucius from the ground.

Lucius stared at the pale upturned palm for a moment before taking hold of it. He was immediately lifted from the ground and transported to the *Breninmaur*. The darkness had disappeared, replaced by the warm hues of a rising sun in the east. Lucius stood breathless in the city square looking up at the Tower of Evingrad standing proudly before him. A few short weeks prior he had faced off against Kiret here. Despite all the enmity he had experienced in Evingrad, it was the only home Lucius knew, and he missed it dearly.

"How does it feel to be home again?" Sêrhalon's voice dashed his reverie.

"Good. Better than I could have imagined." Lucius said. His shoulders sagged, and he turned to the grinning, pale entity beside him. "This isn't real, is it?"

"No, it isn't, but it can be. I can bring you back here and make it so this journey never happened. Your hearing will be restored, your body mended. You can live in peace here, tucked away from the world's cares."

Lucius swallowed hard. The offer was more than tempting. He didn't want to hurt anymore or face an uncertain future as an heir to a kingdom he didn't know. But the thought of Kraegyn's evil spreading kept him from falling headlong into a blissful existence unshackled from the world outside the *Breninmaur*.

"And what about Kraegyn?" Lucius asked, more to himself than the Wretched One.

"Others will fight in your stead to destroy the dragon. You need not worry. The world is full of Yéwa's faithful," Sêrhalon said with a bemused smile.

"You're very good at this," Lucius said, turning to face the Accuser. "Playing on the hopes and dreams of the weak with half-truths and empty promises. I don't want anything to do with you."

Sêrhalon's confident smile vanished. With a clap of his hands, all of Evingrad shattered like glass and rained down all around them. Lucius ducked to avoid the shards of the world he loved from piercing him, but nothing touched him. He looked up and saw the dark clearing in the marsh once more. Sêrhalon glowered and curled his upper lip as he bore his silver eyes into Lucius.

"You are a fool and a weakling," the Wretched One sneered. "I offer you peace and instead you spit in my hand."

Lucius picked up his sword from the ground then squared his shoulders. "Enough chatter, Sêrhalon. The time has come to fight."

Sêrhalon laughed. He raised his index and middle fingers, then slowly pointed them downward. The pointed end of Lucius' sword followed the demon lord's gesture and pinned itself to the ground at his feet. He gripped the sword's hilt and tugged with all of his might, but it would not budge.

"You are an insect to me, Lucius. Yéwa has not defeated me. What makes you stand any chance?" Sêrhalon asked.

"Perhaps, you're right. But you haven't defeated Yesu. I know he still lives," Lucius said with little conviction. He planted his feet firmly and continued to pull on the sword. His fingers were raw from the failed effort, but he refused to stop. "I know your fate, demon—I've read the Ultimum. You may prevail this night, but I fight nonetheless."

"Yes, I see you're eager for a duel. And I'm willing to oblige you," Sêrhalon snickered, watching him like a mouse caught in a trap.

Twigs snapped and leaves rustled softly behind Lucius, beyond the tree line of the clearing. He turned quickly to look, but only saw trees and bushes swaying gently in the night. Sêrhalon clasped his hands and let out a low whistle. A low growl nearby sent Lucius' heart racing. He tugged harder on the hilt, feeling the sword give a little from its fixed position.

"You know what I love about this bog, Lucius? There are all manner of creatures willing to bow to my will," Sêrhalon said, turning his back on Lucius. "My favorite beast is the bog bear—lumbering and slow, but oh so ferocious when it's aching for a meal."

Another growl resounded in the swamp, closer and louder this time. Lucius' arms burned from the incessant yanking, but the sword loosened more with each tug. He only hoped Sêrhalon's minion did not attack while he remained helpless.

"Goodbye, Lucius," the Wretched One said. He raised a hand in the air, walking away from Lucius and into the trees. "I don't foresee we shall meet again."

Lucius heaved with all his strength and yelled as pain rippled from his arms to his injured back. "Yéwa, help me," he groaned.

A heavy grunt startled him. He whipped around and faced the large bog bear on the edge of the clearing. The bear moaned and sniffed the air impatiently. It stood on its haunches and roared before falling on all fours and running full stride at Lucius.

He grabbed the hilt again and pulled once more. The bear's heavy paws pounded behind him, closing the distance between them. Lucius estimated fifteen seconds were all he had before the bear mauled him. He could make a run for it now, but the bear would easily outrun him. The sword was the only hope he had.

Five seconds left. He grit his teeth and yanked until the sword popped from the ground, sending his body backwards onto the moist ground. Lucius caught a glimpse of the bog bear's crazed eyes and bared teeth before rolling out of the possessed animal's path. The bear swiped its massive claw, ripping through Lucius' tunic and the flesh of his upper back. Lucius blinked away tears of pain as warm blood oozed from the gash.

A split second passed and the bear pounced on him. Lucius had barely risen from the ground. He somehow managed to raise his sword in time to block the bear's lunging bite. Holding the sword horizontally in each hand, Lucius stopped the bear's jaws from clamping down on his face, but the creature's large frame toppled him to the ground. His body writhed beneath the bear's bulk, struggling to hold the sword with both hands in the animal's mouth. It snorted and growled at the bit in its mouth, chomping at the sword in a maddened frenzy. Lucius' left palm bled profusely as he gripped the blade and pushed the thrashing bear's head away from his face. His vision blurred, and his breathing became erratic when the bear loosed the sword from his grasp.

I'm going to die. This is it.

With a whip of its head, the bear flung the sword aside and reared back to swipe its claws at Lucius. He wanted to struggle free from the bear's grasp or shield his face with his arms, but his body was sapped of strength. Three arrows whistled through the air and pierced the bear's right flank. The animal fell down beside Lucius, but immediately rose again with a fierce roar. Lucius willed himself to get up and find his rescuer.

Siegfried entered the clearing at full speed with bow in hand. He slowed his pace briefly and loosed two more arrows at the bear. One of the arrows caught the animal in the neck while the other landed in its shoulder. The embedded arrow only made the bear angry. It charged at the elf at full speed, roaring incessantly at its new target. Lucius watched as Siegfried closed the distance between himself and the beast. The bear slashed at Siegfried's midsection, but he jumped into the air and shot another arrow into the bear's back. He landed gracefully behind the growling animal and nocked another arrow.

Lucius stumbled towards the battle and searched the damp ground for his sword. A pang of nausea surged through him when he knelt to retrieve the weapon. Blood continued to pour out from his hand and upper back. He ignored the pain and broke into a light run toward Siegfried. His brother dodged several swipes from the bear in what closely resembled a dance to Lucius. Despite Siegfried's successful defense, the elf struggled to find an opening and draw another arrow. After another well-timed dodge, Siegfried hopped a few feet back and pulled the drawstring taut. The arrow never flew. With incredible speed, the bear lunged at Siegfried and sunk its fangs into his left arm.

Lucius ran harder as his brother's scream pierced the swamp air. He closed in and flung his sword in a downward arc at the bear's neck, hoping to sever it completely. The strike cut deep into the bear's hide, but Lucius failed to separate the beast's head from its body. A guttural wail erupted from the bear, and it released Siegfried's arm. The bear trotted a few feet from them and snorted several times. Lucius drew back for another strike while Siegfried unsheathed the dagger from his belt.

"I'll distract it for a moment, then you kill it," Siegfried ordered.

"Wait, I don't—"

"Just do it!" Siegfried cried. He dropped his bow and slowly approached the bear.

Lucius followed him and kept his eye on the growling bear. Blood pooled on the possessed creature's neck and matted down the fur on its nape. It watched them approach with keen interest, sniffing the air and swaying from side to side as they drew close. Siegfried cursed at the bear in the elvish tongue, flailing his good arm in the air while his left arm hung limp at his side. The scene would have been hilarious to Lucius if their lives weren't at stake.

The bear swung its heavy paws at Siegfried like a cat trying to swat a fly. Siegfried weaved his body between the strikes, doing his best to annoy and distract the beast as Lucius stepped in closer. Lucius' head throbbed from the pain swelling up in his body, but he steeled himself for the attack. He waited for the bear to take another swipe at Siegfried and then dove at the animal's right flank with his blade stretched out in front of him. The sword plunged deep into the bear's ribcage. A pained growl escaped the bear's throat, and it reared back onto its hind legs, pushing Lucius onto the ground. Standing at full height, the bear opened its mouth to roar, but only a raspy noise came out. The possessed animal collapsed then puffed a few breaths before it lay still in the clearing.

Lucius pushed himself up onto his elbows and knees, attempting to stand despite every inclination of his body to lie prone for eternity. Siegfried helped him to his feet then nursed his wounded arm and watched the fallen bear cautiously.

"Is it dead?" Lucius asked, closing his eyes to keep the swamp from spinning around him.

"Yes," Siegfried replied. "Are you all right?"

"I'm fine. Let's get back to the cabin."

He ambled toward the carcass and tugged the sword from the bear's side. The minor exertion proved too much for his ailing muscles. Lucius' legs went limp and buckled beneath him. Before he hit the damp ground, swirling darkness blurred his vision, ushering him into a sea of black.

Dreams of Kraegyn and Sêrhalon danced amid gray, clouded imagery before he awoke to the sight of Alistair and Siegfried looking down at him. He recognized the messy interior of the druid's cabin and wondered how much time had passed. Pulsing pain erupted throughout his head, chest, and back like a thousand mallets drumming onto him. Siegfried looked down at him with doleful eyes while Alistair dabbed a moist rag on his forehead. Lucius could barely hear the sound of words being spoken, and he wondered if he'd lost his hearing completely.

"He's burning up," the druid said, glancing at Siegfried. He turned to Lucius with a forced smile. "Sleep now, my boy. You are in dire need of rest ... sleep ..."

The druid's voice trailed off, and Lucius soon returned to the dark void where dreams awaited him. But this time he dreamt of the beautiful palace and the unopened door again. Yéwa's voice called to him from within the ball of light.

The time has not yet come, Lucius ... soon ... rest now.

TWENTY-EIGHT

Trial by Fire

The chirping melody of a lone thrush flying over the grassland of Ithileo greeted the Aldronian army as they crossed the Dulan River. Thousands of soldiers on foot and horseback marched northeastward into the province of Ragnara, where the northern forest of Ithileo and the southern shore of the Sea of Lagrimas provided a serene backdrop before the cruel black Onyx Mountains riddled the landscape in the east. Behind the front lines of armored pikemen and archers, Silas rode alongside his field marshal, Rainier. A day had passed since Silas joined the march and taken lead of his father's forces. The men were weary of marching across the wilderness and anxious for combat—a feeling Silas only knew too well.

The long march gave Silas plenty of time to dwell on the coming battle—and also on Violet. He regretted leaving her and Avani to travel the remainder of the Barren Road alone, but he quickly dismissed his guilt by reminding himself of the obligation to his mother and sister. Vengeance against the Draknoir had been a powerful motivator for the past few years, but feelings of love caused him to waver, even now when he marched upon his enemy. Silas could not pass an hour without thinking of the night he and Violet kissed. The soft touch of her lips repeated more than a dozen times in his mind. How he wished they met in a less turbulent time, where love would not have been a hindrance to duty.

Within the hour, the last of the Aldronian ranks reached the Narshé, a lake bordering the same forest where Silas' men were ambushed. At the forest's edge, Silas spied movement— two dark silhouettes dashed back and forth before disappearing into the forest.

"My lord, did you—" Rainier said.

"I saw them, marshal," Silas cut in. "Draknoir scouts."

Shouts from men on the front line reached his ears, and he looked to see the cause of their consternation: the scouts had reemerged from the forest with a large force flanking them on both sides.

"How many can you see, Rainier?" Silas asked.

Rainier pulled out a spyglass and examined the scene. "I would estimate anywhere between seventy-five to a hundred thousand strong, your Highness. They've got quite a few Onyx lizards as well."

"So we are outnumbered," Silas sighed. He glanced around at the soldiers marching alongside him. Their faces revealed an eagerness to fight, but the long trek to Ithileo had likely tired them and he worried the odds were not in their favor.

"Organize the men, marshal," Silas ordered. Rainier nodded and ordered all the men to line up in ranks; infantry led the front, archers positioned at the rear, and light and heavy cavalry flanked each side of the Aldronian forces. The field marshal commanded everyone to continue marching to meet the Draknoir head on.

Silas and his forces marched around the eastern shore of Lake Narshé advancing toward the enemy, who also marched in their ragtag formation. Silas ordered Rainier to halt the march then weaved his way through the ranks to the front, where the infantrymen shot him quizzical looks. Royalty seldom fought on the front line, but he could not resist being the first to impale the Draknoir filth with his sword. Rainier rode up alongside him and offered him a helmet.

"Thank you, marshal," Silas said. He placed the battle-worn helmet over his head. He gazed at the northern shore of the Sea of Lagrimas, searching for the familiar sails of

Aldronian corsairs and frigates. "I see no sign of my father's ships, Rainier."

"Perhaps they were delayed, your Highness. Baron Stendahl assured us that our routes would intersect here on the plains of Ithileo," the marshal replied.

"I only fear something ill has hindered him. Baron is a brilliant strategist like my father. He would be here now if he assured it," Silas said, biting his lower lip. "We must fight without them."

"Is that wise, my lord?"

"No, of course not. It is beyond wisdom, but we cannot turn back. We fight, marshal."

"Yéwa help us," Rainier whispered.

"Let us hope he does," Silas said, before turning his attention to the men. "Onward!" he yelled.

On the northern banks of the lake, a Draknoir overlord and a band of warriors lined up at the front line. The overlord handed the Nasgothar standard he held to a subordinate on his left and snatched a horn from another on his right. He blew the horn, which caused a great commotion among the warriors behind him. War cries and chest-pounding salutes ensued among the Draknoir ranks—a brutish display meant to taunt the Aldronians. In the center of the Draknoir horde, Silas could make out the slithering shapes of Onyx lizards rearing back as their riders yanked their reins. Longbow archers, not unlike those who killed his Drachengarde brethren, assembled before the lizard riders. The painful memory of watching Asher die in his arms filled Silas' mind and stoked the dormant rage within his soul.

"Men of Aldron, slay these beasts!" Silas yelled. He gave the command to charge by unsheathing his sword and swinging it in the Draknoir's direction.

The Aldronians cried out in unison as they charged onto the battlefield with swords drawn and arrows nocked.

Silas tapped his heels into the sides of his mare, spurring the horse forward. Rainier and the rest of the cavalry followed suit, brandishing their claymores and crossbows as they rode into the fray. In a matter of seconds, both armies collided into a tangled mess of Draknoir and men, fighting to slay one another. At the rear of the Draknoir lines, the Onyx lizards wailed as they pushed through the ranks to devour Aldronians in combat. Silas ordered the archers to loose arrows on the foul beasts as he cut down two Draknoir on either side of his horse.

Arrows whizzed past him, killing two Draknoir riders while pikemen moved into position and stabbed the legs of the vicious lizards. The tactic caught the attention of the Draknoir overlord, who signaled the riders to attack the Aldronian archers in full force. The reptilian steeds bounded through the air and rushed toward the Aldronian archers. Their massive jaws wrapped around the waists of the archers, and Silas watched in horror as his men were thrown like rag dolls across the battlefield. Silas rallied cavalry to his position then led a charge toward three lizards attacking the left flank. He slashed his way through a band of Draknoir wielding pikestaffs, but many of the horsemen in tow were knocked off their saddles, leaving only him and Rainier to face the lizards.

One of the lizard riders caught sight of their advance and steered his mount toward Silas. The lizard reared backward, and its gaping jaws snapped near Silas head. He dodged the bite and thrust his sword into the roof of the beast's mouth. The Draknoir rider fell backwards onto the ground as the Onyx lizard convulsed violently from its fatal wound. Rainier cut down the fallen rider before Silas engaged the remaining lizards on the fringe of the battlefield.

He swiftly disposed of the last two lizards with Rainier's help and saved the contingent of archers, but the battle was far from over. In the center of the battlefield, more Onyx lizards overpowered the infantry. Without support, the Aldronian lines would be split, and the Draknoir would quickly overwhelm them.

"Aim your arrows at the center line!" Silas ordered.

The archers released a volley at the lizards, knocking down several of the riders, but the large steeds were still on their feet, punishing the Aldronian ranks.

"Come on!" Silas glanced at Rainier before riding off to aid his men.

A heavy blow from his right knocked Silas off the saddle and into the surrounding battle. The close-quarter combat was fierce all around him. Four Draknoir warriors tried to attack him in his prone position, but the Aldronian archers hastily killed the brutes.

Silas stood up and gripped his ribs, fearing they might be broken. When he retrieved his sword from the ground, he caught sight of the assailant—the Draknoir overlord. The ugly fiend held a spiked mace and crude buckler in each hand, approaching Silas with firm resolve. The overlord had locked his beady eyes onto Silas like a wolf hunting its wounded prey. He pushed fellow Draknoir out of the way and swung his mace at any Aldronian who tried to prevent his advance.

Silas waited for the monster to draw nearer, hoping the archers would take him down soon. The overlord dropped his mace and unsheathed a long scimitar when he was ten paces away. Silas gripped his sword and waited for a volley, but none ever came. The Nasgothar warrior rushed at him. Silas braced himself for the attack, taking a defensive stance. The overlord swung the long scimitar down vertically at Silas. He blocked the attack, but the force of the blow nearly knocked him down. Hot breath from the beast's mouth blew onto Silas' face as their swords locked for a moment. He surprised the Draknoir when he turned on his heel and swung at the overlord's poorly protected stomach. But the blade only struck the buckler, which the Draknoir deftly raised to block the attack.

Silas exchanged strikes with the large Draknoir for a few minutes, unable to land a decisive hit. He searched the battlefield for Rainier, who still fought tirelessly nearby. The marshal had rallied a group of riders to clear the closest threats to Silas and the archers. Every few seconds a nearby Draknoir would try to assail Silas from behind, but Rainier and his cavalry prevented them from being successful. Arrows rained down around Silas occasionally, but only a few landed on the Draknoir overlord. None of the hits seemed to deter the brute's obsession with their endless duel.

Silas desperately needed help to kill the overlord—his body strained to block and dodge the Draknoir's blows. He yelled for archers to bring down the beast, but another wave of Onyx lizards had descended on their ranks. No one else could aid him. Every man on the field was locked in their own struggle, including Rainier, who fought hard to save their archers.

Yéwa help me.

In a rapid motion, the overlord swung the scimitar high, meaning to decapitate Silas' head. He ducked and rolled, narrowly missing the scimitar's edge. Silas spun around rapidly while the huge Draknoir cursed in his guttural speech. The overlord slowly closed in on him with a confident swagger in his steps. Silas stood his ground, waiting for the first strike. It came swiftly.

A downward vertical swing fell at his left shoulder, but he sidestepped it and swung at the monster's chest. The Draknoir blocked with the buckler again, but left his right side open for Silas' next attack. Silas thrust his sword into a soft spot in the warrior's armor below the breastplate. The overlord growled in pain and kicked Silas' stomach, causing him to double over onto his knees. The overlord's yellow eyes widened when he saw the large sword still stuck in his ribcage. A loud roar escaped the overlord's mouth, and he frantically swung the scimitar at Silas like a maddened animal.

Silas grabbed a fallen soldier's sword and parried the Draknoir's frenzied strikes. Not an ounce of strength had diminished from the overlord despite the sword protruding from his side. A hard kick from the monster's steel boot to Silas's injured ribs sent him to his knees. The overlord slammed the buckler against Silas' face, and he fell backwards onto the corpse of another Aldronian. The bitter taste of blood filled his mouth as he anxiously tried to rise to his feet. The overlord planted his foot on Silas' chest and pinned him to the ground.

Silas tried to push the Draknoir off, but the creature's weight overpowered him. The overlord smiled maliciously as he raised the scimitar for the killing stroke. Silas frantically clawed the ground for a sword and clutched the hilt of the nearest weapon. At the same moment the Draknoir swung his blade down, Silas swung upward at his enemy's exposed thigh. Silas' blade connected first and severed the beast's leg. The overlord immediately toppled to the ground, awestruck at the loss of his limb. Silas rose to the moment and swiftly decapitated the Draknoir overlord. The few Draknoir minions who witnessed their leader's demise retreated from the battle—their morale suddenly waning.

Despite Silas' hard-won victory, the Draknoir still had the advantage on the battlefield. The horde's numbers exceeded Aldron's, but as more Draknoir became aware their champion had fallen, they began to flee. Panic spread through the Draknoir ranks, and before long the Aldronians pushed their enemies into full retreat back toward the Onyx Mountains. A few warriors and lizard riders held their ground, but they were easily decimated without their dark kin providing support.

Silas watched as his men triumphed over the servants of Memnon and smiled in spite of himself. He ambled over to the fallen overlord and pulled his sword from the Draknoir's side. Rainier trotted over on horseback, bearing cuts and grime all over his face and armor.

"Your Majesty, shall we pursue the Draknoir?" Rainier asked.

Silas thought for a moment. "No, Rainier. The men are spent, as am I. Let the Draks run back to Nasgothar and cower for now."

"Yes, sire." Rainier turned the horse around and relayed the order to the men.

Silas exhaled deeply and sat on the tail of a dead Onyx lizard. He stuck his sword in the ground then wiped the blood from his mouth on his hand. Pain swelled from his ribs, but he briefly lingered on the injury before a deafening roar startled him from behind.

All the men on the field turned to the south and saw it. The silhouettes of two dragons flying in the clouds above the Sea of Lagrimas. Adrenaline surged through Silas' chest when he realized how vulnerable his men were on the open plains. He grabbed his sword and the Draknoir overlord's iron buckler. The men stared at the dragons in a petrified stupor, unmoving until Silas ordered them to find cover.

Rainier galloped near him with Silas' horse in tow. "Come my lord; there is cover in the forest!"

"I am the leader of the Drachengarde, Rainier. It's my sworn duty to rid the world of these devils," Silas replied. He watched the dragons slowly descend just above the water. "Lead the men to the forest. You'll be safe there."

"But, sir—"

"Do as I say, Rainier! Go!"

Rainier nodded, heading to the nearby forest while ordering the rest of the army to follow, but many of the Aldronians stayed behind to aid their Prince.

After failing to persuade them to flee, Silas let the men stay, but ordered everyone to bear shields for the coming fire. The men assembled behind him in a tightly packed semicircle—each man holding his shield to protect the soldier beside him. They stood still for a time, waiting for the dragons to fly closer to their position.

"Archers, draw your bows," Silas ordered. "Shield yourselves from the first flames then loose your arrows. Aim for the eyes and wings if you can."

The dragons passed the shoreline, now only a half mile from Silas and his army. Unexpectedly, one of the dragons roared at the other and broke away from its partner's side. It flew northeast, toward Nasgothar without looking back. The remaining dragon continued its flight to Ithileo. The dragon's red scales shimmered in the afternoon sunlight, and its large horns cast a devilish shadow over the ground as it approached. Silas' heart thumped loudly in his throat, but he feigned courage for the sake of his frightened men.

"The first blast will be the most powerful," Silas whispered to them. "Our greatest chance to defeat it will be before the second blast. We must fell this beast before then. Do you understand?"

All the men nodded and held their weapons and shields at the ready.

"Brace yourselves." Silas crouched and shielded his body with the buckler. The red dragon swooped down in an instant and exhaled a stream of fire on the shielded semicircle with all the force of its massive lungs.

The iron shields deflected the fire, but some of the flames still slipped through the cracks of the shielded formation and singed the men's bodies. When the dragon passed over them, Silas dropped his smoldering shield and ordered the archers to release their arrows. The few who had not suffered burns followed the order, sending a small volley at the dragon. But the flying behemoth was undeterred by the dozens of arrows that pierced its face and backside. It continued on a course to the forest, where Rainier and the rest of the army took refuge. Silas chased the dragon through the corpse-strewn battlefield, screaming to divert its attention. A sudden feeling of relief and panic washed over him when the red dragon banked to the right and came straight at him. He stood defenseless as the huge demon approached with jaws gaping wide.

Thousands of arrows flew out from the forest and quickly descended on the dragon's wings, piercing the thin membranes connected to the arms. The dragon screeched in pain, but continued with amazing speed at Silas. He ordered the men behind him to shoot the dragon's wings, praying it would be enough to cease its charge. The men fired their crossbows and longbows at the beast's wings. Silas watched the arrows perforate and tear through the membranes, causing the dragon to lose its balance and fall on its face.

The crashing dragon rolled uncontrollably toward Silas, who jumped out of the way to avoid impact. Piles of dirt and grass were kicked up by the dragon's enormous tail as it attempted to stand. It let out a guttural roar and whipped its large spiked tail at the Aldronians. Several men flew through the air and crashed into the waters of Lagrimas. The monster then clasped its jaws on a fleeing soldier and swallowed the man whole.

Silas stood from the ground and approached the raging dragon slowly, hoping to somehow kill it before being detected. But the plan failed as the dragon turned its horned head toward him and hissed. He barely sidestepped the creature's snapping jaws. The dragon turned around and flicked its giant tail at Silas' feet. He jumped to avoid the attack and inadvertently mounted the tail. The dragon swiped the tail from side to side to shake him off, but Silas hung on a long spike and stuck his sword into the tail. He fell off the tail as the red dragon convulsed and roared in agony.

Rainier and the army exited the forest and ran to their brothers' aid. They hurled spears and loosed arrows into the wounded dragon's side. The attacks visibly annoyed the dragon, and it let out a quick burst of fire. The flames engulfed three riders and wounded the rest, including Rainier. The field marshal was thrown off his steed and knocked out when he hit the ground.

Silas clutched his aching ribs and dashed toward the dragon's head. He heard the creature suck air into its nostrils for another fiery blast, but he prevented the attack by cutting the monster's scaly face with his sword. When it reared back in pain, Silas jumped and grabbed one of the horns to hoist himself onto the head. The red beast shook its head frantically to dismount him, using the small claws on its wings to scratch him off. But Silas held on to the horn and avoided the dragon's talons long enough to get a firm grip on its neck with his legs. He let go of the horn, and with his sword in both hands, plunged the blade into the base of the dragon's skull.

The red dragon's wings shot up into the air as its body heaved in spasms. Silas pushed the sword further into the dragon's cranium and with a final gurgled wheeze, the beast's head fell to the ground and its body slumped forward. Silas twitched nervously from the vicious ordeal and his muscles tensed with pain. He dismounted the dragon's head, closely watching the fallen creature for any sign of life. When it made no movement, Silas dropped to his knees and exhaled deeply. The surviving Aldronians nearby came to his side, lifting him away from the dead dragon. His ribs twinged when his men helped him sit on a rock to rest.

A disheveled, lanky esquire walked over to him with Rainier, who leaned against the esquire for support as he walked. The lower right side of the marshal's face had been badly burned. He looked at Silas with dreary eyes and talked in a pained whisper.

"You have defeated a great dragon of Ghadarya, sire. A feat not performed in ages and worthy of remembrance," Rainier said, forcing a smile.

"It is not a great enough feat, Rainier. There are still more to be slain before this war is over," Silas replied. He watched as tired, wounded soldiers limped about and sobbed at the loss of their friends in battle. The urge to raise their spirits tugged at him. He painfully rose to his feet and stood on the rock.

"Men of Aldron, take heed of my words!" Silas shouted. Every man on the field turned toward him. "It was by Yéwa's hand that the Draks and this dragon fell before our feet. And by his will Ghadarya and Nasgothar will fall!" Silas raised his sword into the air. "Long live Aldron and the servants of Yéwa!"

"Long live Aldron!" the men yelled in unison.

His heart was strengthened by the soldiers' restored morale and resolve. The future looked bleak with the return of the dragons, but he chose not to despair. Not when a dead dragon lay on the battlefield and the Draknoir no longer held sway in Ithileo. Aldron will stand strong and his triumphant return to the grand city would bring hope of victory to all.

"Gather what provisions and weapons from the dead you can. Tonight we rest and bury our dead. Tomorrow we march back to Aldron." Silas said to all the men. He sheathed his sword and watched them scatter to search the area. His stomach wrenched at the sight of so many dead Aldronians. He feared the sight would be a common one in his future.

Do not leave us, Yéwa ... not in our greatest need ...

Giant plumes of black smoke rising from Aldron frightened both Violet and Avani as the city came into view from the Barren Road. When they reached the city gates, Violet witnessed frenzied Aldronians running around tending to small fires and badly burned citizens. They both dismounted their horses amid the chaotic scene and managed to find a stable hand willing to take their horses.

"What's happened here?" Avani questioned the stable hand.

"It's awful, my lady. Two dragons attacked the city. I heard one of them fell in the Eastern Yards. The other flew off back to its hellish kin in Nasgothar, no doubt," the shaken stable hand recounted.

"One of the dragons was killed in the city?" Violet asked.

"Aye, madame. Felled by a dwarf no less."

"Thank you for your help," Avani said, handing the stable hand two decas.

Violet turned to the winding street behind them and covered her mouth to avoid the stench of burnt flesh. Gray houses on the street stood ominously with no signs of life stirring inside. They rounded a corner on their path and Violet gasped in horror. The once royal square before the gates of Gilead Palace was a charred mess littered with ash and burnt corpses. The luxurious houses of the city's wealthiest patrons were reduced to rubble. Beyond the square, buildings in the southern section of Aldron still burned like large candles in the distance.

Violet ran to the edge of the square and looked over the walls at Gilead Palace. To her relief, it still stood as prominently as before, but its bastions and eastern wing were tarnished by the black scars of dragon fire. Tears streamed down her cheeks at the thought of how many innocents died in the pillage.

"The dragons have risen from their slumber," Avani said, walking up beside her.

"Then our errand has become much more dire," Violet said, wiping her eyes.

"We must find what we need for the Requiem Sword and leave this place, Violet. Or more cities will be razed by the dragons."

"Yes, you're right, Avani," Violet replied. She turned and looked at the elf princess, tightening her expression. "But first, we will find King Alfryd."

Epilogue

High above the ruins of Arkadeus—the former stronghold of Nasgothar and Ghadarya—Albekanar rode the wind currents then descended with three dragons from different tribes. On his backside rode Lord Memnon, jubilant to see the desolate fortress of his ancestor. Despite their massive size, the dragons landed gracefully in the courtyard. Vines and lichen covered the stone walls of Arkadeus, reminding Memnon of how long the glory of Nasgothar had laid dormant.

Albekanar lowered his head to the ground, allowing Memnon to dismount. The Draknoir sorcerer spun around slowly, gazing at every corner of the courtyard and finally settling his eyes on the dry fountain in the center. He walked up to the fountain, placing his scaly hands on the brim and sniffed the air.

"This fountain once ran with the blood of our enemies. I can still smell the stink of their flesh," Memnon said, turning to Albekanar.

"Yes, in the days of our ancestors, this was our altar to Nergoth," Albekanar replied

Memnon nodded and walked to the arched doorway between two staircases on the opposite end of the courtyard. His green robe flowed elegantly along the cracked ground as he strode. Peering into the darkness beyond the doorway, he saw a faint blue mist hovering above the ground at the end of the corridor. He bared his sharp teeth in delight.

"Kraegyn's spirit still lingers in these halls." Memnon stared at the mist, mesmerized by its glow.

"Ever has our lord haunted this place, waiting for release from the Abode of Shadows," Gerudos, the green-scaled dragon, said.

"He waits for you, son of Scipio," Albekanar said, eyeing the sorcerer.

Memnon turned to them and narrowed his eyes. "I know ..."

The Draknoir lord entered the corridor and followed the mist to its source. He descended in the bowels of Arkadeus, and when he approached a large dungeon-like room, he felt a dark presence inside. His excitement could not be contained as he entered a great chamber reeking of smoke and things long dead. The nocturnal nature of the Draknoir allowed him to view the darkness easier than a human or an elf. Chains hung along the walls of the circular room and dried bloodstains covered many places. He glanced above and saw steel perches intersecting each other all the way to the top of the Eastern Tower, where the dragons would escape their roost.

The blue fog was thickest in the center of the room, which he knew as the Great Aviary of the Sacred Dragons. He approached the mist, and it whirled around to create a thick cloud before him. The cloud shifted to create the face of a creature he had longed to see.

"Kraegyn," Lord Memnon said, bowing before the cloud.

The dragon opened its cloudy eyelids and two radiant blue lights stared back at Memnon.

"Lord Memnon, the hour has come for my ascension from the abyss."

"Indeed it has, my lord. You are Nergoth's chosen and I graciously accept this task appointed to me," Memnon said.

"Muster the dragon tribes of Ghadarya and prepare Gerudos for the summoning. I long to be free of this hell!" Kraegyn's voice echoed in the darkness.

"Right away, my lord. Tell me, is there anything else you desire?"

"Yes ... find the heir of Cervantes—Lucius Nostra. I wish to burn his flesh!"

End of Book One of The Azuleah Trilogy

Note from the Author

Thank you for taking the time to read my book, I sincerely appreciate your readership and I hope you enjoyed The Blade Heir as much as I enjoyed writing it.

Want to know more about the world of Azuleah or my current projects? Then please check out my website at http://danieladorno.com for updates.

If you haven't subscribed to my email newsletter, visit the blog page on my website and type your email under the "Newsletter" header on the right. Every now and then I send short stories along with writing news to subscribers, so don't miss out!

I'd also love to connect with you on Twitter or Facebook, so please stop by and say hello!

Twitter: @lucid_ghost

Facebook: http://facebook.com/danielaadorno82

About the Author

Daniel Adorno is an author of fantasy and science fiction, and he occasionally dabbles in poetry. He was a finalist for the 1st Annual Faith Radio Writers Contest. Daniel lives in Farmington, Minnesota with his wife and 2 year-old son.

Visit Daniel's website at http://www.danieladorno.com.

CPSIA information can be obtained at www.ICGtesting.com
Printed in the USA
LVOW10s0856280914

406234LV00002B/325/P